Christopher Whyte was born in Glasgow in 1952 and worked in Rome from 1973 to 1985, when he returned to live in central Scotland. His previous novels are *Euphemia MacFarrigle and the Laughing Virgin*, *The Warlock of Strathearn* and *The Gay Decameron*. *The Cloud Machinery* received a Scottish Arts Council Book Award.

By Christopher Whyte

THE
CLOUD
MACHINERY

Christopher Whyte

PHŒNIX

A PHOENIX PAPERBACK
First published in Great Britain in 2000
by Victor Gollancz
This paperback edition published in 2001
by Phoenix,
an imprint of Orion Books Ltd,
Orion House, 5 Upper St Martin's Lane,
London WC2H 9EA

A CIP catalogue record for this book
is available from the British Library.

ISBN 0 75381 258 4

Printed and bound in Great Britain by
The Guernsey Press Co. Ltd, Guernsey, C.I.

Oh quante sono incantatrici, oh quanti
incantator tra noi, che non si sanno!

Ariosto, *Orlando Furioso* VIII, 1, 1-2

I

Getting out of bed to open the shutters, on the morning of his patron's feast day, January 8th, 1761, the parish priest of St Hyginus's church was dismayed to see that his congregation's direst predictions about the weather had been vindicated. Mist, of a density unknown to living memory, had descended upon the lagoon in the course of the night, transforming Venice into a city of spectres. People going about their daily business loomed as darker smudges in the all-encompassing grey fog. Poor Don Astolfo could hardly make out the houses on the opposite side of the narrow lane his windows opened into.

There could be no question of cancelling the day's procession. The relics of St Hyginus were to be carried from one end of the tiny parish to the other, then restored to their hallowed place beneath the only altar in the church. But when it set off, the candles borne by the most senior altar boys glimmered faint and dreary through the noontide darkness, like exhausted glow-worms. Under normal circumstances, passers-by would fall to their knees on glimpsing the cortège, remove their caps if they were men, bow their heads if they were women, and make the sign of the cross with an appropriate show of devotion. It did not matter whether or not they had heard of St Hyginus, the manner of his death, the miracles he had performed, and the ailments he could be relied upon to cure. The sight of gleaming white surplices, along with the large brass crucifix heading the procession, was enough to fill them with awe.

Today no one noticed it approaching. A fisherman struggling with a crate of seething, slithering silver, its contents half alive, half dead, careered into the sturdy six-footer who held the crucifix aloft, and left him reeking faintly but unmistakably of fish for the remainder of the day. Hurrying by on an errand, an insolent valet collided with Don Astolfo so violently that he knocked the poor priest's hat off, setting him spinning like the target at a funfair. A sense of irritation and bewilderment had taken hold of each and every individual in Venice. When people squeezed against the shopfronts on either side of the narrow alleyway to let the procession pass, they did so with an ill grace which wounded Don Astolfo to the quick. His notion of his patron's and his own importance took such a pummelling that he vowed never to mark the occasion in a similar fashion again.

He had a further reason for resenting the all-pervading mist. If he was lucky, once his evening prayers were said and his candle extinguished, he could watch his neighbour's daughters from an angle, undressing in a room one floor below his own on the other side of the street. He was able to identify the elder sister without the aid of his spectacles, thanks to the outsize mole on her left breast. Tonight his celibate existence would be denied even that meagre consolation.

The procession emerged from the church by a door on the north side, circled round behind the apse, and passed under an archway, which led to a treacherous footpath skirting a narrow, over-shadowed canal. Remembering that this was their feast day, the more devout of Don Astolfo's parishioners had suspended banners and tapestries from their windows in the usual manner. But the neighbourhood was a poor one. The fabrics on display were threadbare and their colours faded. Given the prevailing weather, the state of the decorations in fact made little difference. If it had not been for subdued greetings and pious imprecations, murmured above their heads as they ambled onwards, the members of the procession might well have believed that they were invisible to the city's inhabitants; ghosts who would have cast no reflection on the surface of the murky water, even if it had been possible to see it.

The crucifix had to be lowered as they proceeded beneath a second archway, then swung to the left, along a street lined on either side with high tenements. The rear door of the local theatre had remained firmly bolted since the fateful day, seven years before, when the performance was halted in full flow, with the last act barely started. The building had lain neglected for so long that the wrought-iron grilles sheltering the lower windows, and the heavy bolt which was habitually drawn across the door, were rusted. No one was prepared to assume the responsibility of scraping and repainting them until the lawsuit had been resolved.

The theatre stood cheek by jowl with the mansion of the Contarini family, whose property it had once been. Both buildings looked on to an open square, their elegant and splendid façades giving no hint of the cramped labyrinth that hid behind them, whose alleyways the procession was currently negotiating.

Don Astolfo had not been present at an opera since that night. But in the years when he was a regular attender, he made a point of spending the half hour before the performance in that square. It was bounded on three sides by canals, with slender bridges arching over them. He took great delight in watching the families of quality arrive in ornate gondolas to disembark with bows, laughter and a fluttering of fans. People of the commoner sort approached on foot. As they mounted the steps in an uninterrupted stream, then descended again from the top of a bridge, they reminded him of nothing more than boats at their moorings, which a passing wave lifts momentarily, then lets subside. Lanterns and torches were reflected in the water of the canals. When it was carnival, masks, cloaks and costumes added vigour and excitement to the whole. Before long the square would be a single mass of seething and gesticulating bodies, until all at once, without any warning or visible signal, they were sucked into the bowels of the theatre, like frothy water disappearing down a drain.

The square marked the boundary of Don Astolfo's parish. As the bridges gave access to the realms of different saints, it would have been the height of bad manners for the procession to cross over them. Nor could the relics have entered and left the square from the same point. That would have been to underline the rigid limits imposed upon St Hyginus's jurisdiction. The priest had long since tired of the habitual jokes about the shrunken dimensions of his parish.

His thoughts turned to Alvise Contarini, the last surviving member of the Contarini family, who had been afflicted with a passion for all things theatrical. He showed more loyalty to the stage than to the altar. His appearances at mass had been sporadic. The priest had heard his confession only twice in well over a decade. The theatre occupied all his waking thoughts and consumed a sizeable portion of the family fortune. Yet Don Astolfo could not find it in his heart to condemn him. The keenest pleasure the priest had ever experienced (except on one occasion, which is not germane to the present matter) had been within that candlelit interior, as he watched, in disbelief, gods and nymphs descending from the skies, borne on a marvellous machine.

At the conclusion of that fateful night they found Alvise murdered. He lay in a pool of steadily congealing blood on the floor of his private study, which looked on to the lane at the back of both theatre and mansion. Don Astolfo lifted his eyes towards the study window as they passed beneath. A shiver traversed his body when he caught the glimmering of candles behind the tinted glass of its lozenge-shaped panes. The shutters had been thrown open. He blinked, then realised as he turned back that a small postern, inserted in the larger door on street level at his elbow, lay open. He had not even glanced at the door, so used was he to it being shut.

There was an obvious explanation. How could he be so foolish? Of course! The news had done its rounds the week before. The seemingly interminable lawsuit as to who would inherit Alvise's estate had at last reached a settlement. Donato Gradenigo, a cousin of Alvise's estranged, now deceased wife, had got his hands on the inheritance. Whether or not he would succeed to the title remained to be seen. Alvise had been a nobleman, a count, accustomed to extravagance and leisure. Donato, sixty years old now if he was a day, had led a contrastingly humdrum existence, divided between his lands in Friuli and a series of unremunerative embassies for the Republic. Don Astolfo had met him only once, on the occasion of Alvise's funeral, and had taken an instant dislike to him.

2

Huddled in a cloak, the said Donato signalled to his manservant to usher in the caller just announced. A spasm of coughing shook him. Since taking possession of the Contarini mansion earlier that week he had contracted a chill more violent than any he had suffered in recent years.

The man who entered was considerably younger. No sooner had he crossed the threshold than, sweeping the three-cornered hat from his head, he bowed profoundly, with the confident elegance of one who has travelled the world and seen many different courts.

Spluttering still, Donato waved to him with his free hand to sit.

'My dear Gradenigo,' said the newcomer, once the seizure had subsided, 'the air of the lagoon is unfavourable to your health.'

'Have no fear, Maestro Limentani, I shall get accustomed to it. I have had to wait seven long years for the pleasure of entering this house and calling it my own. I have not the slightest intention of passing away before I fully enjoy the fruits of my victory.'

Ansaldo Limentani was a skilled diplomat as well as a retired actor. It would have been difficult for anyone, except an old acquaintance, to interpret the expression on his face as he laid his elegant tan gloves upon the table. Donato was shaken by another fit of coughing. The visitor knitted his brows fastidiously.

'Good fellow, this is an unfortunate season in which to take up residence in Venice. The winter fogs render the organism unusually susceptible to coughs and fevers of every description. I have never seen one more impenetrable than today's. If I stretched my hand in front of me out there, it disappeared from sight. Might it not be wiser to postpone your removal till the spring?'

'Leave my constitution to take care of itself, dear Limentani. I have no intention of wasting words with you on a matter of such scant importance as my health. Having endured the gales and rigid frosts of Friuli, I find it hard to imagine this city will lop as much as a day from my allotted span. How fortunate that the two of us should find ourselves in Venice at the same time! As you will have observed, I lost no time in seeking you out.'

'I was astonished that the news of my arrival spread so quickly.'

'The movements of an eminent man of the theatre like yourself are the object of general interest.'

'No doubt you are going to explain to me the reason for your summons.'

'Was my letter not sufficient indication?'

'It merely said that you wished to engage my services as impresario, at the shortest possible notice and in an affair of considerable urgency. Naturally I have been speculating about what lies behind it all. I had been informed of your recent, shall we say, elevation to the rank of nobleman. I am not entirely ignorant of the figure of Alvise Contarini, or of his theatrical undertakings. Perhaps you will have the courtesy to enlighten me further.'

'Not so fast, I beg you. The entire estate has fallen to me, thanks to my dear, deceased cousin Giannetta, who had the misfortune to be joined in wedlock with the individual you mention. Though she became a countess in the process, it brought her scant happiness. For the present I remain a humble commoner, a simple landowner whose estates are distant from the capital. But I am sanguine enough to predict that, in the near future, the title, too, will be settled on me. It is my intention to do everything in my power to hasten that process. Which is where you come in, dear Limentani.'

Now that he had warmed to his subject, the coughing troubled Donato no longer. He cleared his throat before going on, without provoking any apparent discomfort.

'We last met, if my memory serves me right, at the table of the Marquis of Monza, in his town house in Milan. That very evening I had had the pleasure of being present at an exquisite perform-ance of a comic opera of Pergolesi's, for which an ensemble under your direction was responsible. I have not heard singing of such consummate artistry since that night. Every element of the staging, the décor and the costumes, the gestures and the move-ments of the individual singers were dictated by an overarching, unified conception of the piece. You had done your task well, Limentani, extremely well. The effect upon the audience was overwhelming.'

While Donato was uttering the last few sentences, Limentani lifted his gloves from the table, and beat their limp tips gently against his upper lip. When he broke in upon the older man, it was with a strain of impatience at odds with his respectful bearing.

'Unlike the majority of men and women in my profession, I am immune to flattery. Indeed, it irritates me, for it is practically never sincere and, when it is, is generally proffered by the dolts and philistines among the public. A nod or a glance from a true connoisseur is sufficient reward for all my labours. Come to the point, dear Gradenigo. What do you wish me to do? When is it to begin? And what sum do you intend to place at my disposal?'

The older man was taken aback by his visitor's forthrightness. His face flushed. It looked for a moment as if a renewed fit of coughing might ensue. Limentani got up, walked over to the window, and forged ahead without waiting for an answer.

'The very fact that I have called upon you so promptly is an indication of what I will not attempt to deny, namely, that I have already decided, in principle, to accept your offer. The decision surprises me as much, or even more, than it will you. At the close of that season in Milan, I resolved never again to have dealings of any sort with an Italian theatre. I cannot enumerate to you the difficulties I encountered in the execution of my plans. Everyone was in league against me. The singers were vain, intractable and money-grubbing. The composer whose services I had engaged delayed delivering his music until the very last minute, then saddled me with a score half of whose numbers he had poached from his competitors. The boor who directed the orchestra, and whom I had employed on the recommendation of a colleague I placed utter trust in till that time, played the harpsichord as if he possessed the front hooves of a donkey in place of hands. The players were a bunch of louts and good for nothings. More than once I was under the necessity of combing the local taverns and houses of ill repute in search of them, then driving them to the theatre, as a peasant lad might drive a flock of recalcitrant goats from juicy pastures.'

Limentani's lean body and shapely hands acted out the emotions which his words expressed. A shrewd observer, though, who paid due attention to the impresario's eyes, would have been struck by their fixity of purpose. However impassioned his speeches, the man maintained an unflinching inner poise. His performance might absorb his listeners. It never dulled the edge of irony he brought to all his dealings.

'I promised myself that I would finish with Italy. The Elector of Saxony had approached me repeatedly, through a series of different intermediaries, with offers of a most tantalising nature. I accepted. Abandoning my native soil, I crossed the Alps to make the court theatre in Dresden the focus of my talents. My nerves were so frayed by the struggle to realise my artistic aims beneath these skies that one more year – a month – another week with an Italian troupe would have been the ending of me.'

'Yet,' put in Donato, with a superior smirk, 'here you are in Italy, about to assume the direction of a theatre.'

'Man is a far from rational being, and I,' the impresario confessed, with a short, wry laugh, 'am no exception. Invisible bonds, more powerful than the weightiest iron, shackle us to the place where we were born, and to the language our first stammerings were couched in.'

Donato did his best to suppress his rising jubilation. Writing to Limentani had been an act of bravado on his part. He had not dared to hope that everything would work out so smoothly. Before him was a tool perfectly adapted to the use he wished to make of it. The more the fellow unburdened himself, the more secure Donato's hold on him would be. Or so, at least, the old man wished to believe.

'In Dresden I had everything I could desire: respectful and reliable singers, hard-working musicians, an attentive patron who followed my every undertaking with an enthusiasm that came close to disconcerting me. The repertoire was mine to choose. Rather than pandering to them, I made it my business to mould the tastes of those who nightly thronged the theatre. I had no cause to fear the whims of a disloyal public or reckon up the takings, at the end of each performance, to see if I could manage to pay out the fees agreed on at the beginning of the season.'

'I find it hard to credit,' said Donato, 'that an outstanding man of the theatre like yourself ever failed to reap the financial rewards he so richly deserves.'

'Be that as it may,' said Limentani, 'during my first years in Dresden, I felt as if I had been transported to paradise while still in the flesh. Then I got bored. It is as simple as that. Maybe no one who makes his living from the theatre can survive on a diet of unadulterated success. The salt of failure and the pepper of controversy are needed if one's entire existence is not to lose its flavour.'

'So your employer released you from your commitment?'

'Not at all. His Majesty most generously granted me a leave of absence of six months, which began at Christmas. And you, dear Gradenigo, will have the good fortune to benefit from the indulgence of that distant sovereign.'

He returned to his seat opposite the older man. Donato clapped his palms briefly in applause, not without a shade of mockery. It crossed his mind that he had not had to pay a ducat for the scene he had just witnessed. The theatre was a sport and those who devoted their energies to it were all children. Alvise, too, had been a child. That undeniable fact made the horrible circumstances of his death all the harder to account for. All that mattered, however, was that the wayward creature now entering Donato's employment should fulfil the role allotted him. The older man leaned forward.

'Money,' he said, tracing spirals on the table with his forefinger, as if he were going over the flowery script on a bill of exchange, 'is to be no object. You will offer a spectacle so splendid that all Venice will flock to my theatre.'

'There are barely six weeks to go until Ash Wednesday,' replied Limentani. 'That does not constitute an excessive amount of time. With the start of Lent, all theatrical performances must cease.'

'The name of Donato Gradenigo will be on everyone's lips.'

'If I am to engage singers of repute at short notice, their fees will be far in excess of the normal sums.'

'The Theatre of St Hyginus will be the envy of the aristocracy of Venice.'

'I am to have control of each and every aspect of the

performance. I will brook no interference from man, woman or child.'

'The other theatres will be deserted. The very noblemen who own them will be forced to rent boxes from me.'

'Do you realise the quality of the competition? Have you heard that the director at St John Chrysostom has engaged Pacifico Anselmi?'

'The boy is a mere upstart. A child prodigy. I will brook no excuses.'

'His operas are performed the length and breadth of Italy.'

'The ones you stage will be superior.'

'He has contracted to provide not one opera, but two. One tragic, one less serious. You wish me to match that?'

'To match it and surpass it.'

'I will see what I can do,' said the impresario, rising to his feet. A smile he did not struggle to conceal teased at the corners of his lips. 'There is no end to your good fortune, Gradenigo. The Elector of Saxony did not release me entirely from my duties.'

'What?' Donato growled, his eyebrows arching, ready for a tantrum.

'It was a condition of my leave of absence that I should scour the theatres of northern Italy for singers, players and technicians of outstanding talent. As a result I am in a peculiarly favourable position to meet your requests. Even as I stand here, I could recite the list of names I plan to bring together.'

The other man produced a scroll of paper from one drawer of the table he was sitting at and handed it to Limentani. It was a bill of exchange. The impresario opened it sufficiently to read the sum involved and gave a contented laugh. He did not appear to be unduly impressed. Piqued, Donato rose and extracted a leather bag from the cabinet next to the wall at his back. It was so heavy that he strained to lift it.

'This is for immediate expenses,' he announced, plumping it down on the table.

'You surely do not expect me to carry a sum like that around upon my person. Carnival has already begun. The streets of Venice are awash with thieves and pickpockets. A gondolier would scupper his craft to get his hands on so much gold. Be so good as to have both bill and bag conveyed to my lodgings, care of Signora Fofi, by the Church of St Zachary. You will also ensure that servants bearing at least two sets of keys and an ample supply of candles are waiting for me outside the theatre one hour before sunset. When I have eaten and rested, I shall inspect the territory on which I have undertaken to give battle. And this evening I intend to penetrate the enemy camp.'

One of the dull-witted peasants Donato Gradenigo had brought with him from the country saw Limentani to the door. As he emerged into the fog, the impresario's step had all the vigour and enthusiasm of a man ten years his junior.

3

Don Astolfo and his altar boys were nowhere to be seen. They had temporarily suspended their procession, as was the custom every year, and were enjoying the hospitality of the nuns of St Clare in the convent along their route. Noon tolled from a church tower in the direction of the open water between St Mark's and the church of St George Major, where the galleys from Cyprus, Crete, Morea, and the other territories Venice had lost to the Turks once used to drop their sails and lie at anchor. The weather muffled the sound of the bells, as if they came from a more distant source.

Though they had reached their highest point, the sun's rays penetrated the thick layer of mist only intermittently, as daylight will descend through shafts into a mine, unable to illuminate the hidden, horizontal passageways where the men who work there are condemned to pass the larger portion of their waking hours. Limentani sniffed the air, wrinkled his nose in disgust, and set off at a lively pace in a direction which he assumed would lead him to St Zachary's.

Turning a tight corner, he brushed against a young woman who, followed by her maid, was heading for St Mark's Square. Limentani did not excuse himself and the woman exclaimed in annoyance at his rudeness. Taking her maid's hand in her own so that they would not be separated, she stretched her other arm in front of her, to avoid future collisions.

The two emerged into the main square of the city by the north side of the basilica. The fog was thick enough to hide the arcades lining it from view, as well as inconveniencing the traffic of pedestrians underneath them. Pulling the ermine collars of their cloaks more tightly round their necks so that the jewels, both false and genuine, adorning them were hid, the wealthy courtesans who had recently abandoned their beds to mingle with the crowd cursed the time spent making up in front of ornate mirrors. It had all been wasted effort. The mist reduced them to uniform, brief, gaudy blurs in the surrounding gloom. It was a commonplace among them that their clients' humours were always affected by atmospheric conditions. There would be no prospect of good business till the weather changed.

Stealing a fleeting glance at them, Oriana scolded herself for being little better than a whore. She had no way of telling if she would ever see the young man who had held her close all through that night again. That uncertainty had been part of his attraction. Her marriage lasted four months and a week, yet she was compelled to wear mourning for three times that period after her husband's death. Wedded at nineteen, widowed at twenty, life had swept her to one side having only just embraced her in its flow. When her official mourning ended she found herself divided into two. One part said and did things she could take no responsibility for, while the other recoiled in fear and alarm. The former had been in charge the previous night. Today the latter was staging a comeback.

What a turn the events of her life had taken! Her elder sister was a nun. Her younger had become a singer and was in Bergamo or Vicenza now, for all she knew. When Bruno proposed marriage, Oriana expected to be transported to a higher sphere, from which her sisters would be only dimly visible. Indeed, it would not have surprised her if they had entirely disappeared over the horizon, for she expected to be fully absorbed by the responsibilities and privileges of her new life. Once fate struck, it was them she had to turn to for comfort, enduring homilies from the one, and condolences mixed with selected highlights of a budding career from the other.

She could not make up her mind whether she had been in love with Bruno or not. He made no secret of his passion, expressing it in ways she found disagreeable. That was the chief sensation her experience of marriage had left her with: a vague, physical discomfort. An alien form snoring in the bed next to her, perspiring, smelling of tobacco. She longed for the fresh smelling sheets of her old bed. What a fuss he made when he deflowered her! He had been on the verge of tears. Oriana took an infinitely more practical view of the business. It was a bridge that had to be crossed, nothing more. Rather than an incalculable gift to the husband of her dreams, virginity was a burden she felt happy to be rid of.

She was sure the man she took into her bed last night suspected she was a virgin. The signs were intangible: a momentary hesitation before placing a hand between her legs, a glance which had a question in it. The look in his eyes frightened her, not just because his suspicions, or his hopes, were groundless. The eyes did not match the rest. It was as if she found herself all of a sudden not with a man, but with a child of five or six who was playing a part. He should have led her onwards, unperturbed. Instead he turned to her for reassurance. Afterwards she decided his alarm had nothing to do with sex. He showed an expertise in that domain that would have put Bruno to shame. It came from another source she could not fathom.

He was not the first man she had slept with since her husband's death. The boredom of early widowhood had been more than she could bear. Bruno was, like herself, an orphan, so no crowds of relatives arrived to cushion her with advice and solicitation. The only surviving member of his family was an ageing uncle from Padua, who stayed on for three days after the funeral. He explained that Bruno's money was tied up in business ventures. Until the necessary legal arrangements were complete, she must make do with a small allowance. She could remain in the lodgings they had taken upon marrying. But she must reduce her household to a cook and a maidservant. He suggested she let out the upper of the two floors they lived in. Oriana was too shocked, and too excited, at first at least, to protest, though it occurred to her that sharing the staircase might prove inconvenient.

Her maidservant had hardly stopped crying since Bruno died. Oriana lost patience, sent her packing, and took on a pert young creature called Giacinta as replacement. One night, unable to sleep, Oriana opened the shutters and sat, leaning with her elbows on the sill, watching the deserted lane below. The canal water lapping at its end could be heard quite distinctly in the hour before dawn. It gave her comfort. This city was not marooned. It might lift anchor and set sail at any moment, without prior warning. Perhaps she was not doomed to stagnate either. A figure stole from her own doorway. It was the younger son of the fishmonger on the corner. He yawned, stretched his arms, and gazed towards the brightening sky. Their eyes met.

Giacinta's manner, in the days that followed, made it clear she knew her mistress knew. The fishmonger's other son knocked on her parlour door unannounced later that week. He brought a present of a basket filled with grapes for Christmas – neat, burnished globes winking in a nest of leaves. The consummation was swift and businesslike but satisfying. When Giacinta came to tell her he was there again, the following afternoon, she told her to dismiss him.

It was the beginning of a confidential relationship between the two women. Oriana could not remember whose idea it was that they should put on masks and explore the start of carnival. She shrank from wearing fancy dress. Even though a year and a week had passed since Bruno's death, that would have been too much. The mask she wore was black, heart-shaped, and glossy. It covered the whole of her face. You held it in place by means of a knob gripped between the teeth which made talking impossible. It was in any case quite normal for masked figures, both men and women, to communicate by nods and gestures. To hear your partner's voice would have dissipated some of the mystery that made disguise such fun.

The two women paid their entrance money at the door of the Vendramin mansion and stepped into fairyland. The whole ground floor, and the garden beyond, were given over to the festivities. Giacinta disappeared. Oriana was just beginning to feel frightened when a man dressed as a Capuchin monk advanced towards her, the white girdle round his loins swaying as he approached. He made a mock sign of the cross. Though he was not wearing a mask, the ample hood which left the upper part of his face in shadow had the same effect. His lips were what caught her attention. Remembering the kisses of the night gone past, she reflected that she had not been disappointed.

'A smile at last,' commented Giacinta, bringing her sharply back to St Mark's and the arcades they were strolling under. Oriana had been proceeding like an automaton. They turned on their heels to complete yet another circuit.

'Where have you been for the last half hour? Carnival is starting! This is no time for melancholy thoughts! Before we know it, Lent will be upon us. Chase him from your mind, if remembering him troubles you! You can find another gallant easily!'

She had danced with the man. His hands were much bigger than hers, but delicate and not so exaggeratedly hairy as Bruno's had been. The sweet wine they drank went to her head. It felt quite normal to be stepping out with a monk. Many of the people in the room were wearing ecclesiastical costume. Two nuns, who had been whispering in a corner, erupted into the middle of the floor. The taller tweaked at his habit to reveal an unequivocally masculine calf. Were both of them men, or only one? Oriana lost all sensation of time. She was enjoying herself thoroughly when Giacinta reappeared with a Turk in tow. A Turk, that is, who spoke the broadest Venetian dialect. He was quite a chatterbox. Giacinta kept breaking into peals of tipsy laughter at the things he said and the expressions he used.

'Time to go home!' she squealed.

Oriana looked at the monk, who bowed ceremoniously and folded his arms. His hands disappeared into the sleeves of his habit and he inclined his head, in a fashion which indicated that he was ready to follow wherever she led. When they got back, though the coals in the brazier by the door were glowing, the air in the room was chill. Giacinta's bedroom would be colder still. But then, it was much smaller and entirely panelled in wood. She and her pasha would soon warm up beneath the quilt. Their voices, coming from beyond the wall, made the silence between Oriana and her monk all the harder to break. She left a single candle burning. He lifted the habit above his head in one swift movement. As she had hoped, he was naked underneath, entirely naked.

She had not shared her wedding bed since Bruno's death. The business with the fishmonger's son had been carried out on a low couch by the fireplace. This man was a foreigner. She knew that from the moment he took his clothes off. Not a word was spoken. She fell asleep afterwards, with him holding her. Waking in the darkness, she found one arm still around her and was not disturbed, but reassured. His breath had the sweetness of rose-water. His eyelashes trembled in the candlelight, like motes of dust in a sunbeam slanting through the darkness of a church's nave. She wondered if he was of noble birth.

4

He awakened long before she did the following morning. The closed shutters gave no hint of what kind of day it was outside. The candle lit in the small hours was burning still. By its light he surveyed the room carefully. His gaze stopped at a wooden bird, painted in gold, perched on a shelf opposite the bed.

The town he came from was squeezed between a craggy ridge and a river, with no room to expand or even breathe. The heat in summer was stifling. In winter, the shapely curves of its Italianate domes and façades were blanketed in snow. There, in the square by the cathedral, he had seen a similar bird. As a special treat, one of his father's servants had taken him, with his two brothers, to see the fair held on Christmas Eve. The chill wind was so cutting he had the sensation of constantly being roused from sleep to wakefulness. He grew light-headed and was separated from the others. It did not trouble him unduly. The crowd of figures that surrounded him, wrapped up in furs or in layer upon layer of wool, occupied all his attention. For a thaler or two you could buy a cup of spiced wine. Steam rising from the cups mingled with the clouds of mist that issued from people's mouths whenever they opened them. He was studying the tiny icicles decorating the hair at the tip of a beggar's nostrils when a strange sound caused him to turn round.

It came from a puppet booth. He had seen such things before. On special occasions, Italian puppeteers would perform stories from Ariosto and Tasso in the main hall of the archbishop's palace, behind the cathedral. They even came to his home once or twice. He had seen Medoro, turned into a shepherd, carving Angelica's name on a tree trunk while, in another part of the wood, mad Roland hunted for her in vain. Or a pair of gruff crusaders seeking out Rinaldo in Armida's magical realm,

18

showing him how far he had fallen into debauchery by letting him see his reflection in a magical shield. The winsome girl he adored, they told him, was in reality a disgusting hag. Best of all was the siege of Paris, with the monstrous Rodomonte breaching the walls and leading his Saracens into the city to assault the palace of Charlemagne.

This puppet booth was a much humbler affair. The strange sound he had heard was an animal speaking. All the puppets represented animals, except for an enchanter. Though the words were in local dialect rather than Italian, the puppeteer was skilled enough to give each voice the appropriate inflection. A horse's neighing had caught the boy's attention. This spectacle also had a source in literature, in Homer's tale of Circe and her island. The animals claimed to have been human before being imprisoned in lower forms by the enchanter's power. A horse protested, then a camel and a lizard. A golden bird came next. In his child's eyes it appeared to be much larger than the bird on Oriana's shelf. It did not speak but moved its glorious wings up and down, with an increasingly powerful, rhythmical beating. The cords that both guided and restricted its movements fell away while he watched, and it soared into the air above, climbing higher and higher into the dark December sky. As they beat, the wings shook off showers of golden snowflakes which melted on the uplifted cheeks of the astonished bystanders. The bird shrank to a pinprick and vanished behind the cathedral tower.

No one would believe the thing he had seen. His brothers laughed at him, then clenched their fists and punched him when he refused to give in. This latest folly from the most enigmatic of his children alarmed their father. An excessively lively imagination did not bode well for the future. The child's grip on reality risked being weakened by such fantastic deceptions. Unwilling to punish the boy himself, his father had the servant who had taken them to the market soundly whipped. The chaplain assigned him an unusually heavy penance when, speaking to the grille in the confessional, the child insisted that his tale was true: the wooden bird had freed itself from its shackles and flown off.

He lacked the strength to hold out against such concerted

opposition. It was easier to give in and pretend that they were right. Resolving that never again would he fall victim to a similar delusion, the boy became a rigid positivist. He decided that every phenomenon in the material world had physical causes which observation could discover. He took his scepticism to even greater lengths. Human personality did not exist. The self was an illusion, and experience merely the effect of external forces upon an organism as limited in its powers as plants or insects are. By his sixteenth birthday he knew all there was to know about natural philosophy. With the connivance of a Masonic bookseller who kept a stall next to the corn market, he obtained scattered volumes of the works of Voltaire and the French encyclopaedists and devoured their contents by candlelight in a private cabinet his father's servants were forbidden to enter.

Yet since crossing the Alps the previous autumn, a truth too long suppressed had begun to trouble him. The Mediterranean air ate away at the certainties which had given him security for so many years. He stopped trying to deny what he had always known. The golden bird of wood had flown into the sky.

Church bells echoed in the mist outside. He tried to count the chimes but failed. When he stroked the cheek of the woman next to him, her eyes opened.

'What is the name of the church?' he asked softly. 'The one the bells are coming from.'

He had no idea what part of the city he had slept in. Because of his monk's cowl, he had had to keep his eyes firmly on the paving stones the previous night, trusting entirely to his guides.

'St Hyginus,' answered Oriana, in a voice heavy with sleep.

The hair rose on the back of his neck. Coincidence upon coincidence! First the bird, and then St Hyginus!

'What is your name? I know nothing about you.'

'And I no more about you,' she said.

'It is Andreas. Andreas Hofmeister.'

She tried the alien syllables on her tongue.

'Could you tell I was a foreigner? Or is my Italian good enough to pass for being from here?'

'You do not talk like a Venetian. And before you spoke a word, I knew you came from far away.'

'How?'

'Your eyes. Your body,' she said dully, still only half awake, then rang the bell on the bedside table.

Giacinta, who had been waiting at the ready, brought in fruited bread and steaming chocolate on a tray. Oriana avoided meeting the maidservant's gaze. Once she was gone, they sipped the gooey liquid in silence.

'Where did the bird come from?'

The change of topic startled her.

'What bird?'

'The one over there, on the shelf.'

'My sister gave it to me.'

'Why?'

'She is an opera singer. Or would like to be. She wanted to give me a singing bird in a cage. I thought that would be too cruel. So she bought me a wooden one instead.'

'Where did she get it?'

'In a shop by the church of the Holy Apostles. What interests you so much about the bird?'

'I saw one like it when I was a child. In Salzburg, the place where I was born.'

'Where is that?'

'Far to the north. Beyond the Alps.'

'Who rules there?'

'A Prince–Archbishop. But I spent the last year at the court of the Empress of Austria in Vienna.'

Her eyes widened in surprise and, perhaps, alarm.

'Are you here on a mission?'

He smiled.

'Of sorts, yes.'

He drew her close to him.

'I was unwilling to believe what they told me about the loose ways of the women of Venice.'

'I am not loose. What's more, I am not from Venice.'

'Where, then?'

'From an island in the lagoon named Burano. My husband was Venetian.'

His features were extraordinarily mobile. He had frowned at

the word 'husband'. Now he was fitting it all together, the past tense she had used, the house he found himself in.

'What is your mission?' she asked. 'Is it dangerous?'

'The honest answer is, I do not know. It concerns a young woman of more or less the same age as you.'

'Are you to marry her?'

'Not at all. I have never set eyes on her. She is lost and my business is to seek her out.'

'And can I help you?'

He had not expected such an offer.

'Why would you want to do that?'

She shrugged her shoulders.

'I have an empty life. My husband died more than a year ago. Since then I have lived like a spectre moving among living creatures.'

'Are you to be trusted?'

'As much as I am able to trust you.'

He thought about that, then went on.

'There are two ways you can help me. But you must act with the greatest secrecy.'

She nodded.

'I need to know everything there is to know about St Hyginus's. Not the church, the theatre.'

'The theatre that's closed?' she asked, incredulous.

'Yes, that one. It must be near to here.'

He hesitated again.

'This afternoon, I have a rendezvous with another foreigner to Venice. Her name is Baroness Hedwiga . . .'

'You are seeing another woman? And you want me to spy on her?'

'Don't be foolish! You have no reason to be jealous. The creature does not interest me in the slightest. But what she knows could be extremely valuable. Her full name is Hedwiga Engelsfeld von Nettesheim.'

Oriana was pouting.

'The theatre is easy. The German baroness will be more difficult.'

Andreas got down from the bed and gestured towards the habit he had doffed the night before.

'How am I to get home? I cannot walk the daytime streets dressed as a monk.'

'I shall lend you some of my husband's clothes. But you must bring them back as soon as possible.'

'Don't worry. After all, I shall have to recover my costume!' was the rejoinder.

Giacinta had slipped out to the market. Oriana chose a set of clothes that matched and helped him on with them, patting and tugging till they showed her guest's figure to the greatest advantage. She had done this so often with Bruno. To do it with a different man unsettled and excited her at the same time. It was sad to see his naked form disappear beneath the clothes. She saw him to the door.

'Goodbye,' he said. 'What are you called? You haven't told me yet.'

She would have preferred to give him a different name, a new one. But nothing came into her mind.

'Oriana,' she answered lamely. 'My name is Oriana.'

5

'It is time we continued the procession,' Don Astolfo told Mother Hilary, the head of the convent. 'I want to get the relics back into the church before nightfall.'

'Given the weather we have today, it will make little difference whether the sun has set or not. We are already surrounded by darkness on all sides. Have another almond cake,' she said, and topped up the frothy red wine in his glass.

In general, Astolfo preferred white. But every time he visited the nuns of St Clare, quite contrary to expectation, he was won over by this particular vintage, which came from an estate on the mainland. Modest though it was in size, the community collected rents from a number of properties south of Treviso, and could afford to be generous to its guests. The clergyman was reluctant to break up the feast, since many of his assistants never saw food of such quality from one year to the next. The altarboys had gorged themselves on pigeon pie, mutton pasties and fresh oysters. The one who had been carrying the crucifix was slumped in a corner of the room, holding his belly with both hands. The expression on his face conveyed a mixture of bliss and discomfort. As Don Astolfo watched, a younger boy came round with a basket of biscuits studded with pine kernels and raisins.

'You are very good to us,' he told Mother Hilary. 'Your hospitality has quite reconciled me to parading through the parish on a day like today, when nobody can see what we are doing. Not that they would pay us much attention, if they could,' he added glumly.

'St Hyginus is watching,' she admonished him. 'Our patron welcomes all the homage we can give him, however indifferent those absorbed in worldly cares may be.'

Don Astolfo lifted his glass to St Hyginus.

'Shall we take a stroll in the cloister?' she proposed.

'Indeed. It will help clear my head after this excellent meal. But then we really must be on our way.'

Mother Hilary trotted after him. They made an odd-looking pair, the lanky, ascetic priest, with not a pick of flesh on him, accompanied by a woman much the same age, who bore with equanimity full responsibility for the twelve souls in her care. She was not dissimilar in shape to the balls of dough that had been patiently kneaded and rolled out the previous day, so as to make the sweetmeats which the altarboys were polishing off at that very moment.

'There is something I want to discuss with you,' she whispered.

Don Astolfo pricked his ears up. He had been hearing Mother Hilary's confession week in, week out for as long as he could remember, and the course of it was so predictable he barely registered the details of what she said. Her accounts of goings-on in the parish, on the other hand, were infinitely valuable to him. He was at a loss to tell where she got her information from. A secret agent could not have been more discreet, or more protective of his sources. Time and again further enquiries had proved the accuracy of her reports.

What they referred to as the cloister was in fact a garden of medium dimensions. Today Don Astolfo could only just make out the well-head at its centre where rainwater collected. But he was thoroughly familiar with the place. It was his favourite spot in the whole parish. A privet hedge cut across it in two diagonals, and it contained fig trees, medlars and an apricot whose leaves he loved to gaze at, as bit by bit the frosts beat them to a pure, shimmering gold. You could enter directly from the refectory. Another door led into the apse of the minuscule convent chapel. One side of the garden had a low wall with a water gate at its centre. Steps led down into the adjacent canal, though no guests came or left by gondola now. They were used exclusively for unloading provisions.

'It's about the theatre,' said Mother Hilary.

Thanks to its position, and the low roofs of the houses adjoining it, the side wall of the theatre was visible from one end of the garden, under normal conditions.

'What about it?' he asked. 'Has he been seen again?'

'Oh, that would be nothing to complain about!' said Mother Hilary. 'We're perfectly used to his antics by now. Mind you, when a new sister arrives she has to be told what to expect, so as to avoid alarming her. Have you called on him recently?'

'Not for a week or two. He still refuses to take the sacrament. Again and again I have urged him to unburden himself, to tell me everything he remembers from that night. He shakes his head in sorrow and will not.'

'How long has he been immured in there?'

'Seven years. Can you possibly have forgotten?'

'No,' said Mother Hilary quietly. 'I have not forgotten. It was seven years ago last November. The night is engraved in my memory. But I lose count of the years, now I am growing old.'

'There is no evil in the creature. No madness either. He has no reasonable cause to hold himself aloof from all society, as if he were accursed. All he does is work at his blessed models.'

'And you bring him the materials he needs?'

'It is the least I can do to help him.'

'He has been singing again. Like a caged bird. Trills and roundels of unbelievable sweetness. It surprises me that he can manage them nowadays.'

'Such skills are not easily lost.'

'To the best of my knowledge, he has no terrible crime on his conscience. Is it a secret connected with his early life that continues to torment him?'

'All his kind have good reason to torment themselves over what happened in their early years. But no, I do not think the crux of the matter lies there.'

'He had an exceptional tutor. Only an excellent training would allow him to be so agile still.'

Don Astolfo drank down the last drops of his wine, which he had brought with him, before continuing. It was cold where they were sitting. He felt the dampness from the canal seeping into his bones. But he enjoyed his heart to hearts with Mother Hilary too much to bring this one to an end until he had to.

'Don't laugh at me, but I suspect he is keeping guard.'

'On what?'

'I cannot tell. It is merely an impression. As if, were he to abandon the place, something terrible would occur. Or something terrible might escape.'

'He is not alone.'

'What?'

The priest's voice rose in a howl of astonishment and disbelief.

'At least, not if Sister Martha is to be believed. The one who came here in spring of last year. She has an opera singer in the family. When she first noticed the singing, she was not frightened the way the others had been. She was used to hearing her sister practise and so she was able to appreciate the extent of his skill. But then, two days ago, she heard a different voice. A woman's.'

'You are sure it was not his?'

'Martha has a fine ear and can distinguish. I would be more easily deceived.'

'This does not bode well.'

'It was an untrained voice, singing in a dialect she did not recognise.'

'What does that mean?'

'I got her to repeat a line or two to me, with what she could imitate of the words. And do you know, Don Astolfo, the song comes from Naples?'

The priest shook his head in perplexity.

'Mystery upon mystery.'

'I recognised the tune. My dear father came from that city. He did not sing the song himself, but friends who visited the house we lived in had sung it. I was able to repeat it to Martha and she confirmed that it was the one she heard. It happened on a sunny day. I love those brilliant mornings at the turn of the year when beads of dew tremble at the tips of the branches, and the reflected beams set the whole cloister brimming with light, as if it were a goblet spilling over. Martha had taken her sewing outside to save her eyes. On hearing the song, she looked up and saw a girl combing her hair at the open window. She had long, auburn tresses, abundant and shimmering.'

6

If Domenico had put solid food in his stomach that day or even the day before, the accident would not have happened. The weakness and malaise that overtook him distorted his sense of time. He had been lying on his bed a lot anyway this last week, as often as not falling asleep and wakening an hour or so further on. He fancied that if he spent as much time as possible in a horizontal position, it would stop him getting so horribly hungry. There was nowhere he had to go, nothing he had to get up for. Hardly any point in staying awake, in fact. And so, this afternoon, when it was so essential he should keep his appointment, the bells from St George of the Greeks had broken in upon a peaceful dream.

He was supposed to be at the coffee house, waiting for Ansaldo Limentani. Domenico could not afford a gondola. And he did not know this part of Venice well enough to be sure of his way. He ran helter-skelter through the fog. It gave a different resonance to the clattering of his feet along the pavements. Twice he found himself at a dead end, with only water in front of him, and had to turn back and try a different route. His heart was pounding in his breast, so it was not surprising that, when he came upon the old woman, the one he had noticed time and again on different corners, selling fruit and flowers, he should career right into her. Or rather, not into her, but into the crate of oranges propped up next to her seat.

It was just as well he came from Bologna and not from Venice. He could not understand a word of the torrent of abuse she poured out. That it was abuse there could be little doubt, given the fury of her expression and the menacing way she waved her arms at him. The accident would make him even later, but there was nothing to be done. He felt obliged to help her put her wares in order again. The old crone might be even poorer than himself. At

28

least she could eat the stuff she failed to sell. He could not eat music.

'Forgive me, forgive me, old mother, I did not mean to do it,' he stammered, as he knelt down and gathered together the bright bulbs, which had rolled in all directions.

It did not take as long as he expected. Later, thinking back upon the incident, it puzzled him that he should have been able to see the oranges in spite of the mist. Although there was no rational explanation, it thinned out at the crossroads where she had set up her stall.

When he escaped at last, her back was turned to him. She was rearranging the fruits in the crate, checking to see if any had been bruised. No doubt she would hide them beneath the better ones and do her best to sell them anyway. Domenico had expected the old woman to smell. But the collision left a fragrance in his nostrils, as if her body had become sufficiently impregnated with the scents of the flowers and the aromas of the fruit she sold to counteract the effect of the rags she was dressed in.

The momentary distraction did him good. Turning a corner, he recognised his surroundings, and reached the coffee house in under two minutes. To his relief, Ansaldo was nowhere to be seen. His instructions were to present himself there one hour after the midday meal. Presumably he had lunch earlier than the impresario! In the days when he had had lunch, he reflected sadly.

He sat down and polished the buttons on his jacket with the cuffs of his embroidered shirt. Since losing his post as a private tutor, he had been careful not to wear it, in view of just such an opportunity as had presented itself. He needed to look his best. To his horror, the owner popped a tray with steaming coffee and a dish of biscuits down at his elbow. How was he to pay? He had been saving his last coins to buy grilled fish at a stall on the waterfront, when he could resist the hunger no longer. He had left those at home. There was something in his pocket, nonetheless. Pulling it out, he saw it was an orange.

How strange! It would never have crossed his mind to rob the old woman. And he could hardly have put the fruit there without realising. On an impulse, he bit into it. The peel was bitter but the zest was fresh and energising. He sucked at the dent in the flesh so as not to lose one drop of the precious juice. Could one eat orange peel? Probably not. It would be unwise to experiment, given his current debilitated state. He stripped it off and contented himself with the fruit.

The door was pushed open. Limentani strode in. Domenico had not expected to recognise him but the athletic pose, the chiselled features and the piercing eyes were somehow familiar.

'You look dreadful, dear fellow!' exclaimed the older man, sitting down.

Domenico mumbled in confusion then fell silent. He was close to tears. Limentani threw his gloves on the table and patted the younger man's hand.

'Coffee for me!' he shouted to the proprietor. 'And bring a generous bowl of fish soup for this fellow. I'd hazard a guess he has not eaten yet.'

'We do not have fish soup, sir.'

'Then send out for it! And don't waste any time!' In lower tones, he added, for Domenico: 'I am going to have to beef you up if you are to cope with the amount of work we have ahead of us.'

Domenico was pulling himself together. Partly it was the effect of the orange, partly the prospect of the soup.

'I cannot tell you how delighted I am that . . .'

'Tut, tut, none of your protestations. I have not forgotten the exquisite performance you gave in Cardinal Albani's villa near Bologna. When was that? Three summers ago? Four?'

'Three,' said Domenico, guardedly.

'And were you in his service at that time?'

'No, not at all. I had just become acquainted with the cardinal. It was the singer who engaged me.'

'Yes, of course. Gabriela Dotti! Do you know, she is to be one of the company as well?'

'What company?'

Limentani rubbed his hands with glee.

'It is an act of the purest folly on my part! But then, what kind of lives would we be left with, if we cut all folly out of them? The theatre is itself a species of madness, do you not agree?'

'I am a musician,' put in Domenico, with an odd blend of

modesty and pride. 'Until now my experience of the theatre has been only as a spectator.'

'That will all change. Today is Tuesday, am I not right? Well, in a week's time we are to reopen one of Venice's most illustrious theatres, the St Hyginus, which has been shut for over seven years. You have heard of St Hyginus?'

'The one where they had the marvellous machines?'

'That's right! You are by no means as ignorant of the theatre as you would have me believe. And I intend to entrust the musical directorship to you.'

Domenico's jaw dropped. Was the man mad?

'You look surprised. You think I am crazy. Perhaps I am. But consider, dear Domenico. I may call you by your Christian name, may I not? After all, if we really are to mount a season, we shall undoubtedly fall out a hundred times between now and Ash Wednesday. So the sooner we get on familiar terms, the better. Consider the following. I am assured of your talent. You played for one whole evening before me in Bologna. I have spent my working life assessing musicians under less favourable conditions. You possess all the qualities one could wish for. Precision, fantasy, diligence. That was obvious when I heard you at the harpsichord. As an alternative, I could engage some stubborn individual approaching middle age, set in his ways, who would fight my ideas every inch of the way, spend his free time attempting to seduce the lead soprano rather than studying scores, and demand in payment twice what I am able to give him. You are young and, in theatrical terms, unformed. You will not stint on time or effort and will listen to what I tell you. When you hear the wage I intend to pay, you will be overjoyed rather than disgruntled. You need the work. I need your skill and your originality. Are we agreed?'

Domenico was struck dumb by this speech. Without thinking, he reached out and grasped the hand the impresario had extended. As if to clinch the contract, the fish soup arrived, rich and steaming, in a terracotta pitcher which, to his famished eyes, looked bottomless. A basket of bread was placed alongside it. All thought of music and the theatre abandoned him. Limentani sipped at his coffee and watched with enjoyment.

'Will that be enough?' he asked, once Domenico had ensured that the pitcher did, in fact, possess a bottom.

'Oh, indeed,' came the answer, amidst a certain confusion.

'I take it you have not been eating a great deal lately.'

'No.'

'When did your employment as tutor to Calerghi's daughters end?'

'A week ago last Thursday,' Domenico said cautiously. He did not want to go into details about the fiasco of his departure from the Calerghi household.

'Nothing to be ashamed of. It is not the first time a tutor has tried to seduce a young gentlewoman given into his care.'

'I did not try to seduce her. That is a calumny. And it was not the daughter, but the mistress of the house.'

'A case of Joseph and Potiphar's wife, then?'

Domenico's sense of humour was returning, now his appetite had been appeased. The ironies of what had happened did not escape him.

'More Susannah and the elders, actually.'

'Her husband was after you as well?'

Domenico blushed, spluttered, then caught Limentani's eye, and they both burst out laughing.

'The truth of it hardly matters. Mind you, if you do seduce the lead soprano, make sure you hear her through her part while you are in bed.'

Domenico kept his eyes firmly on the table. Evidently Limentani did not know quite as much about Cardinal Albani's household as he had feared.

'I thank the stars the family was good enough to forward my message to you. Otherwise finding you would have been impossible.'

'It was not the Calerghis who did it but their doorkeeper. He brought your letter straight to my lodgings without even letting his master see it. It would have been burned if that man had got his hands on it.'

'Enough said. Time to get down to business. Normally I would expect your help in assembling an orchestra. Under the circumstances, I am prepared to take that job on myself. I feel so much energy coursing through me that it would not daunt me to assemble an army, never mind a complement of strings with wind, trumpets and kettledrums.'

Domenico's eyes widened. Was the orchestra to be so huge? The impresario was thinking in grandiose terms indeed.

'Rehearsals will begin in two days' time, on Friday afternoon. You are to rehearse each of the singers individually, and combine them with the players on the afternoon before the opening.'

'How many singers have you got?'

'Let's see . . . Dotti as soprano, Randagio will be the tenor, and I hope Iannelli will come in as bass. That leaves me to track down a contralto, a baritone if possible . . .'

'And what are the operas to be?'

'There you have me, dear fellow. Preferably well-known pieces. Iommelli, Leo, Pergolesi . . .'

'Where are we to find the parts?'

The impresario's brow contracted.

'One thing I will not put up with is having you discourage me, or place obstacles in my way. We will deal with these problems one by one. Work hard and have faith. That is all I ask of you. In any case, we should call for the bill. I had not planned to spend so much time here. They will be waiting for us outside the theatre.'

7

Domenico had difficulty keeping up with the energetic pace of his new employer, who took not more than two wrong turnings on his way from the coffee house to the theatre at St Hyginus's. They approached it via the square. Before crossing the bridge, Limentani indicated a tavern on their right.

'You will take all your meals here henceforth. I shall settle the bill each morning without fail. The place is to be our general headquarters. We shall hold councils of war at its tables as and when needed.'

He cried out in irritation when they found just two servants, with a single lantern, waiting at the side door.

'What does Donato Gradenigo imagine? That you can light a theatre with nothing better than a lantern? You,' he told the older man, who held it, 'come with us. And you,' to the other, 'get back here sharpish with not fewer than eight lackeys, each carrying a candelabra. Do you hear me?' Then, turning back to the first one: 'Open up! Get a move on! What are you afraid of? Do you think the place is haunted?'

Judging from the man's face, that was exactly what he did think. He was bald, with a deeply wrinkled forehead, tufts of white hair along his temples and sheepish, worried eyes. Domenico took the lantern while he struggled with the lock, then pushed the door open. Limentani went first, brushing cobwebs to one side. The dust of years set him choking. There was a scuttling of mice around his feet, then utter silence. Domenico advanced. The old man followed on unwillingly. Limentani seized the lantern and led the way upstairs.

'There is no point in exploring the auditorium until reinforcements have arrived.'

They were halfway up the narrow flight of stairs when there was a vigorous knocking at the door and a voice called, 'Ansaldo! Is that you inside?'

'It's him!' the impresario called out, in delight and disbelief. 'I can't believe it! Luca Schiavoni is to be of our number!'

He greeted the new arrival as a long-lost friend (which indeed he was), hugging him so affectionately that not until they disengaged did Domenico get a chance to survey the man. He was thin and wiry, no taller than Limentani's shoulders, and built like a spider, with a small trunk and disproportionately long arms and legs.

'This fellow,' said Limentani, 'is the most talented designer of theatrical machinery on our side of the Alps. Truly, our enterprise sets out under a favourable star.'

'Better than the one which shone on me last year!' said Luca. 'But that would not be difficult.'

He had a strong Slavonic accent. Domenico decided he must come from one of the Dalmatian cities down the coast.

'Luca,' the impresario explained, 'had a serious fall from a machine he was engaged in building not long after All Saints' Day. For all I knew, he could still have been flat on his back waiting for the injuries to heal. I did not expect him to answer my letter, far less turn up in person!'

'The dead would rise from their biers for the chance of working with you,' said Luca soberly.

'I'll make sure you have your hands full, have no doubt of it. Will you accompany us on our tour of exploration?'

The room which had been the office was on the first floor, at the top of the stairs. A thick layer of dust covered all the objects in it. Luca seized on half-used candles from a shelf and lit them at the lantern, so that each of the party could carry a light. To one side was a glass-fronted cupboard that went up as high as the ceiling, filled with mouldering musical scores.

'That,' said Limentani, 'is your task for tomorrow, dear Domenico. There you have the entire repertory of the theatre. With luck, you can find a full set of parts for a comic and a tragic piece, and that will mean we are in business. You brought two sets of keys?'

The old man with the lantern nodded.

'One goes to me, the other to this gentleman. He is the musical director and is to come and go at his pleasure.'

Domenico accepted the ring of keys with a flush of pride. There was a divan next to the window. He could even sleep there if Limentani would agree. That would mean he could give up his lodgings. He already felt so transformed as to dread the thought of returning. The place belonged to a different life. However, he would have to settle what was owing before he left. He wondered when the first instalment of his salary was due.

There was a door at the far end of the office, concealed in part by a piece of furniture. Limentani put his shoulder to it, shoved it aside with minimal effort, and opened the door. He held the lantern at arm's length.

'Another flight of stairs,' he observed. 'Where do these lead?'

'Oh, you don't want to venture any further,' the old man said.

'Why ever not?'

'There's nothing of interest in the attic, sir. Only broken down furniture and rats.'

The impresario was unconvinced. He shrugged his shoulders.

'Better leave that for another day. But if you ask me, there may be all sorts of equipment hidden there which we could find a use for.'

The sound of several voices came from the bottom of the stairs. The candelabra contingent had arrived. Prey to ever greater excitement, Limentani leapt down the stairs two at a time, already giving out orders. Not eight but ten men had been sent. Within as many minutes he had them ranged around the auditorium, four at ground level, two in front of the stage, and two for each of the tiers above. It was indeed an exquisite theatre, neither too big nor too small. Years of neglect had not been sufficient for the gilding on the woodwork to fade. The fronts of the boxes were decorated with mischievous looking cherubs in an assortment of impossible positions, bearing candles and torches, or waving and winking in the direction of the stage. Limentani's emotion was so strong that his eyes filled with tears. Domenico, too was moved.

'Perfect! exclaimed the impresario. 'Absolutely perfect! And to think of the pandemonium there will be here in one week's time!'

'One week?' the machinist said in astonishment, then clapped his hand to his lips, as if he had been guilty of disloyalty. 'One week,' he repeated, in matter-of-fact tones, which implied that the limit set could not have been more reasonable.

Limentani turned to the proscenium.

'And now . . .' he said. 'How are we to raise the curtain?'

Luca sprinted forward and clambered on to the stage, burrowing beneath the heavy draperies like a mouse returning to its hole. He did not take a light with him. Later Domenico noted that the man had the eyes of a cat and had no difficulty whatsoever in finding his way around in the dark. There was a long and pregnant silence, broken at last by a distant creaking. The barrier of fabric jerked and trembled, like a mountainside about to burst open and release a torrent. And instead, after a certain resistance and shuddering of its folds, the curtain parted to reveal utter darkness behind. All of a sudden Domenico was afraid. Goosepimples prickled on his forearms and his spine. Were they desecrating a mystery better left untouched?

Nobody moved. There was no sign of the machinist.

'What are you all waiting for?' asked Limentani. 'Give me a leg up.'

Two lackeys offered a shoulder and linked palms as if he had been mounting a horse. The impresario picked up his lantern from the edge of the stage, where he had deposited it, and walked forward resolutely into the blackness. Their curiosity stirred, the lackeys followed, forgetting Domenico, who had to scramble up under his own steam. Limentani was laughing, with the laugh of a man who does his best to pass off nervousness with a show of humour. All of a sudden he ducked his head and moved back.

'Just look at this!'

'It's amazing,' came Luca's calm, wondering tones from farther away.

The impresario raised his lantern. The lackeys followed suit. An object hung suspended in the air. An enormous object. It could have been an outsize pigeon on its perch. As Domenico watched, it shifted gently, with a creaking which resounded to the very back of the theatre. He froze with horror. It was of course possible that the machinist had set it swaying from behind. But the creature seemed to have a life of its own.

'What is it?' exclaimed one of the lackeys, in Venetian dialect.

'A great bird,' said another.

'Or a spaceship,' put in Limentani, who had recovered from his surprise.

'A spaceship?' asked Domenico. 'What do you mean?'

'Don't you remember, in Pulci's poem, where they decide to undertake an expedition to the moon? He describes their vessel as being like a fish with fins that can fly through the air.'

'You're way off the mark,' came Luca's voice, emerging into the light of the candelabras.

'What is it then?'

'Cloud machinery,' said Luca. 'The most elaborate I have ever seen.'

He seized one of the lower spars and swung himself up, then took the lantern from Limentani and lifted it above his head. To Domenico it now looked like the upper part of a great tree, whose trunk had been removed, leaving only the network of branches, interlinked, criss-crossing at a dizzying variety of angles, yet distinctly forming the shape of a crown. The entire structure groaned and trembled when Luca climbed into it. As it began to settle once more, the bystanders noticed that strips of tattered, painted card were tacked on, so as to face in the direction of the auditorium.

'It'll have to be pulled down,' one of the lackeys commented.

'Not at all!' said Limentani. 'This is an unexpected piece of luck.'

The machinist was picking his way from strut to strut. He would grasp a beam above with his free hand and swing his weight across, like an ape using creepers to move through the jungle without ever touching earth.

'I've never seen anything like it,' he said. 'I'd love to know who designed it.'

'Why is it still there? Halfway up and halfway down?'

'It got stuck.'

They were all startled. The old man who met them with the keys had not spoken for a long time.

'And can you repair it?' Limentani asked.

'Within a week?'

Luca Schiavoni's voice arrived from far above their heads. His lantern at that height was like a beacon fire lit on a promontory, warning ships of danger. He laughed.

'We can try.'

8

A slender rectangle of tenements belonging to Don Astolfo's parish abutted on the waterfront. On a sunny day, you could make out the bells in the tower of St George Major from their windows, beyond the gleaming surface of the never tranquil waters. Local superstition had it that St Hyginus must unfailingly be 'shown the sea' at least once a year. Though the remainder of the city frequently forgot about the existence of the parish and its obscure saint, the parishioners were firmly convinced in their own minds that to omit this ritual would inevitably bring disaster on the Venetian fleet in the farthest corners of the Mediterranean.

On one side of the lane leading down to the waterfront there was a break in the sequence of tawdry houses. A gateway gave access to a strip of garden, beyond which was another entrance. This was the local brothel. Don Astolfo's heart rose into his mouth when they passed by it on the yearly procession. He had never seen the place by day. The temptation to turn and take a good look at it was so strong he bowed his head and concentrated on watching his sandalled feet taking step after step on the worn paving stones.

Nothing of the lagoon was visible. A compact wall of mist confronted them when they reached the quay. It took on a living, animal quality in Don Astolfo's consciousness. He wanted to stretch his arm out and touch it, convinced that he would find it as palpable as the shaggy, rain-drenched pile of a donkey, trudging alongside them with its load.

At their shoulders a fine new sailing ship was anchored by the church of the Visitation, the latest addition to the already extensive merchant fleet of Michele Calerghi. Although the sun had not yet set, men were loading it by the feeble light of lanterns, stocking the hold with bales of wool and sacks of grain and millet. They were in a hurry to complete the task, for their master insisted that the ship's departure could no longer be postponed. His clients in Dalmatia and the Peloponnese had been kept waiting for the goods and he was unwilling to try their patience further.

So absorbed were the men in their work that they failed to notice a gondola slip out from the narrow canal at their backs, swift and unerring as a serpent's tongue that flicks to trap an insect. It was there and gone in an instant, vanishing with its two passengers into the impenetrable bank of mist that filled the expanse of water between the Doge's Palace and St George's. The gondolier did not raise his voice in song. Andreas Hofmeister reflected that it would have been out of character for any servant of the woman next to him to give a sign of joy, or even of spontaneous volition.

They proceeded so smoothly and effortlessly over the water he could not help wondering if it was a mechanical, rather than a human agency which propelled them forwards. Try as he might, when the fog thinned to reveal the individual steering them on their way, a spectre wreathed in greyish wisps, he could not rid himself of the delusion that this was no living creature, but an automaton. Were they at the mercy of a devilish contraption, devised for the sole purpose of executing its mistress's commands?

Seated beside him, Hedwiga Engelsfeld von Nettesheim spoke of the weather with such undisguised satisfaction she might have been taking personal credit for it.

'No house in Venice could provide the protection from prying eyes and ticklish ears we enjoy here,' she observed with gusto, 'not even my own. Should another boat draw close, my gondolier will give us ample warning of it. There being no danger of eavesdroppers, we can enter without further ado upon a matter that lies close to both our hearts.'

Rarely at a loss for words, Andreas found himself tongue-tied on this occasion. He had the sensation that the interview about to take place would have momentous consequences for his whole existence. His companion jumped to an erroneous conclusion.

'Have no fear, my dear Count Hofmeister,' she said. 'My intentions in inviting you for this short cruise were not amorous in the least. I do not expect you to behave as if you were my gallant.'

She giggled coquettishly, tilting her head at an angle which, in her opinion, showed her powdered hair and rouged cheeks to great advantage.

'I am assured that my charms remain undiminished, in spite of my advancing years and changeable health. But far be it from me to test their power on you. Come, now, tell me. What were you doing prowling in the vicinity of the theatre of St Hyginus's two afternoons ago?'

' "Prowling", dear baroness? What leads you to choose such a disagreeable term? Is it not perfectly normal for foreign visitors to explore each nook and cranny of this city with the utmost interest? I had been told that its greatest charm lies in these forgotten corners, unknown to any but the humblest of its inhabitants.'

'I had been watching you, without your knowledge, for the best part of an hour. You studied the building first from one angle, then another. For a while I thought you were preparing to make an architect's drawing of it. But you did not have the look of an architect.'

'Then may I ask you what you were doing "prowling" there yourself? Is it a habit of yours to loiter in obscure corners, observing individuals who are unknown to you? And why did you practically faint into my arms when at last we came face to face?'

'An irresistible attraction lures me to the streets around that theatre. The place gives me a sense of well-being, of power which I have known only in my happiest hours elsewhere. That afternoon, without warning, a different emanation struck me, like the onset of a fever. A repellent crone had crossed my path shortly before. Do you know who I mean? The flower-seller?'

Andreas vaguely remembered seeing an old woman sitting by a crate of oranges. But he could not recall her features clearly.

'Dear Hofmeister,' said Hedwiga, her voice tinged with exasperation, 'let us stop beating about the bush. We have much to offer each other in the way of assistance and advice. It would be foolish to persist in the deceptive charade that we are merely here as foreign tourists. Frankly, I cannot help but laugh when you accuse me of spying. You are the spy, not myself. Do not lie. My collaboration in this matter could bring you great advantages.

Were I to mention a certain Gottfried Schwarz, would that make you more willing to trust me?'

'Gottfried Schwarz? Goffredo Negri was the name I had for him.'

'The language makes little difference.'

'What do you know about the man?'

'Let the conditions of our treaty be clear. You are to tell me what brought you to Venice and to St Hyginus's, sparing no detail that might be of interest to me. In return, I promise to give you all the help I can in tracing the individual in question. I take it you are looking for Eleonora Calefati?'

Andreas gave such a start that the whole gondola shook.

'Then you know everything!'

'Not everything. I merely possess various pieces of a jigsaw both of us are trying to complete.'

He took a deep breath. He had little to lose. There was nothing secret in what he had to tell her. It was all public knowledge in Naples and still the subject of animated discussion there. Whatever information Hedwiga might pass on to him, as a result of what he was about to divulge, would represent sheer profit.

'The affair I am engaged in was entrusted to me by the highest possible authority. I have in mind no less a person than the Empress Maria Theresa herself.'

'And why did Her Majesty's choice fall on you?'

'When I first appeared at her court two springs ago, my reputation as a sceptic and a natural philosopher had gone before me. My scientific pursuits never interfered with regular attendance at the ceremonies of the Roman church. Nonetheless, Her Majesty was sufficiently concerned to recommend me to the attentions of her personal confessor.'

'A token of exceptional benevolence!'

'Indeed. The Empress's dealings with the world are characterised by a combination of unselfish energy with remarkable common sense and a high degree of shrewdness. Her religious faith, on the other hand, is uncomplicated and unquestioning. She chose as the companion of her private devotions a priest from Upper Austria, a peasant who would have been more at ease chopping wood, binding it into faggots, and driving them homewards on an ass's back, than hearing the confession of the most powerful woman in all Europe. Shocked by the cynicism and debauchery he encountered in the capital, Father Ambrose adopted a severely ascetic style of life. Lacking the intellectual gifts which would have allowed him to take part in theological debate, he devoted the best part of his energies to gathering information on the saintly figures of his native region, in the hope that, thanks to his position, he might achieve canonisation for at least one of them. His choice fell upon the Blessed Lavinia Moll, a widow from Kirchstetten of indubitable piety and the most spotless conduct, who had been lamed in a skating accident while still a young girl, and bore her sufferings with exemplary forbearance. When the Empress gave me into his care, he was on the point of realising this ambition. I submitted ungraciously to daily readings from the saints' lives and from a crude almanac Father Ambrose had brought with him from his native village. Luckily I was able to stifle the laughter his sermons provoked in me the very moment it looked set to explode. But I had to sit through the sessions with pursed lips in case an unwary comment should escape me.

'About that time, an envoy arrived in Vienna from Rome. He was what is known as the devil's advocate, and his business was to do everything he could to disprove the case for canonisation. I took a lively interest in his work, and was instrumental in helping him demonstrate that not one of the miracles performed by Father Ambrose's candidate had a basis in fact. The wonders attributed to her were the fruit of vulgar superstition, nothing more. Thanks to my efforts and those of the devil's advocate, she had to be content with beatification.

'Shortly after this debacle, I was summoned into the Empress's presence. Her Majesty has a talent for turning outwardly un-favourable circumstances to her own advantage. If the alliance formed against her poor confessor had gained the upper hand where Lavinia Moll was concerned, it also gave proof of talents, on my part, which she was determined to find a nobler use for. The Spanish ambassador to the imperial throne, Don Alvaro Sanchez de Almeida, a distant relative of hers for whom she nurtures a great affection, is connected by marriage with several of the principal families of the Kingdom of the Two Sicilies, whose capital, as you must know, is Naples. It was her desire to awaken my interest in a mysterious occurrence which took place in that city seven years ago. Her Majesty was content with half statements and hints, which may well reflect the terms in which she herself heard of the affair. If I had acted the devil's part well in opposing Father Ambrose, I was now to turn my abilities to better ends, she told me. She hesitated to give credit to Don Alvaro's claims that the evil one himself had had a hand in what happened. Nonetheless, she was confident that my skills in rational investigation would be tested to the utmost by this case.

'The events in question occurred in the very heart of Naples, in full view of its most illustrious and enlightened citizens, and caused untold heartbreak to a family in which the ambassador takes a lively interest. The Empress commanded me to depart post haste for Naples, and not to return until I could offer a satisfactory explanation for the mystery. She was confident that I would find the activities of Gottfried Schwarz no harder to account for than the miracles of the saintly widow of Kirchstetten. As proof that I have fulfilled her commission, I am to restore Eleonora Calefati safely to the bosom of her family before the bells of Easter chime.'

9

Hedwiga nodded.

'So you travelled here from Naples. Of course. I was warned you would arrive from the south rather than the north.'

'By whom?'

'That is irrelevant at present. Continue with your tale. Give me, if you can, a full description of Naples. I have never set foot in that city. It will allow me to form a clearer picture of the background to the mystery with which we are concerned.'

'It exceeds my powers, dear baroness, to offer an adequate account of the place. To begin with, the language spoken there is entirely foreign to me. Since I began to walk, the Italian tongue has rung constantly in my ears. My father's cook was from Modena. Our dancing teacher and our singing master were both Mantuans. The family chaplain came from Tuscany. The vernacular of Naples, however, bears little resemblance to the one used on the banks of the Arno.

'Everyone in the city speaks it: aristocrats as well as commoners. And what commoners they are! Though it is the most cultivated of Italy's capitals, famed the length and breadth of Europe for its operas and oratorios, its gardens and its ornate palaces, in short, a magnet drawing painters, sculptors and musicians from all four points of the compass, the tone of life is set by the plebeians. The slums and backstreets have been inhabited continuously since Vesuvius emptied lava and ashes along the shores of the bay, burying Pliny's uncle in the ruins of Pompeii.

'Have you any notion of what that means? Century has yielded place to century, religions and governments have changed, dynasties have faded and been supplanted by others less cankered in their stock. None has succeeded in imposing order on the chaos that is Naples. There are entire neighbourhoods of the city no upstanding citizen in his right mind would ever dream of setting foot in. Nobody less penniless and ragged than the pitiful creatures who live in those slums would dare to venture within their bounds. That human vermin has repeated the same proverbs, sworn the same oaths and practised the same superstitious rituals since the far-off day when one of their number brought a pitcher of chilled wine to Virgil, busy polishing the text of his *Aeneid*.

'I was told how, in the course of a famine two centuries ago, the common people assumed that their representative, named Starace, had colluded with the government in raising the price of bread, mistakenly as it turned out. They took a dreadful vengeance upon him. He was snatched from the convent of St Mary the New, where he and his colleagues were assembling for an audience with the Spanish viceroy. Having heaped insults and blows upon the poor fellow, they shed his blood outside the church of St Augustine. The mob drove a sharpened stake into his flesh and tossed him, agonising, into a ditch. Their victim begged them to summon a priest who could give him the last rites. In response, he was dragged out again, stripped naked and kicked through the streets till he expired. His limbs were torn apart and his bowels and heart extracted while still warm. The leader of the mob offered them to his famished followers, to calm their pangs of hunger. Even today it is a common saying in that city: "Watch your step, or you will meet the same fate as Starace."

'Eleonora departed this world on the first Saturday in December. The weather was exceptionally cold. The winters in Naples are normally brief and temperate. Even the rich dispense with any but the most rudimentary forms of heating in their houses. That year the noble families sat huddled indoors night after night, enveloped in blankets, with hats upon their heads they took to bed with them, their inborn love of gossip checked by the chattering of their teeth and the shivering of all their limbs. The volcano that dominates the landscape of the bay was deep in snow. Fishermen returning home at dawn found the pebbled inlets of the coast carpeted with white. The snowflakes melted directly into the incoming waves. The mob, that same mob which mauled Starace, changed in the individuals which composed it but not in its barbarous disposition, lit a bonfire in the square in front of the Calefati town house. Long before the first carriages trundled up the narrow, cobbled streets of the patrician quarter, they began their own festivity, singing and cavorting wildly to the accompaniment of guitars, zithers and bagpipes. What do you know of Elvezio Calefati?'

'His fortune is second only to that of the reigning monarch, and his sister is the wife of the chief minister. No wonder your ambassador takes such an interest in his affairs!'

'Should I carry on?' Andreas asked, a little piqued. 'Or are you so well informed that nothing I can say will come as news to you?'

Hedwiga waved her hand in dismissal.

'I have gathered together such information as I could. But have no fear. Everything you can tell me is of interest to me.'

'The eldest of the Calefati girls, Caterina, wedded a Hungarian prince from Transylvania that day. The reception was intended to outdo the finest held in Naples since the king ascended the throne. As coach after coach arrived in front of the gates, lackeys in brilliant liveries leant from their perches to beat a passage through the crowd with their sticks. Later that same evening these very fellows, excluded from their masters' celebrations, would warm their chilled limbs at the bonfires of the common people. As if a huge white goose were being plucked for the pot, high in the sky above their heads, outsize snowflakes circled down like random feathers, expiring with a hiss amidst the flames. The air was freezing.

'There can be no disputing the fact that the evening lived up to the highest expectations. Barely forty-five at the time, Elvezio Calefati was universally admired, and not infrequently maligned because of the favours he enjoyed. Envious tongues claimed that hidden enemies were responsible for the tragedy. It is a hypothesis I am inclined to discount. Powers of a different order were at work.

'A boar had been roasted on a spit in the warren of kitchens underneath the courtyard. Waiters paraded amongst the assembled guests, bearing succulent cuts of meat, along with fricassées of every conceivable winged creature, from farmyard breeds to songbirds. People insisted that there was no fish to be had in the whole bay of Naples during the next three days, so relentlessly had Calefati dragged it to supply his tables. The slaughter of eels was compared to the murder of the Holy Innocents at the hands of Herod. Fruits from the newly discovered territories beyond the western ocean, never seen in Naples till that night, were offered to the guests. They had been hollowed out and filled with sorbets and ice-creams flavoured with their pulp. The Prince was said to have obtained them with the help of merchants in Cadiz and Seville, though no one could explain how they reached Naples in such excellent condition. Coconuts were broken open to yield a quantity of milk such as an entire herd of cows could not have supplied inside a month. By a miracle of ingenuity, pyramids of fresh strawberries, decorated with leaves of tangy mint, were wheeled before the guests, as were barrowloads of white mulberries, sufficient to feed an army of silkworms. And all of this in December!'

'Gottfried had done his work well,' broke in Hedwiga. 'What an imagination!'

'Maestro Scarlatti directed a band of musicians in the gallery. As long as the guests were eating, they played Neapolitan airs. But once dinner was over, lines were formed for dancing. The orchestra supplied minuets and sarabandes, occasionally abandoning these more decorous figures for a vigorous tarantella or a sturdy furlan. Everyone present was so absorbed in the different kinds of entertainment on offer that midnight arrived with unprecedented speed. At the first stroke of the bell from the church of St Lawrence, the musicians laid down their bows. An air of expectancy filled the apartments. While it would have been a solecism for a member of the reigning family to appear, rumour had it that the king's current mistress, a certain Giovanna Falconieri, daughter of a vendor of printed ballads, who had risen to be principal soprano at the opera, would join the company at midnight. And this was not all. The principal attraction of the evening had been reserved for that hour.

'The name he went by was Goffredo Negri. He had numerous claims to fame: as natural philosopher, experimental scientist, alchemist, magician, conjuror and charlatan. As well as assisting Calefati in the planning of the feast, he had agreed to mount a display of magical arts for the assembled company. Having made her ceremonial entrance, Giovanna Falconieri took her seat at the front of the room, on one of a host of chairs which appeared, as if out of thin air, in the hands of liveried footmen. Over three hundred guests were crammed into the chamber. The expenditure on candles would have kept ten impoverished families in food and lodging until the end of the century. Caterina Calefati and her Hungarian husband sat on a raised dais at the back. From a vantage point in the gallery on the right side of the room, Prince Calefati watched his remaining daughters, Eleonora and Susanna, huddled in a corner, craning their necks to view the space where Negri would perform. They whispered excitedly to one another behind raised palms. The last bell of midnight tolled. Silence fell. Elvezio grasped his wife's hand convulsively as the magician made his way through the crowd. The outcome of the whole evening depended on this man.

'When I was a boy in Salzburg, one of the cathedral prebend-aries, who later turned completely insane, acquired a reputation for eccentricity thanks to an unusual pet. He would wander along the streets near to the sacred precinct, his open breviary in one hand, while the other held a cord with an outsize lobster at the end of it, trotting over the cobblestones at his heels. Trailing behind Goffredo Negri came, not a lobster, but a pair of creatures which have been described to me as amalgams of a tortoise and a camel. They followed at a respectful distance. No cord was to be seen. We may presume that they propelled themselves along, rather than being pulled. Each was the size of a large dog and had a solid grey shell on its back which rose into two points, terminating in flattened cones, such as you can see on the chimneys of the houses of the poorer sort in northern Italy. The cones lifted and fell, emitting puffs of steam from underneath, as if the creatures were powered by an interior mechanism. Indeed, witnesses have spoken of them as moving forward so smoothly they might have been travelling on wheels.

'Negri's first turns were banal and thoroughly predictable. He apparently intended to lure his audience into a false sense of security. He produced cooing doves from the sleeves of his long, black cloak, eggs from behind his ears and, last of all, a knotted cord with a fish hook at its end from his left nostril. Then he walked past the guests in the front row, extracting incongruous objects from their wigs, their headgear and their laps. Giovanna Falconieri was left to the end. Much to her alarm, a red griffin emerged from her right armpit. Emitting discordant cries just like a turkey, it lifted itself into the air and perched on the upper edge of the frame of a large painting hanging on the wall behind its master. Turning towards the bird, he asked if it had any messages to deliver to the members of the audience.

' "Gabriele Mendola!" it squawked, having first croaked several times, as if to clear its throat. "Can a cuckold's horns truly be sprouting for the third time from your temples? You had better find out what it is in your wife's cauldron that distracts her attention so regularly!"

'There was general mirth. Everyone knew that the Baroness Mendola's newest lover went by the name of Calderone.

' "Mariano Esposito!" the bird continued. "You are making a poor job of tending the king's poultry. Both eggs and feathers end up in your own family's nest!"

'Need I add that Esposito was a notoriously corrupt administrator of taxes, who devoted a substantial part of the sums he collected to building a new town house for himself, and to providing ample dowries for his daughters? You can imagine, dear Baroness, the excitement and titillation caused by what I take to have been Negri's skill in ventriloquism. People were thrilled to see their acquaintances held up to shame. At the same time, they could not mask their fear that they themselves might be the butt of the next joke.

'The magician quickly tired of this game. He clapped his hands, and a flock of giant moths rose up from the floor and settled on the chandeliers which illuminated the room. He called to them with acute, animal cries, and they began to beat phosphorescent wings of black and gold, extinguishing the candles with the breeze that they produced. Next their insect bodies started to glow with light, like living crucibles. Sprays of sparks emerged from their antennae, soaring up towards the vaulted ceiling to descend in incandescent showers rich with all the colours of the rainbow. There was an outburst of applause. The moths disappeared. The chandeliers burned as before.'

'How do you explain a feat of that kind?' put in Hedwiga.

'It could be a collective delusion instilled in the spectators by suggestion,' Andreas surmised. 'What followed is harder to account for. Negri asked for a helper from among the guests. The hubbub of voices greeting the return of normal lighting died away. The merest rustling of a robe could be heard in the silence that fell. No one dared to move, in case by doing so they should draw the magician's attention and lead his choice to fall on them. Negri was displeased. The expression on his face grew bleaker by the minute. His left eyebrow formed an arch, while his right remained quite still. His gaze was still more piercing than before. All of a sudden light footsteps were heard. Eleonora, Elvezio Calefati's youngest daughter, made her way to the front of the room. Her complexion was fair, not dark, and she had auburn hair she washed and combed each morning. Looks of that kind are not uncommon among the women of southern Italy. They are a legacy from the Norman overlords who governed Sicily and Apulia and built the geometrical fortress at Castel del Monte with the help of Arab mathematicians. She was fourteen years old. That night her tresses were gathered in a tower on top of her head, held in place by a finely woven golden net. Even if Negri's request had not cowed them, the grace and energy of her movements would have silenced the onlookers. When she reached the magician's side and turned to face them, she was consumed by fire. Some people say the flames were like a veil she danced behind, others that she began to run within them and vanished into the far distance. Others still, who were watching her eyes, said she seemed to perceive a doorway and walk through it.

'Giovanna Falconieri was sitting so close she had to shield her face from the heat. When she put her hands down and dared to look, all that remained was a pile of whitening embers, moving gently in the draught from beneath the great doors to the rear. The singer cried out in horror. Several men sprang to their feet, their hands upon their swords. Women fainted, or began screaming that they were all doomed to perish in a general conflagration. People rushed forward to apprehend the culprit. The room was plunged in darkness. Servants knocked their masters to the ground. The unfortunate individuals who lost their footing were trampled upon in the pandemonium caused by those whose only concern was to save their own skins at whatever cost.'

'The magician had disappeared.'

'Naturally. Calefati, whose hair turned white that very instant, ordered the chill embers that had once been his daughter, and which resembled nothing more than the remains of a fire left to burn out overnight, should be swept up and placed in an urn. He has them still.'

'Nonsense!' scoffed Hedwiga. 'The ashes are a red herring. Gottfried took with him all of her he needed.'

The side of their craft grated against stonework, returning Andreas with a shock to the lagoon and its mists. Without his noticing, the gondolier had steered them back to the quays. It appeared that the interview was at an end.

'My dear Hofmeister, our afternoon together has been most profitable. Have no fear, I intend to keep my share of our bargain. But if I am to tell you what I know of Gottfried, or Goffredo, as you insist on calling him, it must be in a different setting. Be outside the church of the Holy Apostles the day after tomorrow, at the same hour as our rendezvous today. A servant of mine will meet you there, and lead you to my place of residence. Until then, I bid you goodbye.'

Hedwiga gave him her gloved hand to kiss. When he set foot on the quay, she was little more than a sooty smear against the general darkness. Though he kept his eyes trained on the spot, there was only mist where she had been. The noise of her gondola's prow breasting the black waters faded away to nothing.

IO

Confronted with the severed head of her father Polydorus, Queen Artemisia fainted. It did not matter that this man had invaded her adoptive homeland at the head of an army, or had slain her husband Ilius in single combat. She was so overwhelmed by grief she lost all power of speech and collapsed into the arms of her confidante. Meanwhile the dreadful object was gradually dying the white sheet they had wrapped it in a garish red.

'B minor,' Domenico muttered to Limentani, who did not share his gift of perfect pitch.

The man who played first oboe in the orchestra at St John Chrysostom had a reputation which extended far beyond the lagoon capital. The composer had had the inspired idea of prefacing Artemisia's most important aria with an extended obbligato for the instrument, rendered all the more affecting by an unusual choice of key. Thanks to the oboe's reedy tone, the soloist was able to give the rich melismas of his part a tear-throbbing intensity. The audience, who had been showing signs of restlessness as the second act approached its close, at last fell silent, curious to hear how the singer would cope when her turn came to shape the melody.

'He is exceptionally good,' observed Limentani. 'I must see what can be done to poach him.'

All through the performance vendors had been plying those who could only afford a standing ticket with drinking water, roasted pumpkin seeds and doughnuts. Now they paused in their circuits. Queen Artemisia's bosom heaved in anticipation of the not inconsiderable feats of vocal agility she had contracted to perform. Two or three paces away, her confidante followed every movement with an expression of acute concern, whether provoked by the sight of an orphaned daughter's distress or the unreliability of the singer's memory it was hard to tell. Steeling herself, the monarch took the head from the messenger who had brought it on to the stage. He fell to his knees, in an attitude of profound sorrow, while she became absorbed in contemplation of the horrid bundle. She held it at arm's length, no doubt for fear a stray drop of blood might soil her extravagant costume.

The background was formed by a perspective that took Domenico's breath away when the curtains parted. He had seen something similar, on a much smaller scale, in the town house of a Roman aristocrat, an art lover who was an acquaintance of Cardinal Albani's. To one side of the library on the ground floor, a verandah gave access to a colonnade, barely wide enough for two men to walk down. At the far end lay a garden, with a statue of an antique soldier on a pedestal, neatly framed within an arch. In reality, the statue was less than two thirds life size. The architecture of the colonnade had been skilfully distorted so as to make it appear twice its actual length, thus magnifying artificially the dimensions of the statue. To stroll down it was an unsettling experience. The eye and the legs contradicted one another, as if life were rushing by at a much greater speed than it ought rightly to have done. One had a sense of being crushed.

The stage decorations at St John Chrysostom were of grandiose proportions. The foremost sections were three-dimensional. The walls of the palace chamber where the action was set reached to the height of the proscenium arch, receding on either side only a touch more sharply than they would have done in actuality. They were padded with damask, punctuated at regular intervals by flat pilasters. The roof was deeply coffered, in the ancient Roman style. Embossed roses marked the points at which struts intersected. A double colonnade, beginning behind the singers' shoulders, was prolonged on a painted backdrop, so convincingly one could have sworn it extended several times the depth of the auditorium. The columns terminated in a terrace, from which the feathery tips of cypress trees were silhouetted against a cloudless sky.

Limentani had carried out his avowed intention of penetrating the enemy camp that very evening. Everything had to be done in a great rush. There was no opportunity to have a meal before setting off for the theatre. Domenico was under the illusion that, since he had consumed so little solid food during the preceding days, the fish soup he had eaten that afternoon would keep him satisfied for quite a while. Far from it. His appetite had been aroused, and before he knew it he was hungry again. He could not help gazing longingly into the candlelit taverns they passed on their route to St John Chrysostom. He scolded himself for being so frivolous. Offered the chance of gleaning all sorts of tips that might be of use to him in his new career, he could only think about filling his stomach.

They proceeded from the theatre at St Hyginus's to Limentani's rooms near St Zachary. With characteristic tact, the impresario did not enquire after the foul-smelling street where Domenico had taken lodgings. He pressed a richly embroidered jacket on the younger man. In front, it was cut away above the waist. Behind, the fabric descended to the back of the knees, shaped in a fashion that reminded him of a swallow's tail.

'Next, a mask,' Limentani announced.

The shelves of the mask maker's shop were lined with glistening creations in black and white. Domenico had difficulty turning his back on them, so as to follow the conversation between the impresario and the owner. He had the odd impression that, the minute he stopped looking, mysterious eyes would fill each pair of empty holes, scrutinising him from behind and, as likely as not, mocking what they saw.

'Do I absolutely have to wear one?'

Limentani was shocked.

'Men and women of noble lineage are required by law to wear masks every time they attend a theatrical performance. The merchant classes follow their example. During carnival, anyone who wants to can use them. That is the point. The poorest commoner may pass for an aristocrat. How could you think we would not take part in the game?'

The mist had thinned out when the sun set. Nevertheless, Limentani thought it wise to have a caddie guide them to the theatre. Time was of the essence. The man carried a lantern, and knew the quickest routes and shortcuts through the tight mesh of canals and alleyways that lie between St Mark's and the Rialto bridge. As far as Domenico could tell, there was more theatre going on in the streets of Venice than they were likely to find in any enclosed space, where they would moreover have to pay for the privilege of seeing it. Notwithstanding its mistress's designs upon himself, a puritanical atmosphere had reigned in the Calerghi household. He did not think Michele Calerghi would have responded favourably to the idea of his exploring the temptations Venice had to offer after dark. His former employer was so stingy Domenico lacked the cash for a glass of white wine of the poorest quality, not to mention headier pleasures.

As they hurried along, the caddie first, Limentani behind him, single-minded and intent, Domenico bringing up the rear, the youngest of the three kept looking over his shoulders at clusters and individual figures in the crowd. His heart was in his mouth with the beauty and excitement of it all. He had to keep reminding himself that this was not an exceptional occurrence. He had been released into this world, which from now on could be his own to investigate and sample as he wished.

The commonest masks they saw were painted white, with a long protruding nose like Pulcinella's. A large proportion of passers-by was dressed in black. Many wore a mantle of fabric or lace which fell from beneath the hat to cover the shoulders and the chest. Nothing natural or human could be seen, no hair, no trace of cheek or temple, just the rigid mask and the glittering fabric. Domenico had a notion that several ample bosoms flitting by him were padding, nothing more. The clothing of the lower half of the body, either breeches or the billowing petticoats without which the richer women of the city would never have been seen in public, was a mask, too, in its way, revealing nothing of the anatomy beneath. Everything could be altered so effortlessly, name, sex and social class, it made him feel quite dizzy.

Rather more than halfway to the theatre, they crossed an open space which appeared to be enormous, in the heart of this city where people and buildings were everywhere huddled on top of one another. Like all except the meanest streets in Venice, the square, named after the church of St Mary called *Formosa* or 'Beautiful' that stood on one side, was magnificently lit, at the Republic's expense. A bonfire burned in the centre.

There were plentiful touches of colour in the crowd, especially among men and women of the poorer sort. The girls, especially, put on their finest frocks of green, yellow or red, with white lace petticoats peeping out underneath, embroidered bodices and an apron covering the lap. The men wore caps with feathers in them, or floppy berets, sort of upturned stockings, which did not stay rigid but collapsed at different angles, like an iced cake left to melt in the sun, its careful architecture crumbling unpredictably. They came upon a group of wild men dressed in animal skins, shod in leather moccasins, with leafy garlands on their heads and false moustaches. Two were strumming at mandolins. A third had the windbag of his pipes gripped under his arm. As they came close, he gave a jab with his elbow which produced a nasal groan. His fingers skipped back and forth across the chanter's holes, warming up to play a tune.

Even Limentani could not resist the lure of the spectacle in the square.

'The plague doctor,' he whispered, nudging his companion's arm.

Domenico was scared by the figure. The previous summer an outbreak of the plague had been prevented in the nick of time, by having the incomers who had brought it from the Levant confined in a former lepers' colony on the lagoon. It puzzled Domenico that the symbol of such a terrifying threat should be turned into a mask at carnival. Perhaps it served to exorcise the fear that still pervaded the city, even though it was over thirty years since an epidemic had taken a serious toll of the population. The man Limentani was pointing to resembled nothing more than a gannet. Rather than an exaggerated nose, he had a beak as long as his forearm, which a genuine plague doctor would have filled with herbs and spices renowned for keeping germs at bay. He had a stiff and spotless ruff around his neck, of a kind nobody wore any longer, which marked him out as a ghost from the past. So, at least, people hoped. His black cloak was trimmed down the front and round the ample cuffs with ermine, an indication of the financial rewards awaiting those prepared to brave infected houses with offers of a cure. The doctor never touched his patients. In his right hand he carried a long wand which he used for lifting bedclothes, so as to inspect the sores upon the victim's bodies. Domenico turned away with a shudder.

Ahead of them, animated voices engaged in friendly banter. His eyes were drawn by a man roughly his own height, got up like a baby, in a cascade of linen folds and frills. His face was made up, with outsize tears trailing down each cheek etched in black charcoal. He had a dummy in his mouth and a baggy cap on his head. The figure in charge of him looked like a woman of the people. There was, however, a touch of exaggeration in the floral motifs sewn along the hem of her dress and down her bodice. She raised her voice, shouting at the baby in shrill, piercing tones. The bystanders guffawed at the torrent of insults she was hurling at him.

'It's the *gnaga*,' said the caddie with a tolerant smile. 'You know, *gna gna*, the way a cat goes . . .'

Looking more closely, Domenico got a shock. The double circle of pearls around the nursemaid's neck emphasised, rather than concealed, the Adam's apple. The knotted scarf at his shoulders was pulled provocatively down, disclosing the top of a very hairy chest. Although he had shaved meticulously, a heavy shadow on his jowls underlined the factitiousness of the role the man had assumed.

Just next to them, a group of youths was taunting the *gnaga*, using a dialect so quick and racy Domenico could not understand a word. They appeared to know the target of their humour personally. One of them addressed him by his name. Suddenly a hand was laid on Domenico's shoulder. The fellow next to him, smiling broadly, was about to share a joke with him, and wanted to make sure of his attention first. That very minute, Limentani plucked impatiently at his sleeve from the other side. Domenico was left with an image of lips forming a syllable, a neatly trimmed moustache above them, while the eyes shone bright and tantalising through the slits in the mask, like a child's peeping out from behind a curtain.

As they approached St John Chrysostom, it got harder and harder to force their way through the press of bodies. It was the most prestigious and most expensive of the Venetian theatres, and until recently had offered an exclusive diet of serious and tragic compositions. Domenico wondered what chance they would have of finding a seat, if all the people around them were bound for the same place. The increasingly crowded streets, however, were an indication of their closeness to the Rialto, rather than of the theatre's powers of attraction. Anyone who wanted to cross the Grand Canal had to take this route if they did not want to hire a gondola. The caddie led them off the main thoroughfare, to the right, past the church, then into a courtyard enclosed by buildings on all sides. The entrance to the theatre was tucked into one corner. A man sat in a doorway, selling printed tickets by the light of a candle that smoked in the gentle breeze.

Domenico had frequently seen operas in both Bologna and Rome. Performances there were private affairs. The public was drawn uniformly from the better classes of society and points of etiquette were scrupulously observed. In Venice, the theatres were open to rich and poor alike. He found the resulting mix of clothing styles and faces disconcerting. Limentani sent the caddie to buy tickets for them, then paid him what he was due. When they reached the foyer it became clear that many guests of quality preferred to arrive by water, from the canal on the north side, disembarking directly into the body of the theatre. A lackey conducted the two foreigners to seats on the second floor, where their view of the stage would not be obstructed by the orchestra, in particular by the ornamental neck of the theorbo which accompanied the recitatives.

Limentani had bought a copy of the libretto from a vendor on the stairs.

'This is something we must attend to promptly,' he told Domenico. 'We are required by law to print the texts of all the operas we perform, in advance of the opening night, so that the censors can inspect them if there are protests.' He added, in surprise: '*Artemisia, Queen of the Parthians*! But that is not what I expected to hear at all! Pacifico Anselmi's new piece was to begin tonight. Can he have postponed it yet again?'

They were interrupted by the arrival of a couple who were to share their box, a diminutive old man carrying a lorgnette, his face buried inside a wig several sizes too large for him, accompanied by a smartly turned out matron with a still trim figure, whom he introduced as his 'niece'.

Domenico leant both elbows on the balustrade and surveyed the auditorium. The commoners were crowded between the lowest tier of boxes and the stage, coughing and spitting, jostling each other good-humouredly so as to have a better view once the performance started. The interior was shaped like a cauldron knocked over on to its side, narrower towards the proscenium, fatter at the centre, the flat bottom corresponding to the most prestigious boxes directly opposite the stage. There were no fewer than five tiers, stretching right the way round. Two more boxes at each level were squeezed into the proscenium arch, so that the people sitting in the lowest places overlooked the orchestra, and could have blown down the neck of the bass player.

The place was illuminated by an enormous chandelier, which must surely block the view of the stage from the higher tiers. One of the most magical moments in the whole evening came when the players struck up the overture and, thanks to a mechanism whose existence Domenico had not been warned about, the roof opened over their heads and the chandelier was drawn up into it, leaving the auditorium in darkness.

The boxes had their own sources of light. They were far more than simply a means of viewing operas. It was as if sections of two hundred drawing rooms had been transported here and assembled to form a living wall. The people in them spared little thought for the music or the drama as it unfolded. Each box was a stage in its own theatre, offering its own performance. There was not a face without a mask to be seen anywhere but in the pit. People played cards, received their friends, ate, drank, haggled over marriage contracts and concluded business deals. Here and there a candle flickered and went out. Domenico suspected the inmates might be making love. It was possible to draw a curtain to shield the interior from public view.

With the habitual bad manners of Venetian audiences, every-thing was tossed on to the heads of the standing customers below – the dregs of a wine glass, candle ends, a discarded love letter, abundant spittle. Ladies and gentlemen acknowledged each other's presence with a nod, a deep bow or the wave of a fan. The doors to the boxes were rarely still for five minutes at a time. Visits were made and returned and assignations fixed. Not far to their right, taking exception to a remark of her lover's, a lady in a sumptuous pink robe and a silver mask slapped him resoundingly across the face, gathered her skirts and left. And all of this before the opera had even started!

'Why does everyone come so early?' Domenico asked the old man beside him, who presented himself as Giorgio Venier, and who he hoped would prove a ready source of information.

'Do not imagine,' came the answer, 'that the performance waits until the curtain rises. We have it here before our eyes! All of fashionable Venice is present tonight, to wonder at itself no less than at what appears on stage. Where would the fun be in attending an opera if you were the only person watching? Tell me that, now! What kind of entertainment would that be? Do you think you could get any pleasure out of it?'

Domenico shook his head, wide-eyed.

'This whole building is a stage, the entrance hall, the stairs, the refreshment kiosks. On the first night, maybe, people pay greater attention to the singers. But all of us, yourselves excepted, have followed the fortunes of Queen Artemisia at least five times since Christmas. We know the bits that are worth looking out for.

'Mind you,' and the old fellow leered expressively, 'it's different when the ballet starts. Here in Venice we are used to watching a ballet in between the acts. It is a highlight of the evening. No matter how many times you see a young girl's legs, they will always merit further inspection! And the ladies, though they might deny it, observe the bodies of the men who dance with equal attention. Make no mistake. My niece here could identify any one of them from his backside.'

Domenico was aware that the door to their box had opened. Limentani's efforts at remaining incognito had proved unavailing. This was the first of many visits he would receive in the course of the performance. Domenico was too engrossed in his conversation with Venier to give much heed.

'Look down there!' the old man went on, pointing to a box in the tier below. The youth sitting in it could not be much older than seventeen. There was no trace of a beard on his puffy, bloated cheeks. To his astonishment, Domenico noticed an elaborate beauty spot on one of them, though the poor creature had little enough in the way of looks to call attention to. His jewelled waistcoat glinted in the light from the great chandelier overhead. The powder scattered over his wig gave it an eerily blue veneer. Altogether, his get up was in execrable taste.

'That is Pacifico Anselmi,' said his companion, 'the charlatan who continues to cheat us all. We were promised a fantastic opera set in the isles of the Hesperides, with flying monsters, magical gardens and the drowning of Atlantis at the end. It was supposed to start on the feast of St Stephen, the day after Christmas. I rented these seats for the entire season, so as not to miss a minute of the fun. The drowning of Atlantis! Can you imagine the amount of water that will require? They claim Anselmi is putting the finishing touches to the score. Then why is he in his box night after night? I smell a rat.'

'Ahah!' put in Limentani, ready to join in the conversation now his visitor had left. 'Maybe you have inside information on the affair?'

Old Venier tutted loudly.

'I have no secrets to divulge. In my opinion the creature, far from being a genius, is an artistic hoodlum. Look at the way he is decked out, like an expensive doll! He reminds me of nothing so much as the marzipan cherub with a trumpet, blowing his cheeks out at the top of a wedding cake! He has taken fright. He may hoodwink audiences in Naples or Milan. A Venetian public will not put up with his tomfoolery. The fellow is heading for a fiasco, and he knows it.'

'Is that his protectress sitting next to him?'

Domenico gave a start. He had assumed that the prodigy was being chaperoned by his mother. Her clothes were only a trifle less garish than Pacifico's. The hair on her head was built up into a teetering beehive shape. It looked so weighty and precarious he suspected she would need assistance if she were to return to a standing position without falling flat on her face. Peasant women could carry pots that size upon their heads. The prodigy's companion lacked their poise. He found himself smiling. Gossip had it that elaborate constructions of this kind needed a camouflaged iron frame to keep them in place. A priest with a bent for scientific pursuits, having recently designed a lightning conductor for the bell tower of St Mark's, had declared his willingess to supply smaller models to society ladies, for fear a thunderbolt might strike their hairpieces.

'Precisely. That is Madame Landowska, great-aunt to the king of Poland. I am no harsher a judge of morals than other men of my station in Venice, but I cannot help finding it unnatural that a woman of fifty-four should conduct a relationship with a boy one third her age.'

'How can you be sure that they are lovers?' countered Limentani. 'He hardly looks like a knight of the bedchamber.'

'What do you think she follows him around for? Is it his compositions that keep her at his side?' scoffed the old man.

'When you hear his music,' the impresario answered quietly, 'you may be ready to believe such is the case.'

Giorgio Venier spluttered indignantly and turned back to the woman at his side. Domenico resisted the tempation to ask what he considered to be an acceptable difference in age. His companion was twenty years his junior if not more. Why should there be one law for him and another for Madame Landowska? This was the point at which two panels slid open in the ceiling and the chandelier, with all its candles burning, started its upward journey. The director had taken his place at the keyboard. He nodded to the players, and the first chords of the overture rang out.

I I

There was a certain amount of hissing and shushing, followed by a general murmur of pleasure when the curtain rose. The plebeians below had evidently not seen the piece as often as their betters, or were less easily jaded by its splendours. The first scene showed the forces of Polydorus laying siege to the walls of Queen Artemisia's capital from the sea, complete with galleons, grappling hooks, rope ladders and a fully operational battering ram.

Though he followed the action closely till the city gates were forced open, Domenico could not chase two competing images from his mind. The first, which superimposed itself on the spectacle as it unfolded before him, was of the machine they had discovered at St Hyginus's. The stage around was fully lit, but the cloud machine preserved a core of darkness, as though it harboured a secret menace still to be revealed. As before, it made him think of an enormous bird, which would spread its wings and fly out from under the proscenium arch to terrorise the public. The illusion was so strong he had to blink repeatedly to bring himself back to the less disturbing reality of combat and slaughter in ancient Parthia.

The other image was of the man who had been on the point of speaking to him in the square. Unlikely as it was, he could not help hoping he and his friends would somehow end up in the same opera house. Without admitting it to himself, Domenico had scrutinised the boxes to the right and left of their own, in search of a group of masked figures he might reasonably identify as them. But then, given the way they had been behaving, they would more likely be standing in the pit amidst the lower class of spectators. Who could tell what brand of mischief they might get up to!

He felt guilty for not following their rivals' performance with the concentration it deserved, all the more so as he sensed a growing seriousness of mood in Limentani. The older man was coming to a sober estimation of the task which he had set himself. The theatre at St John Chrysostom had not gained its reputation for nothing. The auditorium and stage were considerably larger than those he had at his disposal at St Hyginus's. And the quality of the singing and playing, he could not deny it, was unlikely to be surpassed by any company he might put together in the next few days. Was he headed for a humiliating defeat?

Shortly after they had closed to mark the end of the first act, the curtains parted again and the ballet started. It took the form of a pastoral interlude, in which Parthian nymphs and shepherds cavorted across the stage. The nymphs bore quivers on their back, and were waving bows and arrows in a menacing but nonetheless attractive manner. The shepherds had elaborate crooks, caps of felt, pleated skirts and criss-cross leggings. All the costumes had a vaguely oriental feel.

'I need to stretch my legs,' Limentani muttered. 'Will you join me?'

Although Domenico had not noticed a significant number of spectators leaving the auditorium, they found the stairs and foyer thronged with people, almost all of them masked, many wearing fancy dress. Could there be some, he wondered, who did not even bother to enter the auditorium, too absorbed with the goings-on front of house to give a thought to the opera? His heartbeat quickened when he remembered the advice he had received from a guest of Cardinal Albani's. The man told him that, if he were ever in a strange city, the corridors of the opera house would be an excellent place to look for . . . He did not complete the sentence.

One of a group of figures standing in an archway called to Limentani. Aware that his air of preoccupation risked being interpreted as haughtiness, Domenico hastened to take part in the introductions, shaking in turn the hand of each person presented to him. The last he took belonged to a figure he found oddly familiar, a tall, burly man with a fashionably wide-brimmed hat, whose waistcoat was covered in delicate traceries of black lace. It was a sign of considerable wealth. Domenico tried to calculate what its value would be, converted into meals. As Domenico released the hand, Limentani, who was presenting

Domenico as his musical director, mentioned Cardinal Albani. Though the man in the waistcoat's face was hidden, the name produced a violent physical reaction. It was as if Domenico's touch had suddenly scalded him. Then he renewed his grip, in acknowledgement and a kind of furtive welcome.

The man's name flooded Domenico's consciousness but made no sense. What kind of complicity could he be seeking?

'My dear maestro, I have the honour of presenting Onofrio Carpi to you,' Limentani said. 'He is the legal representative of our employer, Donato Gradenigo. It is he who will decide the precise terms of our contracts. I would advise you to make an ally of him as quickly as you can.'

There was a burst of urbane laughter from Carpi's companions.

'Our young friend has no cause to worry,' said the lawyer in ringing tones. 'I feel as if we have known each other for some time already.'

Domenico's perceptions were unusually heightened. After all, he had effectively been watching two stage sets during much of the preceding hour: one imagined, one perceived. When he heard the lawyer's voice, it brought home to him, with a sickening certainty, where and under what circumstances he had previously heard it. His cheeks flushed. He must be blushing intensely. He looked away.

There had been a ceaseless movement of figures around them during this exchange and, in spite of his embarrassment, another part of his mind had noticed a figure which passed, then passed again, then stopped beside a pillar. As Carpi released his hand, Domenico, keen not to meet his gaze directly, looked over the lawyer's shoulder. When he did so, the figure that had paused lifted its mask.

Now he could add the rest of the face to the lips and the moustache. It was the red-haired man who had tried to speak to him earlier that evening. Though Domenico felt surprise, there was also an inevitability about it all. He had been certain that the man would reappear. The expression on his face struck home with a peculiar force. It was pleading and playful at one and the same time. Its apparent lightheartedness concealed and revealed a message of a much more urgent nature. The message was a question. Domenico gave the answer without meaning to, for he had already held the man's eyes longer than idle curiosity could justify. The man made a movement with his hand which might signify: 'Afterwards.'

Domenico wondered if his behaviour towards Limentani and the others seemed as rude as he suspected. The battles he had witnessed on stage during the first act were now transferred inside his stomach. Assault followed assault. As he and Limentani mounted the stairs back to their box, he had to concentrate on setting one foot down in front of the other, for fear he might lose his balance and fall over.

'Does music always have this effect on you?' the impresario asked, gruffly but not unaffectionately, once they had taken their places again. He sounded as if he were impressed. 'One would say that you exist on a different plane from ordinary mortals.'

'Forgive me, but I have realised the seriousness of the task that lies before us,' answered Domenico, recovering his presence of mind. 'Does it not daunt you, too?'

By the time Artemisia's great aria arrived he was considerably calmer. He amused himself during much of the second act by trying to visualise what the music he heard would look like written down. It was an effort, but not a great one, and helped keep other images and speculations at bay. At the same time he paid particular attention to the manner in which the keyboard and the theorbo interpreted the figured bass, making mental notes of possible improvements to their version of it.

The third act was dominated by an ineffectual castrato. The man's unease came over in his very presence. He waddled rather than strode on to the stage and could not get his sword to sit correctly. It kept bobbing at his waist like an importunate child. His higher notes were wobbly. Domenico could have sworn that he was cutting swathes through the complex ornamentation he ought to have been giving the melodic line, either because his voice was no longer capable of carrying it out, or because he was so nervous he feared coming unstuck and making a fool of himself. He played the part of a Roman general, at the head of an army Artemisia had summoned to her defence and, of course, the closing scene of the evening saw them happily wedded amid the hurrahs and fraternal embraces of Parthian and Roman troops.

Ungracious though it was, Limentani felt distinctly relieved that the quality of the performance declined during the latter part of the opera. Coming to the theatre at St John Chrysostom was a challenge he had been determined to face. In the last analysis, he was not quite so overawed as he had anticipated. He was ready to reward himself.

'Now,' he said, putting an arm around Domenico's shoulders, 'I invite you to join me as a guest of Signora Putti, who manages Venice's most respected house of ill repute. We shall wine and dine like royalty and then, if the young ladies take our fancy, you and I shall retire to separate rooms and pass what remains of the night in pleasurable dalliance. All at my expense, naturally. Let it be my way of welcoming you to the troupe.'

Domenico mumbled an awkward refusal, which he found a clearer form for when Limentani repeated the invitation. The enclosed square in front of the theatre was one single, compact mass of bodies, greeting one another, commenting on what they had seen, forming groups before they set off, waving farewell and adjusting hats and collars, for the air outside was chill. Domenico watched the impresario disappear into the throng then heard his name called from behind. It was the lawyer. He bent over Domenico, twirling the head of a long black walking stick in the fingers of his left hand.

'I have not forgotten the masque of Ganymede,' he said, 'held in the gardens of Cardinal Albani's villa two summers ago. Nor the delicious role you played in the shrubbery once darkness had fallen. You never learned my name or where I came from. That made our dalliance all the more pleasurable. I was able to pretend you were a sprite from the woods, or a beardless youth from Ganymede's retinue, rather than the young musician who had played so delectably a matter of hours before.'

'We know each other now,' Domenico said, rather sourly, for he resented being reminded of the details of the incident. 'And apparently we are to do business with one another.'

'I hope,' said Carpi, 'we will have occasion to do business of more than one description. Shall we walk a little distance together?'

They were hemmed in on all sides by the crowd which had emerged from the theatre. Without quite admitting it to himself, Domenico had been looking round for the red-haired man. But he could think of no good reason for turning down the lawyer's proposal. Carpi's stature, and the impressive stick he carried, meant that bodies parted as if by magic to let them pass. His step was measured and confident.

'This city, you must know, is a very different setting from that dear clergyman's rural retreat. Our every movement is a feast for interested eyes. Were we to release our vigilance, the slightest misdemeanour could be the object of an anonymous denunciation, deposited in one of the fissures so thoughtfully provided for this purpose by our government. Do you get my drift? In a matter of hours it would be in the hands of the forces of order. A man in my position cannot risk a scandal of that kind.'

'What do you imagine we might do that would cause anyone to inform on us?' Domenico asked guardedly. He wanted to see if the lawyer would put into words a proposition he was merely hinting at at present.

'My dear boy, do not play the innocent with me. What you have already done would be enough to earn you five years in the galleys, were knowledge of it to reach the appropriate ears.'

'Then we are equally at risk.'

'Indeed,' said Carpi, undeterred by the reception he was getting. 'All the more reason for the two of us to stick together. I had learned of your arrival in Venice, you know,' he chortled, 'and found that whole ridiculous business with Calerghi's wife endlessly amusing. I suppose I could have leapt to your defence, if that would not have meant exposing you to even greater opprobrium.'

'As you will see, I have resolved my difficulties without recourse to your professional skills.'

'Thanks to Ansaldo Limentani. Does he know about your inclinations?'

Domenico came to a halt, eager to put an end to the conversation so that he could at least find time to think. If he had been less dazzled by the events of the day and his unexpected change in fortunes, and more capable of cool reflection, he would have realised the emptiness of Carpi's insinuated threats. Limentani was an experienced man of the theatre, who must have encountered every variety of human passion and sensuality in the course of his work. And it was hard to believe he could be unaware of the special penchant that drew the members of Cardinal Albani's coterie together, even though the company, on the evening when he heard Domenico, had been mixed and unexceptionable. He had, of course, been absent from the masque of Ganymede.

Instead, Domenico allowed the man to frighten him.

'You do not mean you plan to tell him about them?'

'Of course not. You may rely upon me. But may I suggest you call in at my office tomorrow afternoon? To discuss the terms of your contract, of course! Our mutual friend Limentani can give you the directions.'

12

With a swirl of his mantle's edge, the lawyer vanished. The crowds from the theatre were dispersing. Domenico had no idea where he was. The mist had thickened once again. He moved to one side of the footpath where he found himself, so as to let the groups of figures wending their way home pass by. At his back, the canal was thronged with gondolas. Suddenly there was a loud hiss. He turned round. At the height of his chest, gripping the end of a pole which disappeared into the water, a three-cornered hat upon his head, was the red-haired man. Domenico had already noticed, while he was in the theatre, the amazing quickness with which one learned to identify masked figures in the absence of a face. A detail of clothing, the angle of a head, the balance of two shoulders was enough.

'Jump in!' the man called. 'We've been looking for you everywhere!'

He let his body take him. The boat rocked gently as hands guided him to a seat. There were four youths in it, one carrying a lantern. Another lantern hung from a hook on the raised stern. Domenico got untold relief from the simple fact of moving upon water, as if it were a more trustworthy element than stone or bricks. He sensed the red-haired man's enjoyment as he propelled them forwards with lithe movements and long, steady strokes. Nobody expected him to talk. The men were friends, at the end of an evening's entertainment, tired and subsiding into silence, broken by occasional reflections on the opera, or a shouted greeting when somebody they knew passed in a nearby gondola, or was spotted at a bridge's head. One by one they were let off, the first near Our Lady of Miracles, two more by the statue of Colleoni, the mercenary captain, on his horse outside Sts John and Paul. The fourth scrambled from the boat two thirds of the way down the canal of St Severus, beyond the Grimani town house, using a v-shaped flight of steps cut into the side of the bank. Domenico took it the red-haired man had often let him off there, for they stopped at the place with no words being exchanged. Shoes echoed lightly on the pavement and the click of a latch was heard, as the last of the friends to depart vanished into the night. No other boats were close. Disturbed by their presence, a bird that had been sleeping fluttered in the branches of a tree beyond the wall. One of them had to break the silence, either Domenico or his new friend.

'My name is Rodrigo.'

'And I am Domenico.'

'Where shall we go?'

A plan formed itself in Domenico's head. The keys to the theatre were in his pocket.

'Do you know where St Hyginus's is?'

'The church, or the theatre?'

'The theatre.'

They set off again. The city was a stage set, rolling past in a sequence of walls which rose sheer out of the water and were irregularly punctuated by windows, by hidden gardens, deserted alleyways, church apses and intersections. Near St Mark's and by the Rialto, the carnival festivities would be at their height, many parties having started when the theatres closed. Gaming houses, dancing halls and brothels would be crammed with revellers. In this poorer, quieter part of the city, the only signs of life were an old woman out looking for her cat, calling through the darkness with a low, repeated whooping, and a serving girl who paused to watch their gondola pass by, before closing her shutters for the night. At one point the smell of baking bread filled Domenico's nostrils. His stomach was too rigid with excitement for him to feel any hunger.

Before he expected it, they were in the square with its trio of bridges which the theatre and Gradenigo's newly acquired home looked on to. Domenico got to his feet.

'Can I take the lantern?' he asked.

'Yes. I'll tie the boat up,' answered Rodrigo.

In a minute he was fitting the key into the lock of the door they had entered by earlier that day. If there had been any doubt in Domenico's mind as to the nature of what was taking place, it was dispelled when Rodrigo, just behind him, placed a kiss on the nape of his neck.

'Is this where you work?'

They ascended the stairs. The door to the office had not been locked.

'Where I will be working, yes.'

He set the lantern down by the cupboard, with its stack of musical scores. Rodrigo put his arms around Domenico, then guided him gently towards the couch. Domenico was at such a pitch of pleasure and excitement he had to struggle to stop himself coming before he got his clothes off. Months had passed since he last held a naked body in his arms, or felt the touch of a hand that was not his own upon his skin. As his lips sought out Rodrigo's, he wondered what the man had been about to say when they were standing close to the *gnaga*, then forgot about it. They had to be careful in their movements. The couch was narrow and sloped a little. Unwary enthusiasm risked having them both end up on the floor. It meant their bodies had to intertwine all the more closely. They paused, as one does having finished the first course of what promises to be a lengthy meal.

'Are you a singer?'

'No, a musician. And you?'

'A boatmaker. I made the boat that brought us here.'

This was said not without a touch of pride.

'Alone?'

Rodrigo laughed.

'No. There are two big sheds, where anything from twenty to thirty men work at one time. Listen!'

Domenico strained to hear. The only noise was the creaking and groaning of the wooden furniture in the room, getting used to having people around once more.

'I can hear nothing.'

'I thought I heard steps. On the ceiling above our heads. Is that possible?'

'No. The place has been abandoned for seven years.'

They fell to kissing again. Rodrigo moved to get on top of Domenico.

'What are you trying to do?'

'Don't you like it? I want to put the blackbird in its nest.'

'Blackbird? Nest? What are you talking about?'

Already beginning to realise, he tried to keep the laughter out of his voice. He had never heard it put so picturesquely.

'But it is the most pleasurable thing of all!'

'What makes you think I want to be the nest, rather than the blackbird?'

Rodrigo paused, perplexed.

'Ssst!' whispered Domenico.

It was unmistakable now, the sound of someone pacing across the room on the floor above. He came out in goosepimples. He was holding Rodrigo and could feel the tension in the other man's muscles, though he gave no sign of fear.

'Who is it?'

Then, incredibly, a voice began to sing. Up and down an A major arpeggio, first of all, with astounding lightness and agility. Next it took a run, filling in all the notes between, as when a fountain is turned on and off, and a jet of water rises for an instant into the sunlight, like a pale feather tickling the air.

'We'd better see who it is.'

Rodrigo pulled his smock on and picked up the lantern. Infected by the other man's courage and curiosity, Domenico said nothing, got into his rather frayed undershirt and took his place next to him. The commode Limentani had pushed aside that afternoon had not been put back in its place. Rodrigo turned the handle of the door it had been hiding, and led the way upstairs. There was light at the bottom of the door there. It was not locked.

Entering the room, they stopped. Rodrigo had one hand on Domenico's shoulders. With the joint of his thumb he was gently, absent-mindedly massaging his friend's neck at the hairline. This man is not afraid, Domenico thought. An erection was still evident beneath his smock. He found that strange, for a whole host of emotions was tussling in his own breast. He did not consider himself to be superstitious. But it had occurred to him that they might be disturbing a phantom. The theatre was new and virgin territory for Rodrigo, a place where he might never set foot again, whereas it was crucial to Domenico's livelihood, and to the future for as far as he could see ahead. He almost felt responsible for whatever they might find.

The room was warm and lit by candles, set in armlets fixed on to the wall panels. The part next to the door they had come in by resembled a forest. It was crowded with costumes, each on its own high stand. Rodrigo took his hand, and they weaved their way through them as if they had been trees. Next they came upon tables, of different heights and sizes. At first Domenico thought they had boxes on them. Then he realised they were miniature theatres. Not puppet theatres, for there was no way to let strings down behind the miniature proscenium arches. What characters there were on stage were two-dimensional, cut out of card, and stood rigid in their places, with no possibility of movement.

A figure with his back to them was humming contentedly as he bent over one of the tables. He was small and portly and wore a wig. He had pulled back the sleeves of his shirt to reveal pink and puffy forearms which were practically hairless. Rodrigo coughed and he turned round.

'Ah, here you are,' he said, with not a hint of surprise. 'You have arrived at last. Let me offer you a glass of wine.'

'The creature is mad,' Rodrigo whispered into Domenico's ear, 'but he seems harmless. Let us humour him. It is good of you to receive us at this hour of the night,' he went on, in his normal voice.

'If you knew how rarely I have been disturbed, in all these years,' the man replied, with a touch of childlike melancholy, 'you would not find my hospitality surprising. Angelo Colombani,' he went on, holding out his hand. 'Whom have I the pleasure . . . ?'

The others presented themselves and all three bowed politely. The chubby, beardless cheeks, the girlish voice left Domenico in no doubt. Their host was, or had been, a castrato singer.

'Why all the models?' asked Rodrigo, whose manner could not have been more unconcerned.

'These are my pride and joy, the solace of my solitude,' said Angelo. 'Let me demonstrate.'

He placed them in front of one of the theatres, then disappeared behind it. The scenery showed a galleon breasting the waves. The turning of wheels was heard, and the boat moved to the right in a most lifelike manner, while the surface of the waves around it shimmered and shifted, just as the water was in the habit of doing between the Doge's Palace and the Customs House.

'Now watch this!' Angelo announced.

The sound of cogs turning and wires pulling grew more agitated. The sea on the stage of the toy theatre began to seethe and heave. The boat rocked from one side to the other, so energetically it looked as if it might capsize. Clouds scudded across the cardboard sky and there was even a flash or two of lightning.

'Excellent!' cried Rodrigo. 'How do you do it?'

'Ahah!' said Angelo, emerging from behind his model with a grin of mischief. 'What makes you think I have any intention of laying such arcane matters bare? Should I betray to you, for nothing, inventions which the Archbishop of Liège, the Elector of Hanover and the Crown Prince of Denmark offered solid gold to buy in days gone past?'

'In days gone past?' Rodrigo asked. 'And would they not be prepared to pay the same sums nowadays? What point is there in barricading yourself away here, when the theatres of half of Europe are eagerly awaiting machinery such as yours?'

'It is true! It is true!' cried Angelo, clasping his hands together, and circling round in a little, prancing dance. 'You have no idea how far my ingenuity reaches! I can show you now! The earthquake of Lisbon, with fires in the churches and the collapse of the principal buildings in the city! Give me another year, and I shall have perfected the tidal wave that sweeps it all away! Or mythological subjects! The flight of Icarus! Look, I have it here,' he said, going over to one of the tables and tapping it with the knuckle of his middle finger, 'so skilfully done the singers can fly through the firmament with not the slightest squeaking of wires! Phaethon riding the horses of the sun! I completed that last autumn! Horses that gallop, and neigh, and ride higher and higher into the sky until the axle breaks asunder, and they all precipitate in flames into the sea!'

His eyes were burning with excitement. In one of his mad

gestures, he had dislodged his wig without noticing, so that it perched to one side of his head, at an angle that gave an unintended comical inflexion to his effusions.

'Then why have you not announced these inventions to the world at large?' Domenico repeated.

'The world?' said Angelo, his features darkening. 'The world? Because the world does not deserve them! The world is a cruel place of malicious rumours and whispering tongues! Do you know what they said of me, the populace of Venice, when my machines reached a sublimity no other city in the world has known? Do you known the calumny with which they soiled my art, the charge they laid upon me? That I used magic! That is what they said! It was alleged that I practised black arts, and had made a league with the father of all mischief!'

He turned to an old-fashioned mirror, the size of a quarto volume, built into its own stand, so that it could be rotated back and forth. It was perched on top of a tallboy at the far end of the room.

'There,' cried Angelo, waving his finger at it, 'there is the source of all the evils I have suffered! He entered my life in the guise of a saviour, yet he it was who brought about my downfall! If only I had been wise enough to resist. But his cunning was too strong, even after he had beguiled me time and again, to my undoing.'

The peculiar fellow collapsed on to a chair and started sobbing. Rodrigo and Domenico looked at the mirror in puzzlement, wondering what it might be guilty of and why Angelo addressed it as if it were a person. Domenico braced himself to ask the question that had been troubling him for some time now.

'Are you,' he stammered, 'are you connected with the cloud machinery? The huge bird-like thing of wood that looms above the stage?'

Angelo, whose attention until now had been directed almost exclusively at Rodrigo, glanced up with an expression of such pain that Domenico reproached himself bitterly for having framed the question. All at once a further mystery confronted them. Another voice was heard, a woman's, untrained as far as Domenico could tell. She was singing close by, from behind a barrier he could not define. The syllables were too distinct to be coming from elsewhere in the building, yet too distant to be in the same room. For the first time in that evening's train of strange events, Rodrigo looked alarmed.

'What is it?' said Domenico.

'The song is Neapolitan.'

This latest wonder was the last straw for Angelo Colombani. He crumpled on to his knees and wept pitifully, like a child that knows the mother who might have comforted it is dead, and that the whole world holds no means of mitigating its pain.

'She is here,' he mumbled through his tears. 'She is here, and I have no way of finding her. What shame, what shame, what shame!'

Without saying a word, Rodrigo took Domenico's arm and edged him towards the door they had come in by. As he closed it behind them, the woman's tones and the heart-rending cries of the castrato could still be heard.

'Is he one of your workmates?' Rodrigo asked, when they had closed the door on the floor below, and the eerie cacophonies could barely be heard.

'What are you trying to suggest? I had no notion he existed!'

'The man is completely mad!'

'Are you going to stay with me? To stay till dawn, I mean? I would prefer not to be left alone!'

'I can stay tonight. But the next night? And the one after that? You had better get to the bottom of this puzzle.'

A sense of utter exhaustion had overtaken Domenico as they descended the stairs. Now, close again to a red-haired man he had not set eyes on until that evening, he found himself aroused.

'And the blackbird?' Rodrigo asked, laughter in his voice.

'There has been so much singing tonight,' Domenico conceded, 'that I hardly think any harm will come if the blackbird is allowed to do its bit.'

13

The pressure of events was such that Domenico completely forgot about his appointment with the lawyer the following day. As the afternoon wore on, Onofrio Carpi's impatience mounted. It was giving place to an increasingly powerful resentment when an unexpected visitor was announced.

He did not number Baroness Hedwiga Engelsfeld von Nettesheim amongst his acquaintance. The figure ushered in a moment later struck him as a strange one. Though he set her age notionally at between forty-five and fifty, she could have been younger, or even considerably older. The clothes she wore indicated both vanity and wealth, but were oddly unfashionable for the period in Venice. Ridiculously exaggerated hoops, of a size no one used any longer, inflated her skirts. All over her was a profusion of lace. Everything was embroidered, her bodice, her cuffs, her kerchief and her collar, so that she made him think of a doll from a forgotten epoch, unearthed in an old clothes shop, dusted down and cleaned for presentation to contemporary children.

There was, however, nothing childlike in her manner. Hedwiga lost no time in getting down to business.

'Good Signor Carpi,' she said, once she had taken her seat, 'we are not known to each other.'

'Indeed. I have not had the pleasure of being presented.'

'My visit concerns a matter in which I am convinced we can be of mutual assistance. I will not waste further time in preliminaries. You are, I understand, the legal representative of Donato Gradenigo, recently installed in a town house which was formerly the property of Alvise Contarini?'

Carpi nodded.

'The theatre attached to it is part of the inheritance?'

'It is. My client intends to reopen it in the course of the current carnival.'

All of this was public knowledge.

'You knew that Contarini had a son?'

The lawyer's face was inscrutable. He cleared his throat.

'Alvise had a childless marriage. I hardly think his wife had any reason to conceal a baby from him.'

'I do not mean a son born in wedlock. Please do not affect a naivety which can only cause us both to waste valuable time. I have a long experience of members of your profession. The incorruptibility of lawyers is a delusion no one who has dealings with them can afford to entertain.'

'If you have come here to insult the legal establishment, dear Baroness . . .'

'I offer no insults, Signor Carpi. You will surely refrain from claiming that it is unheard of for a lawyer, here and there, to fall short in private of the admirable standards which he publicly proclaims. Whether this will be the case with you, only time will tell.'

Carpi gasped. The woman's insolence was unbelievable.

'All I request,' she continued, 'is that we should be plain with one another. Whether you had previous knowledge of the affair or not, Alvise had a son by another woman.'

'Even if what you say were true, my client's claim to the estate remains unchallenged. A bastard son has no right to the inheritance.'

'Unless his natural father stipulates that it should go to him.'

'Alvise made no such stipulation.'

'How can you be so sure? You never spoke to the man.'

'That is true. Nor, I presume, did you. After his murder, no trace of a will was found among his papers.'

'Do you consider it probable that such a wealthy individual could have failed to make one?'

'Alvise's wealth was in large measure dissipated because of his eccentric style of life. Whether he took his eccentricity so far as to die intestate is not up to me to decide.'

'He did not die, good Carpi. He was murdered. Had it not occurred to you that the murderer might himself have removed the will? Or that a third party might have concealed it in a place where the murderer would not discover it?'

'Dear Baroness, I am not a resolver of riddles, but a lawyer. A client approached me in connection with a contested inheritance and I can claim, I think, to have rendered him good service. That is all.'

It was evident that Carpi considered their interview concluded. Hedwiga did not rise from her chair.

'You will not be surprised to learn that my visit to you is not prompted by altruistic motives. I have come to warn your client, now the proprietor of the theatre of St Hyginus, of approaching difficulties, to offer my assistance, and to ask for a favour in return.'

'Do you think you can dictate terms to me?'

'That remains to be seen. It would be unwise in the extreme for you to withhold what I am telling you from Signor Gradenigo, given that his time is running out.'

Carpi drummed his fingers impatiently on the table in front of him. Hedwiga paused.

'Go on, then,' Carpi prompted. 'Let me hear the message.'

'Before long, the rightful heir will make his appearance. To be frank, I have the distinct impression he may already have set foot within the premises intended to be his. My conjecture is that the will, with other associated papers, is concealed somewhere inside the theatre. If we do not find them,' (Carpi's brows knotted at the implied association) 'others will, and will make what use of them they see fit. Were corroboration to be lacking, I have located the individual who, under circumstances there is no need to enter into now, was responsible for, shall we say, disposing of this child of love. My advice to your client is that a thorough search should be made through every nook and cranny of the theatre.'

'And what is your interest in this? You said your motives were not altruistic. What difference does it make to you whose hands the Contarini estate falls into?'

'A search of the kind I am proposing is likely to unearth certain papers not directly concerning the estate, but written in the hand of one Goffredo Negri, who arrived in Venice a few days before Contarini's death.'

Carpi gave a start.

'So the man exists? It was rumoured that an individual by that name had been seen in the vicinity of the theatre, even that he was present at the scene of the crime! Some went so far as to consider him a suspect in the case.'

'Negri will never be brought to trial. Though I am not in a position to enlighten you as to the circumstances of his flight, I can assure you that, at present, he is no longer of this world.'

' "At present"? You mean you have hopes of resuscitating the man?' scoffed Carpi.

Until now, Hedwiga had remained indifferent to the lawyer's haughtiness. Her icy calm was enlivened by the merest flickerings of a smile when an ironic turn of phrase procured her pleasure. Now Carpi had at last offended her *amour propre*. She rose to her feet, not in preparation to depart, but in order to give greater force to the words she was about to say.

'Dear Signor Carpi, since I arrived, you have treated me like an interfering busybody, a decrepit spinster who has nothing better to do than meddle in affairs which are none of her concern. More-over, you have implied that I am on the level of a petty criminal, prepared to stoop to methods you would never dream of in order to obtain my ends. Do you imagine that you yourself are invulnerable? Are the high standards you maintain in the exercise of your profession reflected in every other aspect of your life? Or do you possess secrets which, were they to be made public, might speed you on your way to the galleys? If not the public gallows?'

Carpi looked as though he were about to take an apoplectic fit. He tried hard to speak but, while he moved his lips, no sounds came forth. His hand went to his neckerchief, to loosen it, and he bowed his head, as if to cough up a distasteful pill that he had swallowed.

'Finally lost for words!' Hedwiga crowed. 'You cannot afford to acknowledge the allegation, nor can you yet deny it. Take care! Tell Gradenigo that the price of my silence is the following. He may keep the will and destroy it if he wishes. Any papers found along with it are to be turned over to me. No questions will be asked. I can answer for the witness I mentioned to you earlier. As long as my demands are met, your client has nothing to fear from this person. I will of course expect prompt assistance from Signor Gradenigo in any further researches I shall undertake into the fate of Negri. That apart, he may rest contented with his legacy.'

By this time she had moved towards the bell-pull. The last part of her speech was delivered with one hand upon it.

'As for you, I will leave you to grovel in the mire of your duplicity. I, at least, have no fear of the world's knowing me for what I am. The revelation might strike terror into their hearts, rather than contempt!'

And she was gone.

14

'*The Twins of Syracuse.*'

'Put that aside. It's comic. We could use it.'

'*Adelaide Princess of Burgundy. The Queen of Golconda. Secret Vengeance for a Secret Wrong. The Triumphs of Bellerophon. The Servant Mistress.*'

'Excellent. Put that aside.'

'*Germanicus Conquers the Rhine. Orpheus, or the Wonders of Constancy in Love. You Cannot Guard a House Which Has Two Doors. Mithridates King of Pontus. Aeneas in the Underworld. The Serpent Woman. The Garden of the Hesperides.*'

'Wait! Isn't that the opera Anselmi was supposed to be writing?'

Domenico had got very little sleep that night. He was only just awake when Limentani arrived, expecting him to have gone through the pile of scores already. They had been sitting over them for nearly three hours now. It was all he could do to keep his eyes from closing. He yawned.

'I don't remember. The man next to us said something about the content but I haven't the faintest recollection what.'

Limentani waved dismissively, and Domenico placed the folder along with the pile of rejects.

'Proceed.'

'*The Death of Socrates. Deceit Can Never Pay. The Tragedy of Zenobia.*'

'Marvellous! It's by Terradellas, isn't it? Check on the title page. One of his finest efforts.'

'*Ottokar Defeats the Goths. The Marriage Voucher.*'

'Stop, stop,' Limentani intervened. 'What have you done with the Terradellas?'

Domenico had put it with the rejects by mistake. He leant down and moved it to the diminishing pile of works they might perform.

He had counted the scores before they started. There were seventy-eight in all. This was the third time they had sifted through them, with the aim of whittling the final selection down to four or five at most. Limentani was very concerned that they might overlook something of value to them.

'What's that?' he said, pointing to a mottled portfolio Domenico had laid aside after brief inspection.

'It must have got in here by mistake. It isn't music at all.'

'What is it then?'

'There are some private papers and then sheet upon sheet of numbers and diagrams. What should I do with them?'

'Pop them back into the cupboard. They are of no interest to us.'

Suddenly it struck Domenico that the portfolio's contents might be connected to the strange individual he had encountered on the floor above, in the course of the preceding night. He had not been able to bring himself to tell the impresario about Angelo. Not the least of the considerations which held him back was the necessity he would be under of lying about his reasons for returning to the theatre after the opera at St John Chrysostom had finished. He saw a way of killing two birds with one stone.

'I was wondering,' he ventured, 'how you would feel if I were to give up my lodgings and move in here.'

Limentani's keen gaze focused on him.

'It's not primarily a matter of saving money. We plan to open within a week. All the hours except those I devote to sleep would be spent in here in any case. It seems pointless to come and go when I have everything I need on the spot.'

'Where would you sleep?'

'Over there,' said Domenico, pointing to the couch where he and Rodrigo had spent the night.

'As you wish,' said Limentani. 'Though I am sure we could find something better for you in the building. But you realise it means you will not have a waking moment you can call your own.'

Domenico laughed.

'I am not sure this is a waking moment now. And anyway, I shall be eating and dreaming the theatre until Ash Wednesday. I may as well do so on the premises.'

The old man who met them outside the locked entrance the

previous afternoon had been installed as porter. Having made his way laboriously upstairs, wheezing all the time, he now interrupted them to announce that Don Astolfo had arrived. Limentani ordered him to be admitted, and winked to Domenico.

'The parish priest is coming to bless the building. It can do no harm. I am a firm believer in maintaining the best possible relations with the residents of whatever neighbourhood one happens to be working in. Welcome, good father!' he hailed the newcomer, shaking the priest's hand energetically.

Don Astolfo was wearing a white surplice and a stole. He had a black biretta on his head and was accompanied by two diminutive, wide-eyed altar boys, whose air of disorientation did not abandon them for a moment during the proceedings. They were carrying a thurible and a bowl of sanctified water

Domenico was no lover of ecclesiastical formalities. The pretext for a break, however, was welcome, and he willingly followed the little group down to the auditorium. The porter arrived with a candelabra, stocked it with candles and then lit them, in that ill-humoured way he had of going about all his tasks. Meanwhile, Don Astolfo and his helpers made a great to-do with a tinder box and a little square of combustible material that, when it at last began to glow, was popped into the incense bowl, at once producing a fragrance which was immensely pleasing to the nostrils. The parish priest handled the rather complex mechanism of the thurible with professional aplomb, alternating a movement where, holding one arm high, he clinked the bowl and its perforated lid against the dangling chain, with another where he dipped a short brass club with holes at its end into the holy water, then liberally sprinkled his surroundings.

He managed to do all of this, mumbling the appropriate Latin prayers, while at the same time maintaining a not too disjointed conversation with Ansaldo Limentani. They exchanged pleasantries about the plans for the new season, the supply of fuel to heat the parish house, and a set of vestments the impresario had ordered to be made as a donation in honour of St Hyginus. Domenico watched from a distance. It was enormously evocative to see the cluster of figures circle round tier after tier of the auditorium. When the time came for them to clamber on to the stage, using a flight of movable wooden steps which the porter had found forgotten in a cupboard, Domenico headed off. The idea of seeing the cloud machinery again made him feel squeamish. Luca Schiavoni and his équipe were due to start repairing it that afternoon. Perhaps once they had knocked it into shape it would lose the uncanny air which so disquieted him.

Alone upstairs in the office, he picked up the portfolio. He knew it would be preferable to find a way of telling Limentani about the mad castrato on the floor above. It was irrational to hope that, if ignored, the trouble would simply go away. Similarly, his refusal to look again at the machinery, which he did not doubt was the handiwork of Angelo Colombani, could do nothing to make it disappear. In one way or another, it had to be confronted. He had a flash of intuition. He would ask the parish priest! Who, if not Don Astolfo, could illuminate the theatre's manifold mysteries? He might even be able to explain the contents of the portfolio Domenico was now holding.

His suspicions were confirmed without delay. When the little party arrived to bless the office, Limentani, in the most matter of fact fashion, went to open the door leading to the next storey. The look of alarm on Don Astolfo's face was unmistakable.

'Shall we not continue with our ceremony?'

'Perhaps,' the parish priest said, 'the upper floors can be left until a later occasion. Am I right in assuming there is nothing there that is of interest to you?'

'How are we to know,' said Limentani, 'unless we investigate?'

The porter, standing behind Don Astolfo, looked just as anxious as the priest, who paused a moment, then sat down on the couch.

'To be honest, I am a little tired,' he said. 'Let us leave it for another day. I think I had better be on my way.'

'As you wish,' was the courteous reply.

Limentani had plenty to occupy him, and felt no need to insist. He attributed no real efficacy to the priest's ritual, which was purely a matter of diplomacy in his eyes.

'May I accompany you for a few yards?' Domenico proposed. 'We have been working in this stuffy atmosphere all morning. A breath of air will do me good.'

Once they were outside in the square, Domenico slowed his step so that they fell behind the altar boys. Then he came directly to the point:

'Father, can you tell me what that man is doing on the floor above our office?'

Domenico could have sworn that the priest's foot froze for a moment, inches above the paving-stone. The reaction was fleeting, and Don Astolfo did his best to pretend nothing was amiss. Domenico was not deceived.

'A man? On the floor above?'

'Angelo Colombani? Do you really know nothing about him?'

'Have you told anyone?' There was genuine distress in the priest's voice. He did not look round but started walking again, at an accelerated pace. 'Does Maestro Limentani know?'

'Not yet, but it cannot be kept from him much longer. What can you tell me about Colombani?'

'Dear child, this is a matter of great delicacy, which must be treated with infinite care. It is not something I can broach with you here in the public street. To be frank, it is not a matter I find it easy to discuss at all. Let us meet tomorrow, at the end of the morning. Not in the parish house, that would be far too obvious. In the convent of the nuns of St Clare. Mother Hilary knows as much as any other living creature about the fate of that tragic individual. She will give you a clearer account of his doings than I can ever hope to do.'

15

Limentani was a little taken aback when Domenico declined to accompany him to the tavern at lunchtime the following day.

'I hope you are not about to undergo a religious crisis!' he said, on learning that Domenico intended to call at the local convent instead. 'The last thing we want is for you to slip on a dog collar and start rehearsing clerics and eunuchs in the liturgy of the Holy Mass! Profane art is your responsibility at present, dear fellow, not the choruses of angels!'

With a troubling sense of what he was withholding, Domenico carefully lingered until the impresario was out of the building, before removing the portfolio of papers from the cupboard and wrapping it in a felt cloth. He had not mentioned it to the parish priest the previous day. Now was his chance to learn more about its contents. His surprise was all the greater when he discovered Don Astolfo was not to be of the company.

He was ushered into the only room in the convent to be regularly heated. The sight of a healthy fire in the chimney was welcome, for it was a clear, sunlit day, with a sharp-edged wind blowing from the Alps. The snow-topped mountain caps were just visible from the Fondamenta Nuove, to anyone willing to brave exposure there. A nun laid a single place at table and set lamb stew and polenta in front of him, filled his glass with red wine and left the carafe next to it. Only then did Mother Hilary come in. She took her place on a stool next to the fire and encouraged him to tuck in to the food.

'When is Don Astolfo coming?' asked Domenico. 'Should I not wait for him before I start?'

Mother Hilary dropped her eyes to the hands that restlessly smoothed the white apron she wore at her daily tasks.

'He prefers to be absent. The topic we are to discuss still causes him great distress. I think it is better to avoid upsetting him unnecessarily.'

'He tells me you know more than he does about the mysterious guest upstairs.'

'Whether more or not is hard to say. I know a great deal, yes, for in his time of greatest need he sought sanctuary within these walls. And I could not find it in my heart to refuse.'

'When was that?' asked Domenico.

They were briefly interrupted by a younger sister. She bore a large earthenware pot, and offered him a further helping of stew. He accepted with alacrity, while Mother Hilary busied herself with the fire. Its luminous architecture had grown especially brilliant and was on the point of collapse. She poked vigorously at it, then tossed a log or two on to the smoking ruins that were all she left. Next she inspected her palms, blew the dust from them, joined her hands in her lap and turned back to Domenico. She looked calmer and more resolved than when she first entered the room.

'It may seem strange to a young person like yourself that I should take such an interest in worldly matters,' she began. 'It worries me that I may be a cause of scandal to you. The normal expectation would be for the principal of a convent, such as myself, to have nothing in her head besides the adequate provisioning of the community, the cleaning and maintenance of its buildings and, above all, the spiritual welfare and improvement of the sisters in her care, in so far as that is not entirely the concern of the priest who ministers to them. But I was not destined for the religious life, nor did I enter it by choice. I was too much involved with the affairs of the world before I took the veil. That may be why they have not seen fit to leave me in peace since I did so.

'My father was a rich merchant in Bergamo, a man I loved with all the fierce contradiction of my untutored heart. We were perhaps too similar to one another to live in harmony for long. He chose a husband for me, as a test, I think, of my loyalty and obedience. I found the partner he proposed abhorrent. When I refused, I had no alternative but to renounce the world and make Christ my bridegroom.'

She took a pause for reflection.

'I was a late recruit. By the time my father came to accept that I would not give in, I had passed my twenty-fifth birthday. Who can tell if it was desperation that led him to try and force a husband upon me? Many girls of my station had long been married at that age, and had two or three children at their knee. I had drunk fully of what brilliance and sophistication the society of Bergamo had to offer. A high point of that period in my life was when I heard a male child everyone hailed as a prodigy singing in the cathedral. His fame had spread throughout Lombardy. It was public knowledge that he would not lose his voice or grow a beard with the approach of manhood. I never found out what his real name was, though I have seen the hamlet where his parents came from. He was not baptised Angelo. They called him an angel because of the beauty of his singing.

'There are many, particularly in the northern countries of Europe, where the Protestants hold sway, who curse as an abomination the operation he had been subjected to. They find it all the more shocking, and yet appropriate, that it was at the court of the Popes, and in their churches, that the custom of emasculating first took hold and gained, so to speak, respectability. You must not think, Domenico, that it is cruelty which leads parents to force this destiny upon their son. Imagine what takes place. Word goes round that a surgeon has taken up residence, or is staying for a week or so, in a nearby town, and that he is capable of performing the operation without undue pain or risk, at a low price. If it is successful, and if the boy proves an apt and willing pupil, he will not only be taken off his parents' hands, so that they can devote what meagre resources they have to feeding the remainder of the family, but he will also earn a place at a school of music, where he will be lodged, fed and educated till his fifteenth year. If he does not make his fortune thanks to a career on the stage, he can at least find gainful employment as a musician or a tutor, and will never know the want and misery his parents struggled with. I can understand what makes them do it, and feel no urge to judge them. Do you?'

'I am not sure,' said Domenico. 'The child is not consulted, nor can he have any notion what the operation will mean for his future and his chances of eventual happiness. Of course, were they to wait until he could decide, then it would be too late.'

'And have you never heard a castrato singing? When the transcendent loveliness of a voice which can be obtained by no other means filled you with ecstasy, when it set you, so to speak, before the gates of Heaven, did you feel guilty? Did the pleasure you experienced make you an accomplice in the crime?'

'I can certainly say I have never felt guilt when a tuneful voice gave me pleasure. But what happens to his intimate life? His loves? What woman would look twice at an emasculated creature?'

'My son, you do not know how wrong you are. If anything, a voice which is considered unnatural renders such singers more, rather than less attractive to the women in the audience. You have not the faintest notion how many proposals a castrato will receive in the space of one single season. Did you know that Buffoni stole his mistress from the king of Sweden, and lies with her to this day?'

'That must be love indeed, to make her leave a king for a castrato. But tell me more about Angelo. How did he get from Bergamo to Venice?'

'The day I heard him, he was performing for a high mass. When the crucial words arrived, telling how our saviour took on human flesh and blood to save the world, it was the boy who sang them. I shall never forget the intense devotion his art inspired in me that afternoon. The mystery of the incarnation has never been closer or more palpable. But I was young and rich in foolishness. Within days I could no longer remember his name, and had lost any recollection of his features. Not until several years later, when a scandal broke out sufficient to galvanize every gossipmonger along the course of the Po, did I make the connection and realise it concerned him.

'To study in a music academy, for a child of poverty, is an enormous privilege. No one pretends, however, that the treatment he will receive there can in any sense replace the loving attentions of natural parents. You are a musician yourself. What I am saying cannot be new to your ears. There have been numerous cases of uprisings, of veritable mutinies on the part of pupils, both those who have been castrated and those who have not, against the rigorous regime they have been forced to live under. The population of the academies is divided. Those who will never be men in the fullest sense are generally given better food and lodgings than the others, because of their delicate constitution and the greater hopes placed upon them. Due to this privileged position, the remaining pupils, the normal ones, look on them with hatred and contempt. That double oppression has led many to run off or, even worse, to take their lives.'

Shuddering at the idea of such a crime, Mother Hilary drew the folds of her habit tightly round her, though the room they sat in was by no means cold.

'Angelo Colombani had an accomplice in his escape, an escape that many termed an elopement, whether with justice or not I am unqualified to say. At the age of thirteen, he began to sing frequently in the house of the Marquis of Monza, in Milan. The Marquis's musical evenings were attended by the flower of Milan society. Leading churchmen could be encountered there, as well as ambassadors and visiting noblemen from different countries. In the course of one such evening, Angelo Colombani made the acquaintance of a German aristocrat, whose name in his own language it is beyond my skill to repeat. He became known in Italian as Goffredo Negri.

'Nothing untoward was said about him at the time. Once he and Angelo had made their getaway, it transpired that no one knew exactly what his title was, the location of his estates, or how he had been introduced into the Marquis's circle of acquaintance. Everyone agreed that he was gifted with exceptional charm and eloquence. He spoke four languages with the skill of one who has been born to each of them, and was a connoisseur of sculpture and painting as well as music. I have been told that at the last concert Angelo gave in the Marquis's house, Goffredo Negri leapt to the harpsichord and begged to be allowed the honour of accompanying so outstanding a singer.

'Until he disappeared, those responsible for the running of the academy had made little fuss about Colombani. The Marquis was a sponsor and benefactor and it was perfectly in order for one or more of the pupils to entertain his guests on a regular basis.

Indeed, he had the pick of them. The fact that this one singer was invited back again and again suggests how exceptional his talent must have been. When the bird had flown the cage, however, those who had the charge of guarding it trumpeted its value to the four points of the compass. He was destined to be the greatest castrato singer of his age. So at least they told us. He could memorise an entire operatic role within a matter of hours and, once it had been committed to memory, could reproduce it even months afterwards, without a single mistake. Normally it is the task of the instructors to devise the ornaments with which pupils decorate the melodies they sing. The melodies themselves are written down in bare, unadorned form. With Angelo there had been no need to do this. He invented his own ornaments and cadenzas. In the heat of performance, thanks to the promptings of a brilliant fantasy, he would extemporise trills and mordents that no nightingale, even on the balmiest May evening, could have rivalled.

'I have no way of gauging the accuracy of such claims. But if Angelo's subsequent history is anything to go by, the predictions of his tutors were entirely justified. Other whisperings emerged in the wake of their flight. People sought high and low for evidence of Negri's life before that time, given that Colombani's was well enough known and held no secrets for us. Who can tell if half of what they uncovered may be true?

'It was said that he spent years studying in the library of a Benedictine monastery in Bohemia and had been expelled from there because of an unnatural relationship with a young monk. Perhaps it was this story that led malicious tongues to hint that Negri dabbled in the black arts, and that this explained his marvellous facility in languages, as well as his effortless musicianship. Be that as it may, there was no opportunity to test the truth of these accusations, or to bring either of the accused to trial, since they disappeared without trace for the better part of five years. By the time he set foot in Milan again, Colombani had become such a celebrity, and was the master of such wealth, that no one chose or dared to murmur against him or his protector.'

'What need did he have of a protector, when he could command such fees?' Domenico asked.

' "Protector" may not be the best way to describe him,' Mother

Hilary replied, in some confusion. 'But how else am I to put it? "Master"? "Friend"? "Companion"? "Tutor"? Whatever the nature of the bond that linked those two benighted creatures, no word in my vocabulary can sum it up. Where had I got to? Ah, yes, the gap of five whole years . . .'

'Wait,' Domenico interrupted. 'Don't think I don't believe you. But where did you learn all this? How did you come by your knowledge?'

'Good child, you must be patient. All will become clear in due time. Do not encourage me to jump from place to place, otherwise what I have to say will lose any semblance of order. Incredible as it may sound, Negri and Colombani spent much of that period in the Empire of the Turks. Angelo told me that they travelled as far as Istanbul, the city of the Sultan. Imagine! More than a year went by without him being able to hear mass or have access to the sacraments! Who but the Antichrist would willingly have led him into such circumstances?

'No sooner had they returned to Italy than he made his debut in Rome, in the opera of Darius. His triumph was immediate. There followed a private audience with the Pope and a series of engagements which took him as far afield as Paris and Madrid. He was ranked second to none of his contemporaries. He appeared on stage with both Senesino and Farinelli, on different occasions, naturally. If the listeners' accounts are to be trusted, he surpassed them both. The only sombre note sounding through that brilliant period is the constant presence of Goffredo Negri at his side. Half of what Colombani earned was given to him. Travel arrangements, professional engagements, musical preparation, the ordering of costumes, all these details were entrusted to Angelo's shadow. For that is what Negri was, a shadow, a darkness haunting the singer's back, one he could no more divorce himself from than, with a deft stroke of one of the many swords he carried in his roles on stage, he could have severed the shadow from his heels.'

Domenico had considerations of his own to make about the possible nature of the relationship between the castrato and his shadow. He felt no inclination to share these with Mother Hilary, and so the silence that fell between them remained unbroken for a while.

'I do not know what led them to part company,' she went on, once she had gathered her thoughts again. 'Rumour had it that Negri was an inveterate gambler, and that he was capable of dissipating the lion's share of what Colombani passed on to him in the space of a single night, while the singer slept innocently in the lodgings they had taken, so as not to be tired for the following day's performance. There were other voices which claimed he had grown tired of the older man's tutelage. He had ideas of his own about the interpretation of the roles he played, and was determined to put them to the test, even though Negri disagreed. What is certain is that it was Colombani who initiated the break.

'They were in Florence, and the grand duke of Tuscany had specified, when inviting the singer to stay in his villa near Carmignano, that his disreputable sidekick should not accompany him. A passionate quarrel took place between them that same night. By dawn of the next morning, Negri had disappeared with all his baggage and, one can presume, a sizeable portion of their mutual savings.'

'Where did he go?' Domenico interrupted.

'No one knows. Some said the Low Countries, others Cologne, others still Naples. In any case, his departure was a disaster for poor Angelo.'

'But that's ridiculous! How could it be? Going by your description, nothing could be better for him than to get rid of the man. He was free to develop his art along the lines he chose for it, without external interference.'

Mother Hilary took no heed of his objections and carried on unswervingly with her account.

'The opera that evening was by Iommelli, who had set a celebrated version of the tale of Orpheus to music. Colombani naturally took the part of the prince of poets. The decoration of the stage aroused especial admiration. After losing Eurydice, and descending into Hades, Orpheus was confronted by Pluto and Persephone suspended in mid air, thanks to a wonderful machine, as if in an enormous cavern, while a sea of flames played under and around them. The symphony opening the second act had ended, there was a short chorus of damned spirits, then Colombani entered, while at the same time the horrific spectacle was unveiled. Holding his golden lyre, the singer stepped into the centre of the stage, opened his mouth . . . and produced nothing but a croak. His voice was gone.'

'For ever?'

'So it proved to be. He never sang upon a stage again.'

'How appalling! Had Negri cast a spell upon him?'

Mother Hilary raised her hands in horror.

'Do not speak of such things, even as a joke! That was precisely what the Florentines concluded. It was worse than that, in fact. Rather than deciding Negri had taken revenge on his protégé by administering a secret potion, or merely that the singer was so dependent on his support that, deprived of it, he could not face an audience, they said he had only ever been able to perform thanks to Negri's magic. The talent was not his, but Negri's! Such are the lengths which human calumny will go to! I know it is not true, because, as I told you, I heard him when he was still a child, in the cathedral at Bergamo, and even then his singing deserved to be compared to that of an angel. The fiasco in Florence was terrible. A mob gathered outside his lodgings, jeering, demanding that he be either exorcised or excommunicated. The grand duke and his family wanted nothing more to do with him. When he left the town soon afterwards, the urchins ran after his coach, hurling rotten eggs, vegetables and excrement at the windows.'

16

The fire was once more requiring attention. By the time Mother Hilary had done her task and replaced the poker, the expression on her face was more serene, as if the greater part of the story she had to tell was behind her.

'So did he run after Negri and beg to have his gift restored?' Domenico asked.

'How could he? He knew no more than anyone else where the man had gone. He spent the remainder of that year in a Carthusian monastery close to Parma. It was there he discovered a second talent, no less outstanding than the first, though it is one that brings lesser rewards than does singing. The fame it earned him was as the melancholy sweetness of a reed instrument, compared to the blaring trumpets of his earlier career.'

'He began designing models of staging,' put in Domenico.

'How did you know?' And then, without letting him answer, she added: 'Of course, you saw them in his room. Don Astolfo has described the place to me in detail, though I have never set foot in it myself. The abbot of the monastery was happy to give him hospitality, in spite of the rumours raging about his life. He never again had the courage to appear upon a stage, and directed his talents instead to devising scenery where others could perform. The theatre was in his blood, you see. Even in the company of the holy brothers, in a place completely withdrawn from the world, it was more than he could do to chase it from his mind.'

She rose and rang a small bell on the table in front of Domenico, asking the sister who came at once to bring her a shawl.

'Let us take a walk in the cloister,' she said. 'These are dark and gloomy matters, and it will do me good to see the sky and feel the light of day upon my cheeks before I continue. The cloister will be filled with sunshine at this hour. It is a sheltered spot. Even when the weather is cold, the wind that blows from the north gains no admittance there.'

She was right. The walls of the little garden had absorbed what heat there was in the sun, reverberating it back into the enclosed space. It was nearly warm enough for them to sit out, though they did not. Mother Hilary cut across the garden in one direction, led Domenico round the perimeter, then inspected the state of the fig tree and the medlars without pausing in her talk, before cutting across it in the opposite direction and repeating the same movements on the far side. The familiar surroundings and the concise geometry of the place soothed her, though not quite sufficiently to prevent her coming close to tears at one point.

'Colombani was prey to the vanity which characterises all singers. The mixture of fame and infamy he enjoyed meant that a range of noteworthy men and women sought him out in his retreat. People of culture and breeding were less hasty in jumping to conclusions about the crisis he had faced, and were loath to judge the circumstances he had lived in until then. He rarely refused their visits. The chief minister of the Duchy of Parma called on him several times. And so, within barely a year of the break with Negri, his first machines were inaugurated in the theatre of that town.

'Money did not concern him and, though his skill was exceptional, he could hardly have gained greater notoriety in his second career than his first had won for him. Nevertheless, offers of employment poured in from the most distant corners of the peninsula, as well as further afield. He accepted and rejected them with an eccentricity that marked all his doings from that time on. He spent a season in Turin, at the invitation of the king of Sardinia. and worked in Munich, beyond the Alps, for the better part of a year, at the behest of one of the princes who have the honour of electing Charlemagne's successor. Why he should have accepted Alvise's proposal to come and work in our small parish, in a poor neighbourhood of Venice, is beyond my understanding. His inventions made St Hyginus's, however briefly, the foremost theatre in the city. Gossip had it that a lady of high breeding gave herself for one night to a senior official of the Republic, merely in order to have the opportunity to attend an important première there.

'Look,' she said, pointing, 'you can see the upper part of the building across the rooftops. It is visible from my tiny realm of fertility and peace, in the midst of this stern world composed of nothing but water and stone. Angelo, in turn, could see this garden from the upper windows of the room he lives in. You know the secret of his presence there, so I need not conceal from you the fact that, when he is unwary, one or other of my sisters glimpses him. The community within the convent takes it as an article of faith that the theatre is haunted by his ghost.

'He insisted on living there during the time he worked for Alvise, so as not to separate himself, even for the space of a night, from his precious machines. When the theatre was inactive, he could sometimes be persuaded to retire to Alvise's country villa on the mainland. But generally he preferred his lonely eyrie, absorbed in plans for a device that would cause geniuses to sweep like birds across the space beneath the proscenium arch, or allow Moses and the Israelites to find a dry path through the Red Sea under the spectators' astonished gaze, while the waters towered in glassy ramparts of quicksilver to either side of them.

'I am a sinful woman. Here in Venice the rules governing the behaviour of those who dedicate their lives to serving God are laxer than in other cities. My disobedience has never run the length of endangering my virginity, make no mistake of that! I shall take it with me to my maker, as intact as on the day I promised it to him. But when the whole city was murmuring of the wondrous things to be seen within four walls, only five minutes away from here, it was more than I could do to resist the temptation to be present. Many other nuns and priests in Venice have done the same, and taken the transgressions further. That does not make my sin any the less serious. I donned a cloak and mask and went to the theatre, week after week. And as a result I was in the audience on the night of poor Colombani's second catastrophe.'

She stopped and lifted a corner of her habit to her face. Domenico saw that her eyes were full of tears. He waited patiently for her to recover her composure, noting with interest that it was the bitterness of Colombani's fate, rather than the memory of her own transgressions, that moved her.

'The subject of the opera was Hercules. Included were both the episode of his enslavement, in woman's clothing, at the court of Queen Omphale, who made him spin thread along with her other handmaids, and the unwitting betrayal of his foolish wife, Deianira, who placed around his shoulders the shirt of fire Nessus had devised to put an end to him. Everyone present watched these scenes with a modicum of impatience. We were waiting excitedly for the closing tableau of the opera. Having read the libretto, we knew that the gods and goddesses, the heroes and the heroines of all the myths were to appear as stars in the firmament, and that Hercules, his labours done, would ascend to take his place among them. How am I to convey to you the sense of anticipation that filled the theatre? Audiences in Venice, as you know, are famous for their indifference to doings on the stage, too taken up with their own petty bickering and conversation to pay heed. Yet from the moment the curtain went up on the last act, not a word was to be heard anywhere in the auditorium.

'The machinery was visible to us, for, with all the singers already in place, it was too heavy to be raised entirely out of sight into the vault above the proscenium. All that could be made out was the lower edge of a bank of clouds, of a kind familiar to us from the skies above our city. You must know how it is, on an afternoon in early summer, when the pale blue sky to the north fills gradually with spirals of white and pale pink smoke, as though a barrage of cannon fire had been released along the horizon, and traces of the detonations ascended lazily into the air. They end up with the shape of outsize, insubstantial pineapples. The clouds designed by Colombani were similar to those, only darker, more substantial and more menacing.

'A solemn symphony struck up in the orchestra as, inch by inch, the machinery was lowered. There were gasps of wonder on all sides, even though this latest triumph of Colombani's imagination had yet to be disclosed to us in full. We all knew that, behind the clouds, the divinities were sitting ready, waiting to be exposed before they burst into triumphant song.

'A cry from those standing nearest to the stage gave the first alert. Something was amiss. Tilting to one side, the bank of cloud trembled, then trembled again. One last, rude shock and, unable to recover its earlier, majestic pace of descent, it came to a standstill. The rising murmur of concern on all sides turned quickly to derision and dismay. The unseen figures operating the machinery called to one another in subdued, breathy tones, unwilling to acknowledge that the accident was past concealing, tugging and straining at the different ropes which controlled the complex mechanism. All of a sudden the clouds, which were painted on moveable flats attached to the front of the machine, shifted to one side. The singers were revealed to us, no longer serene and Olympian, but in a disorder prompted by fear and anger. Some looked to the right, others to the left, or leant across to speak to one another, trying to devise a way of getting down from their precarious perches, forgetting the burning candles they held in their hands, which were supposed to symbolise the generous beams with which the stars they represented illumine the night sky.

'There could so easily have been a fire. On that night of multiple disasters, God spared us at least that trial. The symphony had come to an end. Doing his best to save the situation, the director, from the harpsichord, ordered his players to repeat it from the start, in the hope that the fault might be only a temporary one. But it was useless. Someone behind the proscenium, with more presence of mind than his fellows, ordered the curtains to be closed, and the symphony unravelled like a piece of ragged cloth a family of sharp-toothed rats has set to work upon.

'The auditorium was plunged into darkness. The ushers whose responsibility it would have been to restore light to us at the end of the performance were not at their places. A presentiment of disaster took hold of us all. Though some cried out indignantly, or mocked at Colombani, the greater part assigned a deeper significance to the failure of the machinery. They were proved right, alas!

'I hurried home as quickly as I could, tormented by the idea that this was a specific punishment for my own wrongdoing, for the criminal giddiness with which I had repeatedly abandoned my station, disguising myself like an ungodly woman in pursuit of foolish pleasures I had publicly renounced so long before. Slipping the cloak from my shoulders, I cast my mask into the fire, the very fire I was sitting by while you ate lunch today. Try as I might, I was unable to calm the turmoil of my spirits. I felt that I was suffocating. On an impulse, I walked out into the cloister, to see if the night air would restore me. That is where I encountered Colombani.

'I should say that I had not spoken to him before that night. He had appeared in front of the curtain on several occasions when I was present, once the opera was finished, to acknowledge the applause. Don Astolfo had also told me what he looked like at closer quarters, and I had seen him twice in different settings, once at the market, another time at mass. Practically nothing of what I have told you so far comes from his lips. In the days he spent under our roof, he was too distraught at the events of that one night to talk about his past. My account of the preceding years is the fruit of careful listening and hearsay. When he arrived at St Hyginus's, and his creations began to adorn its stage, everyone in the district, from pensioned widows to shopkeepers, made it their business to discover all they could about his earlier life. The slander of diabolical pursuits had followed him as far as Venice. I persist in thinking it was the fruit of jealousy, and had no basis in fact. When I saw him, however, after midnight, in our convent garden, that was the first thing that came to my mind, and I called out to Our Lady and all the saints for protection.

'He arrived from the canal,' said Mother Hilary, indicating the place to Domenico with a wave of her hand. In the fading sunlight of a winter afternoon, he found it hard to picture anything sinister or fearful setting foot within those walls. He closed his eyes momentarily, in order to concentrate on her words, so that the beauty of their surroundings would not detract from the story she was telling.

'He was sopping from head to foot. I never asked him what route he had come by. It was clear he had half swum, half waded the last part. He was breathless from the effort of clambering over the gate. When he caught sight of me, he fell to his knees at my feet and burst into tears. I could make nothing of his confused mumblings, but they gave me the opportunity to reach a calmer assessment of what was happening. I realised he must be in a state of shock and humiliation, near to madness even. Helping him gently to his feet with words of comfort and solicitude, I led him indoors. Already I could make out his obsessively repeated prayer for "sanctuary", "sanctuary". To admit a member of the male sex within our convent at that hour was an act of enormous impropriety, I will not deny it, even if this particular individual was less likely to imperil the sisters' purity than many others. He was a soul in torment. Charity is the foremost among all our duties. It must take precedence over what the world demands or thinks. That is my firm belief. And the word that came to his lips again and again rang in my ears like an admonition. He invoked a right hallowed by centuries of use. It was one I, for all my fearfulness and uncertainty, could not deny him.

'We keep a fire burning in the guests' sitting-room throughout the winter months. It was the work of a moment to stir the embers and add further fuel. I had lit a candle on first arriving home, and had not extinguished it when I walked into the garden. Turning to face Colombani, I saw that the front of his jerkin was stained with blood. Not just a spot or two, a veritable stream, as if he had grasped the body of a mortally wounded man in his arms.

' "What is this?" I whispered. "What evil thing has happened, beyond the failure of your machine?"

' "Oh mother, mother, do not judge me!" he implored. "Do not chase me from your presence, on this night when every other creature has deserted me! I have triumphed at last. He is my prisoner now. Never again can he return to tempt me or torment me. But oh," and he fell to his knees again, his words faltering amidst abundant tears, "I did not wish blood to be shed! Oh, no, not that! And the blood of an innocent man!" '

'Wait,' Domenico interrupted, 'when he spoke of triumph, he was thinking of Negri, there can be no doubt. But Negri had disappeared from his life years before! Who did he mean? Had someone else been killed?'

Mother Hilary nodded emphatically.

'Alvise Contarini. They found his body the next morning.'

'The man was crazy. He lost his senses as a consequence of the disgrace, mistook his employer for Goffredo Negri, and struck him down.'

'Such a construction can very easily be put upon the facts. But in my opinion, it would be mistaken. A spirit that has reached the depths of desperation Colombani plumbed in those grim days would not be capable of guile. He had the air of one who has succeeding in confronting his personal demon and has wrested victory from the jaws of catastrophe, even at the price of his own soul and happiness. I was at his side, comforting him, exhorting him to pray, encouraging him to have hope again, or to accept that, even if it was more than he could conceive of at that time, sooner or later a glimmering of hope would illumine his existence. He insisted resolutely, never wavering from his position, that he had committed no crime. At the same time, there were clearly elements in what had happened which he felt he could not share with me, which he was, indeed, determined to protect me from.'

'But why did he mention Negri, after all those years of separation? Was not that a sign of madness?'

'When I heard his words, I began to wonder if Negri had arrived in Venice, and could perhaps have been present in the theatre on the night of the disaster. My supposition was confirmed when several individuals reported seeing a figure, which answered to his description, in the neighbourhood of St Hyginus's during the days immediately preceding the catastrophe. But nothing could be proved. There was no sure way of telling whether Alvise had received only one, or two visitors in his study on that fateful night.'

'And that is all you are able to tell me? You know nothing more?'

'Don Astolfo was my unfailing guide and helper throughout those days. We waited for the commotion to subside. Angelo was smuggled back inside the theatre, which had been locked up like a coffin with the lid nailed on, because what it contains is not to see the light again until the day of judgment. He has lived there ever since. The local people know about his presence. It would be impossible to keep such a secret from them. But they are discreet and they have faith in their parish priest. No one could contemplate betraying an individual who enjoys his protection.'

'And did Colombani confess his crime to Don Astolfo? Is he no wiser than you, concerning the happenings of that awful night?'

'The secret of the confessional,' came the solemn answer, 'is one even the most reprobate and profligate of priests in Venice take care to honour. Surely you have not forgotten how a saint of the church was cast from the great bridge of Prague into the icy waters of the river, for refusing to reveal to his emperor the things he had been told of in confession. I have no idea what words may have passed between Colombani and our priest. But my impression is that he is just as ignorant as you or me in this affair.'

Mother Hilary led the way indoors again, returning to her place by the fire. Domenico had been away from the theatre much longer than he had intended. The time had come for him to leave, but he found it hard to put an end to the conversation. There was so much he had learned, so much he needed to digest, and so much he still wanted to find out.

'When I visited Colombani,' he said, carefully choosing the singular pronoun, conscious of the deception he was practising, 'I heard singing. It was most peculiar, for it seemed to be coming from inside the room where we stood. And yet there was no one to be seen. It was a woman's voice and the song, if I am not mistaken, was Neapolitan.'

'My son,' said Mother Hilary, 'it is foolish of me to conceal any element in this puzzle from you! I understand that now. The habit of years makes me unwilling to disclose any of the secrets Don Astolfo and I have harboured for such a long time except when it proves absolutely necessary. Recently a girl appeared at the window of Colombani's room. A girl with long, auburn tresses she loves to comb out in the sunlight. She must come from Naples, for the songs she sings are from that city.'

'But this latest enigma sheds no light on the business at all. If anything, it makes it more congested!' Domenico complained. He lifted the portfolio from the table top where he had placed it. 'Mother, I found these papers amongst some musical scores, in a cupboard in the theatre, on the floor below the one where Colombani lives. I can make nothing of them. Some sheets are covered in handwriting, others in diagrams and calculations that could be the work of a mathematician or a natural scientist, if they do not have a more sinister intent. Would you be so good as to look through them, or to show them, if possible, to Don Astolfo?

Although it is unlikely, I cannot help hoping they may offer us a clue to this tangled knot of mysteries.'

'Leave them with me, my son. I shall see what I can do once I have regained my presence of mind. To speak of these events brings back most vividly the painful emotions which accompanied them at the time of their occurrence. They cloud my understanding and disturb my judgement, like the great mysteries of the faith. But while the wonder the latter induce is salutary and humbling, the former provoke dull dread and despair, which are often the prelude to some greater sin or tragedy.'

17

As soon as he set foot inside the theatre, Domenico realised that something untoward was afoot. Two lackeys he did not recognise, in a livery he knew was Gradenigo's, bustled rudely past him. There was a general air of rummaging, poking and probing which he found unsettling. Despite the short time he had spent there, he had already come to feel proprietorial about the place, so that an irruption on the part of strangers struck him as a personal offence. Limentani's voice, in a tone of unmistakable irritation, reached him as he climbed the stairs.

'I still do not grasp the point of all this. What is it you wish to find? Your men are turning the premises upside down, raising clouds of dust, provoking a disorder it may take us ages to set right, and for the sake of what?'

'I have strict instructions from my client, whose import I am not at liberty to divulge,' answered a voice he recognised as Carpi's, with a certain agitation. 'Need I point out that my client is also your employer?'

When he got to the top of the stairs, Domenico saw both men, as well as the scene of chaos which surrounded them. The air of the room was thick with dust. The pile of scores they had sorted through so carefully had been scattered pell-mell across the floor. Every cupboard and casket had been thrown open. Somebody had even ripped the lining of the couch where he and Rodrigo had spent the night, in order to see if anything might be concealed inside it.

'What is going on?' he half shouted, not even trying to hide his anger. 'What do you think you are up to? Are we not to be allowed to work in peace?'

Because of their conversation outside the opera house, he addressed the lawyer more directly than he might otherwise have done. Carpi's reaction was peculiar. He appeared to be so afraid the bystanders might gain some inkling of the bond that linked them that he did his best to ignore Domenico's presence. The younger man was unable to catch his eye. He wondered what could have happened to produce such a change. Only two nights before, the lawyer had been eager to arrange a private interview, under any pretext whatsoever.

'The nuisance is practically over,' Carpi said to Limentani, as the men he had brought with him reassembled.

It was evident their search had been quite fruitless. What random papers they had come upon were cast aside disconsolately by the lawyer, after only a moment's inspection.

'But what is it you are looking for?' the impresario insisted, unable to suppress a smile at the ridiculousness of the whole proceedings. 'If you tell us the object of your search, then perhaps we can help you.'

'I was looking,' said Carpi with a sigh, still avoiding any acknowledgement that Domenico had joined them, 'for something which probably does not exist, and which I ought not to have been cajoled into believing might have existed at one time. It was the idle fancy of a foolish woman and, if she had not caught me in a moment of weakness, I would have paid no heed to her insinuations.'

He removed his hat and bowed, evidently keen to withdraw as soon as he comfortably could. It struck Domenico that, rather than being frustrated, the lawyer was relieved at the result of his ransackings.

'I thought Gradenigo had put this bee into your bonnet,' said Limentani with characteristic acuteness. 'You had not mentioned a woman until now.'

'If he did not provide the hint, it was nonetheless his interests that I came to safeguard,' the lawyer said sententiously. 'Here as in other cases, the sole reason for my conduct is to be sought in the security of those I have the privilege to act for.'

He and his lackeys trooped downstairs. Domenico reflected that Carpi's intervention would at least prevent Limentani from upbraiding him for taking such a lengthy lunch break. He did of course realise that he had unwittingly removed, in the nick of time, perhaps the very papers Carpi wished to get his hands on. It troubled him that he might be guilty of dishonesty in saying nothing to the man in front of him, who treated him so generously. But then he had no way of being sure that the contents of the portfolio possessed any importance whatsoever. They might be as worthless as the other scattered sheets which now littered the floor of their office. Limentani had quite enough on his mind without taking an interest in the fate of Colombani or the murder of a man seven years before they set foot in the theatre. Domenico was relieved that the papers had been entrusted to Mother Hilary and Don Astolfo rather than to the lawyer. They would be safer in their hands.

'What madness!' the impresario was commenting. 'And to think that the company will be assembled here within the hour! I had my work cut out to stop them throwing out the parts you and your assistants have been copying, as if they were rubbish.'

Domenico had spent that morning directing, and helping, two young scribes as they concocted sets of orchestral parts from the scores of the operas that had been chosen. Though there were no indications of wind instruments, it was easy enough to deduce these from the string parts. There were to be pairs of oboes and bassoons in the orchestra at St Hyginus's. Even clarinets had been discussed, if it proved possible to get hold of a pair of those new-fangled contraptions with their smooth, mellifluous tone. Trumpets and kettledrums, which Limentani insisted were to be written in for the climaxes, were another matter. Domenico had had to invent their parts from scratch. The work was nearly complete. He planned to spend the remainder of the afternoon putting the finishing touches to it. The news of a general meeting took him unawares.

'Who is coming?'

'The singers, the prompter, a répétiteur to help you. Everyone except the technicians. They are busy with the clouds,' said Limentani with a smile. 'Which gives me an idea. We shall receive the company down below, in the auditorium. The hammering and knocking may distract us somewhat, but it will be easier than trying to squeeze everyone into this dust-filled hole.'

'You realise,' said Domenico, as he and his employer arranged chairs in a semi-circle, in the very space where within five days crowds would be gathered for the first night, 'the biggest problem we face? We do not have a new opera. Can we attract the interest we need with music that is five, or ten years old? Even if the pieces we are giving have not been heard before in Venice?'

Limentani slumped into a chair, in an attitude of exhaustion that was most unlike him.

'What are we to do, my friend? You are absolutely right and, though I have found a half solution, a whole one would be infinitely preferable.'

'And what is your half solution?'

The impresario's features lit up again.

'Ah! I would be no man of the theatre if I did not have a trick or two up my sleeve, with which to surprise even my most faithful collaborator. Have patience. All will be revealed before night falls.'

18

The Court of Darkness. Or would the court of obscurity be a better translation? Andreas had many times been intrigued by the street names he came across in Venice, derived from a celebrated family that lived or had lived there, a coffee shop, a bakery or a boatyard, a well, a warehouse or the battered remants of an antique statue, to be encountered half way down its length. None, however, was so appropriately named as the shadowy courtyard Hedwiga's manservant led him into. The town house which she rented filled one side with its imposing façade of grey stone, in a sombre version of the Palladian style. For Andreas, a paladin of enlightened thought, an enthusiastic reader of the French philosophers since puberty, the very designation of the place read like a challenge.

From the moment he set eyes upon him outside the church of the Holy Apostles, Andreas had observed the manservant closely. If his features were different from those of the gondolier who had steered their craft two days before, they had the same unnatural stillness and fixity. There was something peculiar in the way he placed his feet upon the ground, as if it were a procedure he had only recently learned, and still had not got properly accustomed to. Such a manner of walking would have been unsurprising in a toddler. It gave an uncanny air to a guide who, as far as Andreas was able to tell, for he studiously averted his face, had long since entered upon middle age.

They set out past Our Lady of Miracles in the direction of Sts John and Paul, then cut sharply to the left. Andreas had not visited this part of the city before. The lane they were following reached an abrupt conclusion in front of a stretch of dismally still water. A small, flat-bottomed boat was tied up where the paving stones petered out. The fellow indicated with a gesture that Andreas should get in, then pushed off using an oar. The canal, if it was a canal, rather than an isolated, stagnant pond, was so narrow no further impetus was necessary to ferry them across. An alleyway on the other side led into the courtyard, which had a scrawny bush of holm oak at its centre.

There was no sign of life around them. Andreas found it hard to believe the houses neighbouring Hedwiga's could be unoccupied for, in spite of the all-encompassing silence, they showed no evidence of neglect or decay. The bell rang eerily in those deserted surroundings and, after a brief interval, the door swung open, as if by a magical command. From what he could make out, the ground plan of the house was a squashed rectangle. The façade corresponded to one of the longer sides. He left the manservant at the bottom of a flight of marble stairs and was met at the top by a lackey in livery, bearing a candelabra with three lighted candles, which smoked excessively. Either they were of poor quality, which would have been odd, since Hedwiga's means were anything but limited, or there was an element hostile to them in the air of the interior, one they had to struggle with, at great cost of wick and wax, in order to give light. The corridor at first floor level skirted an inner courtyard deep in shadow. Long drapes of pale fabric hung over the windows, parting as they fell to reveal a monotonous pattern of corresponding apertures on the other side.

After such dullness, the room Hedwiga received him in was incongruously bright. Andreas had been conscious, as he approached, of a pervasive smell, and struggled to identify it. No sooner had he entered his hostess's presence than it vanished. The room looked northwards. The shutters on the high, elongated windows had been thrown aside to reveal a cloudless sky beyond, which was, however, drained of colour. The daylight entering was chill, uniform and penetrating. He could not help thinking that Hedwiga looked younger than the last time he had seen her. She wore a fashionable velvet cap, decorated with feathers in the latest French style, with pale blue ribbons attached to it falling down behind. Her hair had not been powdered, but was of a natural grey certain women of Andreas's acquaintance took enormous pains to counterfeit by artificial means. Without rising to greet him, she gestured to a chair opposite her own, close to the log fire which burned in a monumental chimney, then dismissed the lackey with a curt wave of her hand. Andreas wondered if he would be offered any form of refreshment. The journey, though not effortful, had left him breathless, his mouth and lips parched and dry. He noticed a glass on the ornamental table to his right, evidently placed there in anticipation of his arrival. It was filled with a sweet-smelling distilled liqueur. He raised it to his lips. Hedwiga, who did not like to waste time, began speaking while he was still sipping from it.

'At our last meeting, you did not make clear to me what brought you to the theatre of St Hyginus, or how you managed to establish that there was a connection between it and our friend Goffredo Negri.'

'That is easily explained,' Andreas said, starting slowly, then getting into his stride, helped, no doubt, by the liqueur, which diffused a warm glow through his chest. 'I have learned in my work that it is a mistake to accept any line of investigation as exhausted, especially when pursued by incompetents, or in a less than recent past. When Eleonora Calefati vanished, or was ravished, all of those who had any association with Negri were rounded up and interrogated. Not a few were tortured, so as to extract more reliable confessions. The men responsible for the investigation believed that the black arts had been employed in the affair, and therefore considered extreme measures to be justified.

'This expedient could not, however, be made use of where Negri's closest collaborator was concerned. A renowned apothecary, he enjoyed the personal protection of the queen, who feared that, if he were to die or suffer mutilation, his competitors would prove unable to prepare the ointments and decoctions she relied on in her various maladies. All of those present at the interrogation of this man were astounded by the sense he showed of his own importance, and by the insolence with which he treated his accusers. The instruments of torture were brought in for him to inspect, but he looked on them with equanimity. Perhaps he had already received assurances from his protectress that, in his case, they would not be applied. Although placed under house arrest, he managed to slip past his guards and flee to Rome. It is far from improbable that the monarch's wife had connived at his escape.

'With the haphazard inefficiency that characterises the administration of that kingdom, no attempt was made to pursue the matter further. The complexities of obtaining an extradition from the Pope constituted an insurmountable barrier to the laziness of the Neapolitan police. Three years later, news arrived that he had died in circumstances of abject poverty. That is where things lay when I interviewed Prince Calefati. You will appreciate that I lost no time in journeying to Rome to seek out the lodging house where the apothecary had breathed his last.

'My enquiries led me to a grimy, ill-smelling hostelry, by the theatre of Marcellus in the Jewish ghetto, not far from the Capitoline hill. It transpired that I was not the first person to arrive there in search of information about the apothecary's last days, nor the first to mention the name of Goffredo Negri. The proprietor, an old man of diminutive stature who scowled at me from beneath bushy eyebrows, rubbing his scarred and scabby palms together all the while, offered to sell me what he claimed was the last of the articles to be found in the fugitive's baggage when he died. He refused to let me examine its contents. The price he named initially was so high that I was forced to barter with him for the better part of an hour, till his greed could be coaxed down to more reasonable proportions. Nevertheless, I believe I got the best part of the apothecary's legacy. From what I could gather, the other articles sold off before I came had been glass containers, sieves, phials and printed books. My share of the spoils was a worn old leather satchel containing written papers, among them letters to the apothecary from Goffredo Negri.'

Hedwiga's face lit up with excitement. She was so impressed that she got up from her chair and paused in front of the chimney piece, bending forward over Andreas.

'So you have held in those hands papers written by Negri himself? Did not an electric shock run through your frame when you touched them? Were not your fingers scorched and seared, as if they had picked up coals from a living fire, even though the fire itself was cooling, and the coals had lost the incandescence that was theirs at the height of the blaze?'

Andreas shook his head uncomprehendingly.

'Nothing of all that, my dear Baroness. The sheets were stained and greasy, whether from the apothecary's touch, or because the kitchen fats had impregnated every object in that poor hovel, I cannot tell. There were strings of mathematical formulas and jumbled up Greek letters I could make nothing of, annotations and jottings Negri intended for himself, and which it would be impossible for another reader to unravel. I suspect the apothecary had taken pains to destroy all those papers which risked incriminating him. One sheet, however, had escaped his vigilance. It bore the name of an inn in Bologna, at the northern limit of the Papal States. In the few lines it contained, Negri informed his friend, or his accomplice, that his journey northwards was practically complete, and that all further communications must be addressed to him care of Alvise Contarini, at the theatre of St Hyginus in Venice.'

This last revelation provoked an even higher degree of agitation in Hedwiga.

'How could he do it? The traitor! The scoundrel! How could he be so foolish? It was Colombani who drew him there, you realise that? Time and again I had warned him against yielding to sweet memories of former times, against attempting to renew an association which could only bring greater ruin to them both! If he had returned to my side with the fruits of his expedition, together we could have brought the great work to completion! I would have been spared these dreary years of waiting, and Negri could have reached a new pinnacle of achievement in his art. And instead he chose to double-cross me, to take his booty to that stupid clown and his employer, for whom nothing was real till it appeared upon a stage.

'He feared me, do you know that?' she virtually spat out to Andreas, her eyes aflame. 'He feared my power and feared I might surpass him! That is why he sought out his old assistant, in defiance of all pacts and understandings. I cannot tell how much of his lore Colombani shared. But I have long been convinced that the purpose of their journey through the Ottoman lands had nothing to do with musicality and vocal technique, and everything to do with Negri's need, his longing for a pupil and a helpmate. He found both those in me, found everything he could have desired.

Then at the last moment, with the winning post in sight, he betrayed me, and all was lost!'

Andreas had never seen, and had never expected to see, Hedwiga overcome by a paroxysm of emotion such as this. A creature of great gifts and equal insecurities, he was instinctively drawn to those he perceived as stronger, more ruthless and dispassionate than he could ever be. The child in him was appalled to witness signs of weakness and frustration in a woman who till then had seemed the embodiment of chill calculation. Bewildered by the talk of Colombani, whose name meant nothing to him, he allowed the torrent of words to sweep over him without even attempting to grasp the deeper significance that lay behind them.

'Don't you understand?' cried Hedwiga, still standing in front of the fire, the upper part of her body arched forwards, gesturing wildly with her arms. 'Colombani and Eleonora are of a kind. Nature made them from the same mould. Of all the thousands of wretches who tumble each day into the world of the living, unawares and unprepared, only a handful possess the energy with which creatures such as those are gifted. And even fewer have the skill to turn that energy to higher uses!'

As she spoke, she grew calmer, and her eyes, still fixed upon Andreas' features, at last began to see them. She caught the look of incomprehension on his face, and it brought her to a realisation of how disjointed and incoherent her phrases had been. She was frothing slightly at the lips. Sinking back into her chair with a moan, she crumpled her handkerchief in her left hand and covered her mouth with it, as though she feared she might be sick. To Andreas, it was as if she had aged a decade in the course of their discussion.

'Dear Baroness,' he put in, after a brief and very awkward silence, 'I can make nothing of this outburst. Be so good as to begin at the very beginning and explain, in an orderly fashion, the nature of your association with Goffredo Negri. And when this dove, this pigeon, this Colombani person enters the tale, give me as much information about him as will allow me to assign him his due role in such a tangled web.'

'Beginnings, beginnings, my dear Count,' mumbled Hedwiga, rocking back and forth. 'What are beginnings? What are endings?

You talk like a child, as if it were possible to trace the root of our actions back to a day or an hour, a decision or a thought. As if, by unravelling thread after thread the fabric on the loom, one could discover the intentions of the woman who carded the wool, the mood of the lichens which were used to dye it, the paths of the sheep from whose haunches it was taken, or the thoughts of the blades of grass they cropped while the wool was thickening on their flanks.'

'Then let me attempt to bring order to this chaos,' offered Andreas.

It was like finding himself in a foreign country, whose language he had only mastered fragments of. Yet he must string those fragments together if he was to communicate, in even the most rudimentary fashion, with its inhabitants. He did not ask himself whether he believed in the concepts he was dealing with, any more than he had forced himself, in the past, to accept or explicitly to deny the tenets of the Catholic Church. He engaged in a suspension of disbelief similar to the one he had practised at the Empress's court in Vienna, when involved in assessing the claims to sainthood of Father Ambrose's candidate.

'Negri set out for Naples on a mission known to you both. His intention was to find Eleonora Calefati and to kidnap her, so that she could assist you in a task in which Colombani had failed.'

'That is not quite correct,' Hedwiga said. 'When Negri travelled south that autumn, we knew what he was looking for, but not whether he would find it, or where. Coming upon the girl so soon was a piece of luck neither of us could have counted on.'

'And having found her, why did Negri return to Venice? Had he not destroyed her? Or if he had taken from her everything he needed, what point was there in returning northwards with her and sharing his prey with others? If she had been burnt, or transmuted by fire, what form did she accompany him in?'

'What happened at the Calefati reception was merely the beginning,' Hedwiga explained, in weary, hopeless tones. 'Kidnapping may be the best word for it, though the term is crude and grossly physical. Let us say that Negri was able to remove Eleonora temporarily to another dimension, from which she cannot return under her own volition.'

'What good was she to him there?'

'You forget, dear Count, that I did not have the privilege of talking to Goffredo after he had made his catch. Spirits such as hers, or Colombani's, cannot be overpowered or forced. They can, however, be imprisoned. Or rather, certain limits can be set on their movements which they are powerless to break. Forgive me, I am being imprecise. Negri could never have done to Colombani what he did to Eleonora. My suspicion is that he revealed so much to Colombani that, rather than master and pupil, they had become equals.'

'So why did Colombani refuse to cooperate?'

Hedwiga gave a hollow laugh.

'I cannot see into that creature's mind. His motivations are a mystery to me. Many years have passed since he learned to wrap his thoughts in a fog impenetrable to my power. When he broke with Negri for the first time, he was numbered among the greatest singers of his day. He paid a price for shattering that bond, and never sang again upon a stage. Not that I think he depended on Negri in order to be able to sing. It broke his heart to leave the man. It is as simple as that.'

'But why did he leave him?' Andreas repeated.

Hedwiga sucked her cheeks in meditatively, as if ruminating her answer, or as if the word she was about to pronounce were so abhorrent to her she had to gather her forces before uttering it.

'Goodness,' she said. 'Do you know what goodness is? I have long since forgotten, though I could learn again. It is a banal thing, that infiltrates and foils the greatest schemes of human and more than human minds. The most grandiose construction can be almost completed, when the meddling of goodness brings it tumbling down about one's ears.'

'The way you are talking reminds me of Father Ambrose,' Andreas mused.

'Of whom?'

'No matter. Your religion ought to be the reverse of his, yet there are moments when I could almost believe they are one and the same. And equally absurd. So Eleonora is still alive?'

He put the question which was most important of all to him with an affected lightness of tone, which he fervently hoped would lure Hedwiga into a direct answer.

'Alive?' she repeated. ' "Beginnings, endings, alive, dead . . ." What terms are these for men and women placed as we are to employ? It is my custom to be faithful to the pacts I enter into, and I think what I have revealed to you in this half hour is infinitely more precious than anything you have told me since we met. Yet you will make poor use of it, dear Count. Your scepticism is like a leather harness which cruelly binds the wings sprouting on your shoulders. They are no use to you for flying, either to Heaven or to Hell.'

'You are talking in riddles, Baroness. Your words mean nothing to me.'

Hedwiga rose from her chair again, this time with a more decided air.

'Then let me furnish you with proof, or at the least a further puzzle. We shall see what your training as a natural philosopher makes of it. I shall reveal to you the manner in which I first made Goffredo Negri's acquaintance, and the only way I have had sight of him through these seven long years.'

She led Andreas to a corner of the room, and released the catch on a cabinet of polished wood at little more than waist height. The lid lifted to reveal a shallow porcelain basin, a jug of water and a cluster of bottles containing powders of different colours and textures. As Andreas watched, she poured enough water into the basin to fill it not quite to the brim then, opening a bottle, scattered a handful of blue crystals across the surface, at the same time murmuring words under her breath he strained to catch but could not.

When the crystals hit the water, it frothed up and hissed, turning a brilliant, cobalt blue. As the dye gradually cleared, the liquid assumed an unnatural transparency, as if it were a sheet of glass. With an involuntary shiver, Andreas realised that he could now see neither the bottom of the basin, nor the reflection of his features or Hedwiga's in the water. All of a sudden a face appeared, at one further remove. It could have been behind another sheet of glass as when, if a tumult is going on in the street, faces impatient of confinement pressed close to the window, peering out to learn as much as they can, become visible to those below. This face was a man's. It had once been handsome but was now merely imposing, even terrifying. He had a large wart in the hollow between his left eye and the bridge of his nose.

His expression changed, growing livelier, more acute. The eyes looked directly out, straining to perceive something they knew must be there but were unable to distinguish. Andreas felt an instinctive urge, which he resisted, to cover his face with his hands, so as to prevent that gaze alighting upon him.

'He knows we are watching him,' said Hedwiga, 'though he does not know who we are. I have tried every strategy I can think of to communicate with him, to shatter the barrier that separates us, but to no purpose. Look what pain it causes him!'

The face slackened. Its owner had given up the attempt to discover who was observing him. As if the surface of the water had been a lens of variable intensity, different parts of the face lunged at the spectators, magnified to such an extent that the very pores of the skin resembled craters on a planet viewed through a telescope. Watching made Andreas dizzy. The thought of being, however distantly and briefly, in the man's power (for there could be no doubt that, powerless to prevent them seeing him, he was interfering at will with the manner of their seeing) filled him with nausea. It detracted from the satisfaction of knowing that at last, in a fashion he could never have explained to those who sent him on his mission, he had succeeded in beholding the features of Goffredo Negri.

19

By the time the remainder of the company got to find out about Limentani's surprise, the meeting had reached such a contentious point that the impresario had more or less decided to abandon the entire madcap project. As far as he was concerned, the cloud machinery at St Hyginus's might continue to rot away in the darkness to which, for the better part of a decade, it had been consigned. A heavy curtain hung between the stage and the body of the theatre. It muffled the knocking and hammering of Luca Schiavoni and his assistants, who were working round the clock to get the huge contraption functioning again in time for the opening of the season. Nevertheless, the racket they made could be clearly heard. A wave of discouragement swept over Limentani, and the background interference jangled on his already fraying nerves, though he could not bring himself to order the technicians to call a halt.

Persuading opera singers to agree with one another, or with their music director, had never been an easy business. Furthermore, this season was beginning late and under anomalous conditions. Gabriela Dotti barely deigned to acknowledge Domenico when she arrived, so grand had she become, in her own estimation, since the evening when they performed together to the delectation of Cardinal Albani's guests. Though the weather that afternoon was considerably milder than during the preceding days, Gabriela wore a heavy mantle with fur trimmings. She entrusted the matching muffler, which protected her fashionably pale and delicate hands, to a little Moorish boy, acting as her servant. Attending to her caprices was not enough to exhaust the lad's energies, and he danced incessantly at her heels throughout the afternoon's proceedings. She also sported a stylish hat in the likeness of a gamebird, with glistening feathers of sheeny black and terracotta colouring. A fascinator veil, with beauty spots sewn into it, tumbled from the brim across her face, yet did not hide the larger beauty spot on her right cheek, or the characteristic pout into which her gaudily coloured lips had set.

The contralto singer, Donatella Reis, could not have been more different. Although her name was German, she hailed from Bologna. Her shapely curves exemplified the generous embonpoint so long considered typical of women from that city. Having recently given birth to her fourth child, she was attended by a wetnurse with whose services, in the stricter sense, she could easily have dispensed. Twice during the discussion Donatella undid her corsage to reveal a breast of dazzling whiteness, popping the nipple into the mouth of her protesting infant. The two middle children were, however, enough of a handful to stretch the wetnurse's powers of discipline to the full with their antics. By contrast the eldest, a boy in tight breeches which looked several sizes too small for him, observed the proceedings with an expression of unrelieved earnestness, pressed up tightly against his father's side.

Donatella's husband had the lean rigidity of the perpetually nervous and preoccupied. He reminded Domenico of a thin deal plank just beginning to warp, or of a sliver of Parmesan cheese, shaved off from a large block of the stuff. He stooped slightly, and looked so frail it would not have been surprising to discover he was full of holes. Combining the roles of spouse and manager, he presented a striking contrast to his wife's sensual curvaceousness. He tutted when Donatella breast fed their baby, not because bystanders might be scandalised, but because by exposing her throat she risked catching a chill, thereby impairing the quality of the rich tones which Ansaldo Limentani had promised a considerable sum to enlist for his season.

The tenor, Umberto Tecchi by name, suffered from a nervous tic. He had become afflicted with this in the course of a renowned episode, when he found himself compelled to defend the honour of his mistress from the aspersions of an Austrian cavalry officer. The woman had a weakness for the gaming table and, on that particular evening, had gambled away the better part of Tecchi's earnings for the season. It was an unlucky night for her in more ways than one. As she and her protector were leaving the casino, they ran into the officer on the steps. He made an extravagant bow and addressed her with a frankness that left Tecchi no alternative but to challenge the fellow to a duel.

Rumour had it that the glum expression his features so often settled into had won him the nickname 'sour the milk' from his playmates when a child. If this had not been the case, the circumstances of the duel would have justified it. Already fully informed of his mistress's infidelities, Tecchi had been struggling to devise a fitting plan for relieving himself of her company forthwith. Now he found himself with no choice but to risk his life defending a putative good reputation not a shred of which actually survived. Fate could not have reserved an unkinder irony for him.

Glum he may have looked, but he did not lack courage. With a skilful manoeuvre no one would have predicted, he ran his opponent through in a matter of minutes. The sight of the poor fellow expiring at his feet, however, so distressed him that, from that time on, the left side of his face was convulsed at regular intervals by an involuntary grimace, accompanied by a clicking of the teeth not unlike the noise which is produced when a military man brings his heels together and salutes. Limentani reassured a disbelieving Domenico that the only time Tecchi was freed of this distressing symptom was when he faced an audience and sang to them.

It was the bass Domenico liked best. He came from Naples and owed much of his fame to his performance of dialect roles in comic interludes set in that city. A modest man and yet a consummate musician, he experienced not the slightest difficulty in learning everyone else's parts on top of his own. If another singer's memory faltered, Salvatore Iannelli was able to prompt them so discreetly no offence was ever taken. He was an instinctive actor and could send his spectators into paroxysms of laughter, merely by the posture of his body when he arrived on stage. That was the only drawback to working with him. The music had to wait until the laughter had subsided. He had been known, perhaps in order to tease the director at the harpsichord (who, a matter of days later, would be Domenico) as much as the public in the theatre, to postpone still further the moment when he started singing by a movement of the arm, or a different tilt of the head, which led to a renewed chorus of mirth.

On one memorable evening, near the end of that celebrated season at St Hyginus's, Domenico laughed so much that the tears in his eyes meant he was unable to make out the keys his fingers were preparing to strike. He had, in fact, forgotten that it was up to him to give the opening chords of the aria, so engrossed was he in watching Iannelli. Until they got the customary nod from their maestro's head, the string players would not bring down their bows. The bass soloist had to wiggle his right eyebrow expressively before Domenico realised the gesture was directed, not at the audience, but at him, and recalled that he was not in the theatre primarily to enjoy himself, but had a job to do as well.

But there was little to laugh about in the company's preliminary meeting. Dissension broke out at the very start. Without even waiting to hear the names of the operas they were to perform, Donatella's husband insisted that, by the terms of her contract, his wife could not be asked to sing in an opera where her part had fewer solo arias than the soprano. As a consequence, any piece which cast the alto in a subsidiary role must be excluded. Gabriela rose from her chair in high dudgeon. Without bothering to protest, she motioned to her Moorish servant to lead the way out. She had not taken her first steps towards the door, however, when Limentani laid a hand on her arm. He angrily reminded Reis that no contract had as yet been signed, although the sum he would pay for Donatella's services had been agreed. Any discussion of the conditions under which she would sing was therefore purely hypothetical.

'Put an end to this foolishness, Raimondo,' the alto told her husband. 'I have the utmost confidence in Maestro Limentani and am happy to sing in any opera he chooses. And if there are fewer arias than you might wish, it will give me a chance to save my voice for our next engagement.'

Tecchi intervened at this point and reminded those present, in mournful tones that, the damp climate of Venice being detrimental to his upper register, he could not guarantee to produce anything higher than a G with that characteristic sweetness of tone which had rendered him famous. His words were interspersed with clicking noises occurring at unpredictable intervals. That afternoon's meeting was not long enough for any of the people present to get used to his handicap, so that each time it afflicted him they were all startled in the most disagreeable fashion. The sounds he made involuntarily had a distinctly warlike effect. Later, in conversation with Domenico, Iannelli compared it to intermittent gunfire coming from the theatre foyer at their backs, and Domenico realised that one of several factors contributing to his general feeling of unease that afternoon was this sense of irregular warfare going on just within earshot, all the time that they were talking.

Limentani was determined to get down to business quickly. The season was to open, he said, in four days' time, on Tuesday evening, with a performance of a farce by Scarlatti, to be followed on Wednesday by one of Iommelli's greatest successes in the tragic genre, *Elvira, Queen of Thebes*.

'But there is a high B flat in the tenor's opening cavatina!' exclaimed Tecchi, so genuinely aggrieved he produced four clicks in the course of a single sentence.

'We shall transpose it downwards,' said Limentani. 'Our director will make the necessary adjustments in a matter of minutes.'

He gestured towards Domenico.

'Whatever opera is selected, I agree to take part only on condition that I am allowed to include the rondo from Garavini's *Dido* in the second act,' said Gabriela. She had remained standing since her earlier protest, and now sat down again with a thump, as if to emphasise the point.

Domenico knew from experience that insecurity, rather than arrogance, provoked this statement. Gabriela was slow at learning new parts and, if she were to shine at her best from the start, she would have to be allowed to squeeze one of her favourite vocal warhorses into the evening.

'Done,' said Limentani, in a voice growing weary.

'The farce you mentioned, Maestro,' murmured Iannelli, 'has both a bass and a baritone role. I suppose that with a bit of editing

I could manage the two. But it will require careful planning and a couple of smart costume changes.'

'That will only be required of you if I have failed to engage another soloist, subsidiary, of course, to yourself, before our opening night. But I am grateful for such adaptability, my dear Iannelli.'

'So you only wish us to prepare two operas. You are letting us off lightly,' put in Donatella in her rich, booming tones. 'It is a rare impresario who treats his company with such consideration.'

'Not so quickly,' chuckled Limentani. 'A third opera will be added in the course of the season. Your musical director and I have still to make a definitive choice.'

'We will of course be guided,' put in Domenico, determined to be as helpful as he could, 'by the musical substance of the piece, and the opportunities it gives our soloists to display their artistry.'

'I cannot hear a word this fellow says,' exclaimed Reis, 'what with the clattering coming from the stage.'

'What is going on there?' asked Gabriela. 'Do not tell me you are planning to rebuild the theatre as well as preparing two operas within the space of four days!'

Limentani rose to the occasion.

'This delightful theatre brought with it, as a dowry, an unexpected treasure which may prove to be a highlight of our season. It will, indeed, be crucial to the selection of our third and most splendid production, for it would be foolish of me in the extreme not to turn the thing to our advantage.'

He paused, enjoying their puzzlement. No one but Domenico had any inkling what the man could be referring to. As if to increase the suspense, the hammering behind the curtain redoubled at that very moment.

'On the most recent occasion when this building was actively dedicated to the service of the Muses, seven years ago, it counted among its technical staff a designer of machinery whose name was celebrated throughout Europe. His present whereabouts are, sadly, a mystery to all of those who wondered at his art. I have in mind none other than Angelo Colombani.'

Several of those present gasped. Gabriela, who had never heard of the man, tried to look shocked, mournful and excited by turns, not certain which emotion would be the most appropriate response to this important piece of news. Domenico was aware of a tingling sensation up and down his spine.

'Concealed by the curtain at my back,' Limentani went on, with a majestic wave of the hand which showed what a consummate man of the theatre he was, 'hang suspended the remnants of his last creation, an assemblage of clouds the like of which has not been seen in Milan, Dresden or even in Naples.'

'And you will have it ready for next week?'

The tenor was so astounded he did not click even once.

'I can promise you that by the time the opening night arrives the mechanism will be fully overhauled, allowing the structure to be hoisted out of sight far above the stage. What use we put it to depends which opera we settle on as our third.'

'*The Greeks Return from Troy*,' said Iannelli. 'That has a splendid final scene where all the gods descend out of Olympus.'

'I had not thought of that one,' said Limentani.

Domenico's blood was running cold. Though he had never heard the opera performed, the contrapuntal complexities of the finale made it renowned, if not notorious, throughout the peninsula. It flattered him to think he might be asked to conduct it. But he very much doubted whether he, or the singers, would be able to do it justice, or even to get to the end without coming disastrously unstuck.

'It is a source of great concern to me,' began Reis, his petulant tones contrasting harshly with the reverence which the very mention of Colombani's name had inspired in everybody else, 'that our dear Maestro should overlook a factor even the most inexperienced impresario would never dream of neglecting. A season of three operas, not one of them new? Three revivals, each of which the more cultivated part of the public is likely to have seen already, and in productions drawing on resources infinitely grander than any we can call upon? It is generally considered to be the death of an opera if its finest melodies are leaked to the public only a matter of hours before the première. What kind of success do you imagine we can hope for if we fail to offer Venice one new tune, and if organ grinders and blind fiddlers can delight our clients at street corners with the music we want them to pay money to hear?'

'I have a tune for the fellow.'

The new voice came from the shadows at Reis's back. As if by previous accord, a mandolin struck up on the opposite side of the auditorium, which was also in darkness, and the first voice launched into a Neapolitan ditty. At the same time, a lithe young man described a circle in the space between the singers, turning cartwheels so swiftly that the black and white lozenges on his costume became a confused blur in everyone's eyes. It made Domenico feel dizzy.

What with one thing and another, Limentani had practically forgotten the carefully laid plan according to which Paolo Sarti was to burst in upon them all without warning. As a result, for a split second, he was no less astonished and overwhelmed than the other men and women sitting in front of the lowered curtain in the body of the theatre.

'Harlequin!' the contralto's eldest son cried out in ecstasy.

Forgetting all his shyness, he ran at the young man's heels, doing his utmost to turn cartwheels in imitation, and bringing off one or two so well it was evident he was not averse to a bit of spirited high jinks when he felt in the mood for it. Brighella emerged into the circle of light, singing to his own accompaniment. His costume identified him unmistakably. He wore baggy trousers, a stylishly cut jacket and a flat cap, all of white material, with short, horizontal blue stitching across the seams of the trousers and down the buttons and buttonholes of his jacket. He held the mandolin high up on his chest so that you could see his fine leather belt with its purse, as well as a dagger poking from its sheath, ready for use.

There came a tittering from the other edge of the circle. Colombine, the object of Brighella's serenade, was being led forward by Pulcinella, who was Domenico's favourite. He had nearly split his sides the other day reading a broadside addressed to the chief procurator, in which Pulcinella took up the cause of the wooden puppets whose theatre had been banned from St Mark's Square. And here was the author of the pamphlet right in front of him! True, the gnarled red mask with its prominent, hooked nose looked a little fearsome. The Reis boy stopped his cartwheels and drew close to his father again. Everybody, with the exception of Reis and Gabriela, was laughing with delight and surprise.

'Has this gentleman given you offence?' asked Pulcinella, once the song was finished. He had taken his stance next to the contralto's husband and was sparring with his fists as if preparing for a fight. He shook his head menacingly, and his tapering cylindrical hat teetered like a building on the point of collapse.

'Dear Pulcinella,' Limentani answered, 'we were sorely in need of a spot of comic relief.'

'It's Paolo Sarti,' said Iannelli unbelievingly. 'I thought I recognised the voice.'

'We've eaten nothing but dregs and scrapings for four days,' wailed Harlequin, who was always famished, and could think about nothing except filling his stomach. 'See if the gentleman can give us some employment,' he hinted, nudging Pulcinella and pointing at Limentani.

'An excellent idea,' put in Brighella. 'I have ten other songs as excellent as that one, and I could do with a new pair of shoes. These ones are worn thin with trudging the by-roads from Bergamo to Venice. Hardly the kind of thing a dandy wants to be seen abroad in.'

An elderly man had taken up his position right next to Gabriela, without her noticing. When he spoke up, in the purest Venetian dialect, he gave her such a shock she nearly fainted.

'You shall never marry her!' he shrilled, throwing one arm about the soprano, waving a handkerchief in her face with the other in order to revive her. It was Pantaloon. He was pretending Gabriela was his daughter and heiress and that he had to stop Brighella from seducing her.

'Well?' asked Pulcinella, in a different voice now, not a caricature at all. He took his hat off and lifted the red mask, revealing the face of one delighted at rejoining an old friend. 'What do you say, Ansaldo? Can St Hyginus offer this motley band a refuge from cold and indigence, and from the harshness of the roads?'

'Wait a moment!' broke in Reis. 'Nothing was said in our

negotiations about these vile comics playing on the same stage as my wife!'

'Dear fellow,' said Limentani between his teeth, for he was finally losing his patience, 'one more objection from you and I will be happy to cancel from my mind the very notion that your wife might ever be a member of this company.'

The baby Donatella was holding began to howl as loudly as his lungs would let him. Harlequin had been pulling faces at the infant and, instead of entertaining it, had terrified it.

'Perhaps we could reach a compromise,' said Gabriela, shaking herself free of Pantaloon and stepping forward. 'I propose a pastiche.'

'A what?' asked Pantaloon, twiddling his long moustache and trying to look puzzled but intelligent. Improvisation was his daily bread and butter, as the company generally worked to only the sketchiest of plot outlines. He was quite happy to play along with whatever the soprano might have in mind.

'Is it something we can eat?' asked Harlequin, brightening up. 'A meat dish? Or better still, meat and pasta together?'

He produced a fork from thin air and held it up expectantly in front of him, so that it caught the light and glittered attractively.

'I abhor pastiches,' Limentani said ill-temperedly.

'I, on the contrary, think it is a splendid proposal,' put in Reis.

'You mean,' said Tecchi, warming to the idea, 'that we choose our favourite bits from the repertoire we already know . . .'

'Domenico does some transposing and stitching together,' broke in Gabriela, 'and hey presto! we have an opera.'

A huge load of additional work for me, and you are spared having to learn a new role, thought Domenico.

'And the plot?' asked Limentani. 'The words? Or should we forget about such mundane practicalities?'

'Given your wide range of acquaintances,' said Reis, 'I am sure you can come up with some dishevelled poet mouldering in an attic who will be only too happy to provide verses in return for a crust or two of bread.'

'More food,' said Harlequin. 'These people keep talking about things you can eat but nothing ever arrives. Is it some kind of torture?'

'Out of the question!' cried Limentani, his eyes ablaze. 'I want nothing to do with such base practices! Do you think you can make a fool of me? I will never agree to cobbling and patching of that nature, do you hear, never!'

'Calm down, my friends, calm down!' said Iannelli. 'Can we not negotiate like reasonable creatures?'

He had noticed that the humour of the more difficult members of the company had improved considerably since the idea of a pastiche came up, and hoped to take advantage of this in order to negotiate an agreement.

'I, for one, am happy to welcome Paolo Sarti and his troupe into our midst, on whatever terms our impresario proposes. And no doubt he, in the interests of general harmony and tranquillity, will be ready at least to consider the proposal you have put forward. In all fairness,' he went on, turning to Reis, 'I feel it is up to you to provide a librettist, since you are so enthusiastic about the idea. Let us not be pessimistic. Most of the arias we sing are specifically designed to be moved from one opera to the other, or even between positions in the same opera, with only minimum changes to the wording.'

'How ridiculous these puffed-up creatures are,' commented Colombine. 'I can improvise a dozen songs between one dance and the next, to words no one has heard before. And the singers are terrified to open their mouths unless a poet has made verses for them that scan and rhyme!'

Just to emphasise her point, she blew up her cheeks and, all of a sudden looking fat and middle-aged, took up the kind of posture several female singers of Limentani's acquaintance, who should long since have been pensioned off and had never been capable of acting anyway, rejoiced in adopting because they thought it was dramatic.

'I must take this child home and put it to bed,' Donatella observed, rising from her chair, as she comforted the wailing child in a businesslike fashion.

She had till then been such a still point in the midst of the debate that, by the very fact of moving, she made everyone feel it had ended.

'Why don't we postpone a decision until Sunday?' she continued. 'After all, we have enough on our hands until then learning the pieces that have been chosen. And perhaps when we have begun working together seriously we will find ourselves, as a consquence, more capable of agreeing with one another.'

20

Limentani could not find it in him to be entirely dissatisfied with the upshot of the first full-scale meeting with his singers. He had hoped, by arranging a theatrical entrance for his old friend's troupe, to sidestep the objections he expected the more self-important members of the company to raise. It was agreed that, since a ballet interlude could not be offered, Paolo Sarti and his colleagues would mount a comic sketch between the acts of *Elvira, Queen of Thebes*, as well as putting on a more extended piece to warm the audience up before the farce. Limentani had been worried that the latter was too slight to constitute a full evening's entertainment. But no one would complain about the price of the ticket if they got Pulcinella, his friends and their antics as part of the bargain. Concerning the pastiche, he had two full days to prepare for renewed battle on that front. Donatella and Iannelli, he felt confident, would back up whatever he suggested. As for Gabriela, she was still in the process of rebuilding her reputation after a disastrous failure of memory while on stage in Parma. The impresario was perfectly ready to make veiled or unveiled references to the incident, if it proved necessary in order to bring the singer back into line.

Lacking the older man's experience, Domenico was troubled by a sense of imminent catastrophe. His confidence by no means matched the talent he possessed, and part of him refused to believe he could achieve what Limentani was asking of him in the limited space of time available. Memorising the scores, which he considered to be essential, proved a tougher under-taking than he had anticipated. His dreams were awash with bar lines, key signatures and ornamentations, so that he awoke on Saturday and Sunday mornings without any sensation of actually having rested. Rehearsals with the singers were hampered by the pandemonium coming from the stage where, as well as checking the complicated system of weights and pulleys which allowed Colombani's wonderful mechanism to soar aloft, then descend again without a jolt, Schiavoni and his team were putting the finishing touches to the sets for the opera and the farce, along with a jack of all trades set which would cater for the needs of the comic troupe.

The thought of the castrato, in the room above the one he slept in, busy with his crazy models, further troubled Domenico. He felt guilty about not revealing the man's presence to his employer, especially once Limentani had expressed such admiration for the contraptions Angelo designed. But he did not like the idea of betraying Mother Hilary's confidences by disclosing everything she had told him to Limentani. Were the impresario to be informed about their unofficial lodger, one question would inevitably lead to another. Domenico told himself that, if he kept his own counsel and concentrated on his work, the creature's presence might continue to pass unnoticed and, who knows, they might get to the end of the season without having to learn anything more about the theatre's previous history or the events of that disastrous night. Yet however hard he tried to persuade himself that this was feasible, he could not quite believe it. Perhaps that explained his feeling that disaster was looming. The danger lay in the past as much as in the present. He would have preferred Schiavoni to leave the cloud machinery untouched, or to dismantle it and take it away piece after piece, to be turned to more mundane uses. Instinct told him that, as soon as it resumed its dizzying vertical journeys, a whole range of related phantoms would be summoned back to life. Indeed, the process had already begun.

Nor could he get Rodrigo out of his thoughts. It was foolish to expect that he would bump into the boatman soon or that, even if he did, the man would acknowledge him. Previous encounters of a similar nature had taught Domenico to look for only embarrassment, or hostility, when confronted with a former accomplice, under whatever circumstances. Even when a passionate declaration of love accompanied the misdemeanours, everything was bound to evaporate in the chill light of day. Rodrigo had said nothing about his feelings, and Domenico took this as further proof that there would be no sequel.

The couch felt lonely now he had it to himself. Returning to the theatre on Saturday night after a hearty meal, with the intention of lighting a candle and sitting over a score until the early hours, he saw a lamp reflected in the dark water. When he realised a man was waiting there in a gondola, his heart leapt in spite of him. It had to be Rodrigo. Domenico all but tripped over, in his hurry to get to the edge of the canal.

It was not. But the fellow brought a message from the boatman. He wanted Domenico to meet him the next morning, outside the church of St Lazarus of the Beggars.

'But what is his family name? Where does he live? Where is his boatyard?'

The messenger shook his head and stroked his beard, then answered in thick dialect that this was all he had to say.

Nothing more could be got out of him. Domenico watched as the lantern receded with the rhythm of the man's strokes, lingering then pulling away until it finally rounded a bend and vanished. As luck would have it, he would be free until late in the afternoon of the following day. It was Sunday, and the entire company had been given instructions to rest in preparation for the first run-through, which was scheduled for one hour after sunset. Limentani had assured Domenico that the entire orchestra would be assembled.

An unusual amount of trouble was being taken over the preparations for the performances. From what he knew of theatre practice, it was more common for the members of the orchestra not to have set eyes on the singers until the curtain rose on the opening night, when they would crane their necks across the bodies of their violins to get a glimpse. For Limentani to take such pains was, in Domenico's eyes, an indication of the standards he was being relied upon to achieve. He found the situation intimidating.

Mass lasted longer than was customary. Don Astolfo officiated. Domenico reflected wryly that the priest could not have an important engagement to rush off to afterwards, or he would hardly have drawled out the Latin phrases in quite such a leisurely fashion. Elbowing his way through the crowd issuing from the church, Domenico broke into a sprint that took him past the cloisters of St Francis of the Vineyard, then dashed over the bridge by St Justina's. The hour stipulated for their meeting tolled from the bell tower of Sts John and Paul just as he reached the walkway which runs straight as an arrow along the canal bank to St Lazarus's.

One of the isolated figures loitering outside the church resembled what he remembered of Rodrigo. Domenico slowed his pace. He was out of breath and perspiring. He was sure there would be unattractive dark circles under his eyes, for he had not blown out his candle until dawn began to thin the skies to palish grey. Doubtful whether he would be able to sleep, he had preferred to devote the night to study.

The figure caught sight of him and waved. They greeted one another formally, without touching. Rodrigo, too, was embarrassed. He turned and walked towards the open water of the lagoon, where the canal joins the Fondamenta Nuove, indicating that Domenico should follow. A medium-sized boat was tied up next to the bridge at the end of the canal. Not until they had both got in, and he pushed off from the moorings with a single oar, did Rodrigo explain his plan. He was going to take Domenico out past the graveyard island of St Michael to Murano. There they could eat fried fish in a shack belonging to friends of his. Then he wanted to explore some reed banks in the lagoon.

He blushed when he said this and it made Domenico want to laugh.

'Are there blackbirds in the reed banks?' he asked, and Rodrigo's face broke into a nervous smile.

The day was overcast but not cold, with enough of a breeze to fill out the sail and carry them along at a reasonable pace. Rodrigo made no attempt at conversation. The only sound was the flapping of canvas and an occasional greeting, called across the water to another boatman Rodrigo recognised. Domenico lay back and watched the banks of cloud above them, soft-looking, grey and furry. All at once they made him think of the machinery in the theatre, and he sat up again with a start. There seemed to be no way of escaping from Colombani's device, even out here in the lagoon.

They were not able to eat for some time. In spite of its modest appearance, the shack had an excellent reputation and there was a long queue of customers waiting to get an empty table. Domenico burnt his fingers on the fish because the smell was so enticing and he was impatient to get a piece into his mouth. He tried not to drink too much wine, given that he would be sitting at the harpsichord once darkness had fallen and he needed to have all his wits about him. He was not sure if an afternoon sleep was part of the plan for the reed banks.

'I have to be back before nightfall,' he said.

'There's plenty of time. Anyway, it would be difficult to sail after dark,' Rodrigo pointed out, as if his word were not enough. 'I haven't brought a lantern.'

And he smiled. His mood until then had been subdued. Domenico wondered if he were perhaps afraid. After all, there were people he knew all around them and, although he did not introduce him, he made no attempt to conceal Domenico's presence. There was no way he could have done so. It did not occur to Domenico that Rodrigo had not expected him to turn up for the appointment and could not quite believe he was there. He was ready for this marvellous creature, who could sit at a keyboard and conjure music from it at will, and would soon be directing an orchestra, in a theatre where people paid for tickets, to vanish without trace at any moment.

Domenico gazed at the fishermen's houses along the waterfront. Dressed in their Sunday best, the womenfolk were sitting on the steps outside the front doors, chatting to one another from one family to the next. Some were busy with embroidery. Others were merely indulging in the pleasure of a good gossip. He licked his fingers. It was hard to believe that, only a week ago, even the smell of incense had made him think of food. When he received communion on the preceding Sunday, he had had to rebuke himself for the blasphemous thought that it was the only free nourishment he was likely to get for many days to come.

Once their meal was over, and Rodrigo had insisted on paying, they made their way back to where the boat was tied up. They had to be patient, for one of the ferry boats which carried people of quality back and forth between the city and the different islands had drawn up next to theirs. Men and women were being handed down into it with a great to do and much ceremony.

Domenico's attention shifted to Rodrigo's boat. The boat itself was relatively new, but a carved block of wood he had not noticed before, evidently retrieved from an older vessel, had been fitted neatly into the prow. The relief was of a woman's head, plebeian and lively, and it looked as if at any minute it might spit energetically into the gutter and reel forth a long string of abuse. It possessed a certain air of mystery that struck him as familiar. All at once he realised where he had already seen it. The head bore a remarkable likeness to the fruit-seller whose stall he had careered into five days before.

His train of thoughts was disturbed by the realisation that, next to him, Rodrigo had gone completely rigid. Domenico looked round. He wore an expression between rage and dismay, and his mouth had fallen open. He was unable to bring forth any words, so strong was his emotion. He put one hand on Domenico's shoulder, and pointed towards the ferry boat with the other.

Two women were being ushered to privileged places in the centre, where it was most stable and they were less likely to suffer from seasickness. A lackey arranged the cushions at their backs to make sure they would be comfortable. Domenico's eyes were drawn to the older of the two. She was wearing a fashionable French velvet hat with pale blue ribbons dangling from it, and was swathed everywhere in slightly greying but elaborate lace, like an antiquated Venus emerging from stale foam. It made him think of a child's toy once cast aside, which has been rescued from the bottom of a cupboard and dusted up.

'Agatha!' broke from Rodrigo's lips. 'Agatha!'

There was such distress in the cry Domenico had to restrain the urge to clap his hand across Rodrigo's mouth. The ferry boat was pulling away. The doll-like woman did not look up at first, but her attendant did, with an air of irritation which also had a semblance of guilt in it. Evidently she recognised the voice. She was younger and plumper than her mistress and dressed in canary yellow. Her flamboyant hat was garnished with peacock feathers and there was a string of pearls around her neck. Now both the women were staring at Rodrigo who, having first recovered the power of speech, next regained the use of his legs and dashed across the cobblestones, with every intention of leaping into the boat and using force to prevent their departure.

Alarmed at the incident, the remaining passengers drew away from the women, as if they were infected, or might be the authors of a crime. The older one called in clipped tones to the rowers, with instructions to pull away. They redoubled their efforts and the boat lifted slightly in the water, their strokes were so determined. Two bystanders laid hands on Rodrigo to restrain him, but there was no longer any need. Domenico thought he might burst into tears. His face was like that of a child who has been abandoned once already, and lacks the strength to protest against further desertions. He shook himself free, drew the back of his hand across his mouth as if he had received a blow, then murmured to Domenico:

'Let's go.'

When they were manoeuvring into their mooring place before, he had refused to let Domenico help him. Now, however, he motioned gruffly towards the other oar, and they pulled in time together. In the absence of any other figure of authority, someone had summoned the beadle from the local church. By the time he had been told about the incident, and approached the water's edge to view the culprit, they had rounded a corner in the canal. The man made no attempt to pursue them.

Domenico was unsure where they were heading for and chose not to ask. Soon the thrifty aspect of the houses near the place where they had eaten gave way to poverty and decay. Rodrigo grabbed Domenico's arm to stop him rowing and used his own oar to guide them into a stretch of water, which proved to be a dead end. He attached the boat's painter to a ring at the foot of a flight of slippery, slime green steps.

'Sorry about all that,' he said. 'I'm over it now.'

'What was going on?' asked Domenico, at last giving vent to his curiosity. 'Who were those women? Where do you know them from?'

Rodrigo paid no attention to his questions.

'I want to show you the place where I was brought up,' he said.

Already a knot of ragged children had gathered to welcome them on to the quay. One of them made a comment to Rodrigo which Domenico could catch nothing of. Apparently he answered in their own dialect, for the child's eyes widened with surprise and respect. They were not troubled any further, but the children followed at a distance, observing their every movement with a mixture of wonder and incredulity.

The whole place was enveloped in a sickly stench of rotting fish. Domenico found it hard to tell which houses were inhabited and which were not. Every single roof had gaps or broken rafters. The cloths which covered the window apertures were rotten and moth-infested. They had to climb over a pile of damp wood, rich with mould, to reach the inner courtyard Rodrigo wanted to take him to. An awning lifted briefly and a young woman with a smutty face, and the eyes of someone infinitely older, looked out at them sullenly.

'That's it,' said Rodrigo.

The house he pointed to had a broken-down door and two windows slightly askew. Long ago, in an attempt at decoration, someone had stencilled a pattern of fruits around the door frame. He had to put his shoulder to the door to force it open. Domenico expected darkness, but the apertures on the far side gave directly on to the lagoon. The shutters hung loose, jagged with fragments of broken glass, and the morose light of a January Sunday filled the interior. The memory of his father's warm and comfortable house, above a portico in Bologna, filled Domenico with a confused sense of shame. Until the week before he had thought himself so unfortunate. Yet he had never had to deal with anything like this.

'Was the place always as run down?' he asked.

Rodrigo shook his head but gave no answer. He was rummaging in a wooden cupboard, built into a corner of the room at shoulder height. With a grunt of satisfaction, he produced a small linen bag, tied with a cord at the mouth. He loosened the knot, put his hand inside and, as if he knew the contents so well he could distinguish merely by touch what it was he sought, brought out two statuettes. It looked to Domenico as if they were made of plaster or moulded paper.

'These were my favourite toys when I was small,' Rodrigo said.

One was a water-seller, the other a woman twisting thread on a spindle. The images were absolutely banal, miniatures of the kind you would buy to decorate a crib at Christmas time. The real people they were based on could be seen trudging the streets of practically any city in the peninsula, in winter and in summer, whatever the weather might be. Most such toys were made in Naples, yet there was something that marked these out in Domenico's eyes. With a shudder, he realised they reminded him of the statuettes that peopled the stages of Angelo Colombani's model theatres, in the loft at St Hyginus's. Was it possible that the castrato could have made them?

Rodrigo perched the figures on the windowsill and burrowed in the cloth bag once more. When he withdrew his hand, two objects glinted on his palm. He raised his eyebrows, inviting Domenico to examine them. The larger of the two, though still very small, was a portrait of a woman, set in a golden frame with a ring attached to it, so that it could be worn around the neck. Though the portrait was of fine quality, nothing special distinguished the woman. She had the face of one of the host of girls of the lower classes who washed clothes, cleaned houses and ran errands for the more prosperous families in Venice. A lock of golden hair was pressed carefully between the glass cover and the portrait, so that it did not obscure her features.

Without a word, Domenico replaced the cameo on Rodrigo's palm and lifted the other object to the light. It was a ring with a precious stone set into it, a sapphire as far as he could see. The rim was carved with a pattern of leaves into which a pair of letters was repeatedly interwoven, an A and a C.

'It's all a mystery to me,' Domenico said. 'When are you going to explain? And why did you leave such precious things amidst these ruins, where anyone could come upon them?'

Rodrigo half smiled.

'It must be nearly four years since I came here last. I did not expect to find them.'

'So what are you going to do with them now?'

He held the cloth bag out to Domenico.

'You keep them for me.'

'Only if you explain to me everything that has happened this afternoon.'

21

Not until they were safely hidden in a reed bank in the lagoon did Rodrigo break the silence which followed. The weather had grown colder since lunchtime. Isolated drops of rain fell, puckering the surface of the inlet where they left the boat. He rowed them out from the cul-de-sac by a different route, which led into the open lagoon. Domenico buttoned his jacket up around his neck and thought longingly of the tavern by the theatre where he took his meals. There was always a fire burning there. How warm and welcoming it would be just now! Rodrigo was pulling manfully at the oars, steering between monotonous sandbanks where cane brakes grew thickly. He turned suddenly into a narrow passage, whose existence Domenico had not noticed. The wind whistled through the dry, paper-thin leaves, which closed over their heads as if they were entering a forest. Driving one of the oars firmly into the mud, Rodrigo tied the boat to it, then helped Domenico to get out without wetting his feet. They lay side by side on their backs, not touching. Here at the root of the canes there was not so much as a breath of wind. Above them, however, the tips quivered unceasingly. Beyond were only clouds. No getting away from those.

'There isn't much to tell,' Rodrigo began. 'The people I lived with in that house were not my parents, but they could not have been more kind to me if they had been. I have no memories of moving, so I must have been very young when I arrived. But I can remember something of a time before.'

'They were your foster parents,' said Domenico. 'And the woman in the portrait is your mother.'

Rodrigo grunted his acknowledgement.

'So I must be the long lost heir to a huge fortune, don't you think? It would make sense!'

He laughed.

'What happened to your foster parents?'

'They were fisherfolk and very poor. Maybe that is why they took me in. When I was fifteen there was an outbreak of plague on the island. It did not spread and was confined to the part we visited, perhaps even to those broken-down houses round the courtyard. A sailor returned from Cyprus and fell ill not long after he got home. All the people that caught it died, except for myself and one other child. The place was cordoned off. No one could get in and no one could leave. They brought us food each morning. But nobody wanted to come close to us or touch us.'

'And were you visited by the plague doctor?' asked Domenico, thinking of the gruesome figure he had seen in the square by Santa Maria Formosa.

'No, we were far too poor for that! We were left to live or die as fate decided.'

'And if they were so poor, why did your foster parents take you in? Why did they accept an extra mouth to feed?'

'The woman who brought me in the first place visited us twice a year. She gave them money for my upkeep. It was not much, but to my parents it must have been a small fortune.'

'And that is the woman you spotted in the boat,' said Domenico.

All of it was beginning to make sense now.

'Every time I have come back, the place has been deserted. No one wants to live in those houses because of what happened. Though if any contagion was left over, it must have been dissipated long ago. I was surprised to see that woman looking out at us. I am sure she is a newcomer. None of the islanders would want to settle there. They say the place is haunted.'

'And what about the other woman in the boat? The older one? Did you recognise her? They were together.'

'I had never set eyes upon her until today. And all I know of the one in yellow is her name.'

'Agatha,' murmured Domenico. 'Was she kind?'

'She made me very angry. When she came she would not speak to me, but only to my foster parents. More often than not they

146

would send me out because I misbehaved so badly. And it prevented me hearing the things they talked about.'

'Didn't they tell you more about her?'

'My foster mother said on one occasion that they had been forbidden to repeat anything of what she said. If I found out, I would be taken away from them. I promised I would keep silent but it didn't make any difference. She was too scared. After they died, a priest came in a boat and took the two of us away, the survivors.'

'And did you tell the priest your story?'

'I didn't speak for nearly a year after that time. They thought that I was dumb. The other child, a little girl, and I were separated at once. After a week or so in the priest's house, I was set to work in a boatyard. Not the one I work in now, a different one. And do you know what made me start to speak again? A wooden head.'

'The head on your boat?'

'How quick you are! You mean you noticed it?'

'Yes, it reminded me of someone. A flower-seller I nearly sent flying the other day, not far from the theatre at St Hyginus.'

'An old boat was being broken up. The planks were badly warped and they smashed them to bits for firewood. They were going to throw the figurehead away when I spoke up. All of a sudden, without any preamble.'

'What did you say?'

'"Don't". Nothing more than that. I said "Don't" and reached my hands out for it. And everyone was so amazed they gave it to me. I have built it into every boat I have had and it has always brought me good luck.'

'And what do you remember from the years before? You said you could remember a time when you were not with the fisher-folk.'

'I would like to be able to place the woman in the portrait, but I can't. The portrait and the ring and the figures came with me when I first arrived. A sort of heirloom. Softness and closeness, that is all I remember. And being in a tight space. Smells, too. Different from the smell of fish we lived with for so long.'

This was when Domenico, who was growing impatient, and aware he had no time to spare, did as he had been wanting to do since he caught sight of him outside the church of St Lazarus, and placed his palm on Rodrigo's crotch. The two moved closer, and their lips met. Their embraces were hurried, but not furtive. No church bells could be heard here. The only guide to the passage of time was the gradually fading daylight. Domenico was determined to feel Rodrigo's skin pressed against his own, and to acquaint himself with its particular fragrance once more. He felt he deserved as much before facing the trial of a full rehearsal.

And nevertheless he was angry with himself for being late. The wind was against them on the return journey. He communicated his sense of urgency to Rodrigo without words and he, fearful it might turn into irritation at his seamanship, mismanaged the small sail, delaying their arrival further still. Domenico more or less leapt from the boat when they reached the square at St Hyginus's, barely catching Rodrigo's promise to be present on the first night of the season. He was equally impatient with the small boy who stopped him on the threshold of the theatre, with a message from Mother Hilary.

'What message?' Domenico asked shortly, as the child held out the portfolio.

'She told me to give you this. She would like to talk to you about it but she is unwell.'

From inside the sound of string instruments tuning up could be heard, along with the squeaking of an oboe's reed, as the player tested it before inserting it into his mouthpiece. Domenico's agitation grew. He felt in his pocket and thrust a coin into the small boy's hand. What was he to do with the portfolio? Limentani's voice reached him, then the booming tones of Donatella Reis. He could not tell how long they had been waiting for him to appear. He sprinted upstairs and quickly stuffed the papers into the cupboard, leaving them jutting out at the top of a pile of rejected scores.

The rehearsal did not proceed well. There were problems already with the opening symphony, for the parts had been copied in great haste and had bars missing from them here and there. The ensemble kept falling apart and Domenico had to call a halt each time and try to work out what had been omitted and where. Limentani said nothing when he arrived late, which was in itself a sign the impresario was discontented. Only six of the promised chorus of ten turned up, so there were no contraltos for the opening scene, which gave the whole ensemble a mean and scrawny tone. Immediately after her first aria, Gabriela had a long dialogue with her confidante, who was sung by Donatella. Domenico's fingers had still not warmed up from the journey back and he kept stumbling as he accompanied the recitative. That made it hard for him to correct the singers when they made a mistake in pitch, or skipped a line and hurried on towards the conclusion. He felt he was doing considerably worse than they were.

Somehow they muddled through the first act of *Elvira, Queen of Thebes*. Iannelli was not in form (he always delivered less than his best in rehearsals) but Tecchi sang passably well. Thinking it would be good for her morale, Domenico suggested that Gabriela should perform the rondo from Garavini's *Dido*, which he had learned was one of her showpieces. They still had to decide just where to insert it in the following act. If they went over it now, the disputes as to its eventual placing could be postponed, at least for a while. She accepted the proposal with alacrity, for her voice was completely warmed up at this stage and the ornamentation held no fears for her.

All at once the general atmosphere improved. Domenico, to his own astonishment, was deeply touched by the piece, and the chorus members broke into spontaneous applause. Limentani, who had been listening anxiously from one of the boxes throughout the whole rehearsal, got to his feet and clapped as well. Domenico knew that a break was in order. But he was also aware that they had spent much more time than he anticipated on only one act from the two operas they were meant to be preparing. Maybe the best thing would be to carry on till everybody dropped. After all, today was Sunday and they did not have to sing before a paying audience until Tuesday evening.

The impresario had a different plan.

'Sit down, everyone,' he ordered.

There were barely enough seats for the soloists in the main part of the auditorium, reserved for standing customers. The chorus members, however, made no fuss. They helped each other to clamber on to the part of the stage in front of the curtain and settled in the boxes on either side. Perhaps they had been warned of what was in store. Limentani whistled, softly but distinctly, and the curtain started to rise.

An assistant had just finished lighting the sets of candles placed in high brackets, at three different levels on either side of the stage. He used an extendable taper like an outsize drinking straw, whose sections retracted into one another until it was reduced to more or less his own height, and he could snuff it out. Luca Schiavoni stood with his back to them, his hands raised as if he, not Domenico, were the conductor, and he were about to give a signal for the first chord of a ceremonial overture to be struck. He brought his hands down in a decisive gesture. Instead of music, there came a distant, barely perceptible scraping and creaking. Many of those watching let out gasps of astonishment as Angelo Colombani's monstrous machine descended, with faultless smoothness, from the vault above the stage. The repairs were complete. New flaps were in place, though they had still to be painted. The clouds, or constellations, or whatever was to be represented, occupied the whole rear of the playing area. Two assistants perched at opposite ends of it bore candelabras, whose candles flared when they set off, then fluttered in the breeze produced by the descent. At the very centre stood another assistant, carrying in his arms a red velvet curtain. As the cloud machinery came to a halt, he released it and it scattered like a waterfall at sunset, catching the reflection of the candles in its folds as they opened out and settled on to the floor of the stage.

The impression was so powerful no one dared applaud. Instead there was a kind of awe-struck murmuring. Tecchi tried to say something but merely produced an agitated series of clicks.

'Excellent,' called Limentani, the only person present to have retained his composure.

The praise was drowned out by an unexpected thud. The thud repeated itself. Everyone looked around, startled. The obvious conclusion was that something had gone wrong with the machinery. But it still hung there, motionless and perfect, like a bank of seemingly eternal clouds upon a windless day. The sound was coming from the opposite end of the auditorium, where the main entrance to the theatre was situated. It had not been opened since the night the machinery got stuck. An unexpected guest was demanding admission. The thuds turned into a barrage of knocking, increasingly impatient and impertinent. No one dared move. The old janitor, for whom alone the building held no secrets, pulled back the great bolt and began to heave open one half of the majestic double doors. His low tones could be heard, along with two other voices. At first Domenico thought both the newcomers were women, and his mind flew to Agatha and her companion, in the boat earlier that day. But his keen ear soon told him the rehearsal was being interrupted by a middle-aged foreign woman, accompanied by a youngish man, who spoke in high-pitched and effeminate tones.

The entire company now faced the back of the auditorium, as if the stage was positioned at the entrance to the theatre, rather than opposite it, and they constituted the audience. Pacifico Anselmi emerged from the shadows, dressed in a long coat sewn with gleaming spangles, which would have looked better on a carved figure, decorating the summit of the portable baldachin in a gaudy procession of church dignitaries. In his hand he carried an ornate walking stick, with a sumptuously large and painted pommel at its top. After him came the great-aunt of the king of Poland, Madame Landowska. The heel of one of her shoes had broken off as she was being helped out of her gondola on to the quay. She hobbled and was panting, and the perspiration that resulted had begun to dislodge her make-up. Nonetheless, she was determined not to let her protégé elude her vigilance for as long as a minute.

Despite his sense of self-importance, Pacifico was only seventeen. Domenico detected a touch of insecurity in his bearing, which the composer overcame by beating the end of his stick on the floor when he came to a halt. He swept his gloved hand in a circle which took in the entire company, as well as the enormous construction filling the stage.

'I have broken definitively with the management at St John Chrysostom,' he announced in ringing tones. 'You,' he went on with emphasis, evidently looking round for Limentani, but unable to locate him, so that the notional singular had to become a plural, 'will put on my operas.'

He turned to Madame Landowska who, it appeared, ought to have been carrying the scores, in spite of her damaged shoe and her breathless condition. Fortunately, two lackeys rushed forward at that very moment, bearing the material in question. Domenico could not be sure if they had intended to transport the mound of folio sheets in this fashion, like a crown upon a ceremonial cushion, or if they had been fighting with one another for the privilege, and had adopted a more seemly posture the minute they realised how many pairs of eyes were fixed upon them.

Ansaldo Limentani would normally have risen to the occasion. Even he was so flabbergasted, however, by this turn of events, that he met Pacifico's announcement with silence. The prodigy saw himself obliged to proceed with his monologue. Drawing the glove from his right hand with his left, fussily teasing each finger from the cloth that enclosed it, he gestured with bare fingers in the direction of the stage.

'This exquisite device,' he cried, 'this paradisiacal construction, this marvel of science and imagination, whose exhumation has been the talk of every salon in the city, is perfectly adapted to represent the opening scene of my new opera' (he pronounced the title with a special emphasis) '*King Montezuma and the Conquest of Peru.*'

'*The Conquest of Peru*!' chanted Gabriela, whose notions of history and geography were equally vague. 'Peacock feathers! Camels! And a row of sphinxes! Will I be expected to put on blacking? My skin is so delicate I could not possibly agree to do that.'

The oboe player gave out a brief, celebratory fanfare, managing to make his reedy instrument sound remarkably like a trumpet.

'And *The Garden of the Hesperides*?' piped up Umberto Tecchi. 'Was not that the opera you were supposed to write?'

'Merely a rumour put about to deceive the masses,' said Anselmi. 'My actual subject matter is infinitely more original.'

By now Limentani had taken stock of the situation and descended from his box. Rubbing his hands together, he approached the young composer and embraced him heartily.

'You really mean to say they have released you from your

contract? And that we can perform both your operas in this theatre?'

'Both of them,' Pacifico assured him. 'The scoundrels at St John Chrysostom insisted that an indemnity had to be paid. Madame Landowska was happy to step into the breach and deal with that trifling inconvenience. She is determined that considerations of a practical nature must never be allowed to interfere with the operation of my genius.'

Limentani acknowledged the Polish aristocrat with a deep bow. She, in her turn, honoured the impresario with an ungainly curtsey, after which she allowed him to kiss her hand.

'That means there will be no need for a pastiche,' put in Domenico, with considerable relief.

'An opera by Pacifico Anselmi! *Two* operas!' mused Donatella's husband. 'Who could ever have thought we would be so fortunate, after the inauspicious beginnings of this trumped-up season!'

Limentani ignored the remark.

'Forget about *Elvira, Queen of Thebes*, everybody. We will postpone the solemn re-opening of the theatre till Friday night. On Tuesday and Wednesday Paolo Sarti's troupe will entertain the public, followed by the Neapolitan farce we had already planned to perform. Do not think our work is over for the day, ladies and gentlemen. Domenico will take you through that piece while I accompany Maestro Anselmi and his lady patron to the office upstairs, so that we can discuss the details of our agreement. Luca, how quickly can you transform Thebes into Peru? Can the decorations be transported across twenty centuries and to the other side of the Atlantic Ocean, so as to be ready for a première in four days' time?'

Luca Schiavoni shook his head ruefully from side to side at this latest piece of madness on his employer's part. It was a good thing they had not got beyond repairing the basic structure of the machinery, which could still be turned to whatever uses they might think fit. At the mention of Peru, his mind had filled with tales he had heard of a wondrous ceiling fresco showing the Four Continents, painted by Giambattista Tiepolo for a German Prince Archbishop, on the other side of the Alps in far-off Franconia. He had seen pirated engravings of the section representing the

Americas and was sure he could get hold of travellers' accounts of the continent at relatively short notice. There would be no shortage of inspiration. And he was sufficiently experienced as a designer of stage sets to know that Thebes and Peru did not have to look quite so different from one another as a lay person might suspect.

'It shall be done,' he said, 'as you command.'

'It must be done,' said Limentani.

22

'She has been unwell for the better part of a week now,' said Giacinta in a low voice.

Gabriela looked annoyed. Visiting her widowed sister was something of a chore, and she had put off doing it for as long as she decently could. What finally persuaded her to come this afternoon was the story of Pacifico Anselmi's defection to St Hyginus's, which she was sure would impress Oriana infinitely. And there were other novelties, of a more intimate nature, which she wanted to share. If Oriana was unwell, she had no idea where else to take her news. She had a strong need to unburden herself to someone.

'What is the matter with her?' asked Gabriela, trying to sound concerned rather than irritated. 'Is she running a fever?'

'She was, until last night,' replied Giacinta. 'She has hardly opened her eyes today, except for half an hour this morning, when I got her to sip some hot broth. She is in a very weak state. It would be dangerous to let you speak to her just now.'

They were squashed into the small servant's chamber, whispering to one another so as not to waken the invalid. Gabriela considered it the height of indignity for a woman of her rank to be received in this way. Then, with one of the flashes of self-knowledge which affected her infrequently, yet were among her most attractive traits, she realised she was angry with Giacinta for saying nothing about the splendid hat which she had put on specially for the occasion. She accused herself of heartlessness.

'Do you have money for everything you need?' she asked, reaching for her purse. 'I am preparing for a role which is sure to make me famous and am perfectly ready to help you in whatever way proves possible.'

'Then let's go away from here to a place where we can talk,' said

Giacinta. 'My mistress is fast asleep. I am sure she will not wake until the evening, if we do not disturb her.'

Gabriela's immediate reaction was that it would be a serious error of judgement for her to be seen on the streets of Venice in the company of a servant girl. Then she remembered that she was wearing a mask. The anonymity it conferred on her made Giacinta's proposal perfectly acceptable.

Five minutes later the two women were seated just inside the door of a wigmaker's shop, which also functioned as an informal meeting place. The wigmaker's apprentice was sent out to fetch a bottle of sweet wine and two glasses. Giacinta began to weep, without the slightest touch of theatricality, in a manner Gabriela found profoundly affecting. The servant girl sat quite upright, staring vacantly in front of her, making no sound. The tears formed themselves spontaneously on her cheeks, like humidity seeping from a chill, dank wall. It was impossible to remain indifferent to the spectacle of such misery.

Gabriela took her hand.

'It's all my fault!' murmured Giacinta. 'I am the one who brought this on her!'

'What on earth do you mean?'

'I persuaded her to go to a masked ball in the town house of the Vendramin family. We both came home with partners. Mine was a buxom creature, dressed up like a Turk. Yet we had great fun together. If it had not been for your sister's illness, I would have met up with him again. Carnival is so much more enjoyable if you have somebody to go to parties with, especially if that somebody holds you in his arms all through the night. The only thing I know about Oriana's lover is that he was disguised as a monk. I did not hear him say a word. He joined his hands gravely, bowed his head like a real monk and followed us home. She says he promised to return after that night but never did. And now she has fallen in love with him. Your sister is pining away! I thought she was going to die.'

Gabriela tutted in disbelief.

'How can you be sure? It may be a perfectly ordinary distemper, of the kind everyone in Venice catches at this time of the year. You know how damp and chilly the city is in January.'

'No, it isn't that. You see, he left his costume behind. When your sister first became unwell, and could not rise from her bed, she insisted I went to the cupboard where it was concealed to fetch it for her. She lay there, fondling it as if it had been her mysterious guest. She even used its hood to dry her tears. It is lying there even as we speak. It covers her as if it were a shroud.'

At the thought of her mistress's predicament, Giacinta's tears began to flow without restraint. Gabriela decided that the sensible course would be to make light of her fears.

'Surely the worst is over. You told me that the fever had abated. When my sister recovers her health, she will also recover her senses. What could be more normal than for a woman in delirium to imagine she has fallen in love with the last man to hold her close?'

The tears stopped. Giacinta snuffled. She was growing calmer.

'I shall return in a couple of days' time. No doubt it will be possible for me to speak to her then. Do not worry, you will not be left alone with this responsibility. If necessary, I shall try and talk some sense to her. And you can tell Oriana, on my authority, that she will have no difficulty finding a replacement. If my own good fortune is anything to go by, that is.'

Giacinta felt a twinge of curiosity. It was part of her livelihood to listen to confidences of this kind. Every woman she had waited upon indulged in them. Dealing with them had become, to all intents and purposes, a professional reflex for the servant girl. Gentle prompting was in order.

'You mean that you have found a partner since coming to Venice?'

Gabriela smiled and nodded.

'How long ago did you arrive?'

Gabriela was tempted to lie. She felt a little ashamed that she had let so much time pass without enquiring after her sister, especially now she knew that she was ill. If she shortened the time excessively, however, Giacinta might think she had seized on the first man who came her way.

'Eight days.'

'That *is* good fortune! When did you meet?'

'The day before yesterday.'

'And how?'

'He is an admirer of my singing. It is the custom in Venice for tourists and members of the leading families to be admitted to theatrical rehearsals, especially when such an importance piece as Pacifico Anselmi's *King Montezuma and the Conquest of Peru* is being prepared.'

In spite of herself, Gabriela could not help hoping that the mention of Anselmi's name would have an effect on Giacinta. It did not. The girl's face was completely blank. It was a scant consolation to reflect that her sister might prove just as ignorant. She could have made a fuss and explained to Oriana who Anselmi was and why he was so celebrated. To do that with a servant girl would be stooping too low.

'The impresario I am employed by, Ansaldo Limentani, is a capricious creature. He has made a rule that nobody is to be admitted to the theatre while we are working there unless they are directly involved in the production. But there is a way round every prohibition. My admirer slipped a generous bribe into the hand of the janitor. And, can you imagine, he did so with the sole purpose of hearing me!'

Giacinta was sceptical. Her relief at finally being able to share her worries, and the emotions it released, were subsiding. Her native shrewdness reasserted itself. She made an instinctive assessment of Gabriela's character. Flattery was clearly the best way to manipulate the singer, who was vulnerable to praise from any source. Considering it beneath her to exploit such an obvious weakness, Giactina concentrated on the facts.

'When did you first speak to him?'

'He was waiting for me outside the theatre on Monday. I allowed him to accompany me to my lodgings in his gondola. Although he was wearing a mask, it could not conceal the delicacy of his profile. He is extremely handsome.'

'And did he . . . ?'

Gabriela coloured with indignation.

'What do you take me for? My morals are more steadfast than my sister's, let me tell you!'

Giacinta was unsure whether to give this assertion credence or not. She patiently awaited further disclosures.

'He is a connoisseur in everything regarding music. He has attended operas by all the most fashionable composers, in the Empress's own theatre in Vienna. You see, he is a foreigner. He speaks Italian perfectly, but with a German accent. I find it utterly appealing.'

The sweet wine was going to Gabriela's head, making her more inclined to confidences than she might otherwise have been.

'He has a special interest in the theatre at St Hyginus's which, if he is to be believed, has an extraordinary history. Do you know that its former owner was rumoured to have been an alchemist?'

Giacinta raised her eyebrows. She was finding all of this harder and harder to believe.

'My admirer, whose name is Andreas, is a kind of spy! What could be more exciting? Of course, that is not the word he used. He is currently employed by the Vatican to investigate the circumstances of the former owner's death and to ensure that, now the theatre is being reopened, those nefarious practices will not start up again.'

'How fascinating,' Giacinta commented drily. She was growing anxious about her mistress and was ready to terminate the discussion, not least because she could make neither head nor tail of the nonsense Gabriela was uttering.

'And he has requested my assistance.'

'Your help?'

'I am to listen carefully for mention of incidents from the theatre's past and make a note of them at once. And I have also agreed to keep my eyes open for any obscure documents or mysterious writings which may be lying around inside the building.'

'In exchange for what?'

'Exchange?' Gabriela shrugged her shoulders. 'It is a worthy cause. Why should I not lend a hand with it?'

Giacinta looked unconvinced. She nodded to the apprentice, who approached Gabriela for payment. The feather on the opera singer's hat bobbed expressively as she rummaged around in her purse, looking for the appropriate coins.

'You are not to breathe a word of this to anyone,' she murmured in Giacinta's ear, as they parted on the threshold of the shop. She had taken to the girl. Her sister rose in her estimation for her choice of servant.

'Not even Oriana?'

'You may tell her the gist of it once she is well enough to listen. But do not give her the impression I was boasting. Use my good news sensibly, to show that she will find another partner, a better one, the minute she sets foot outside her lodgings. After all, the carnival will soon be at its height.'

Gabriela had not been entirely forthright in her revelations to Giacinta. She made it sound as though her mysterious admirer's request for help was nothing more than a tempting proposition, which might not lead to direct action on her part. Insecurity, though, was the unfortunate reverse side of her vanity. She was eager to do everything she could to please this unexpected conquest. And that was why, only a matter of hours after Giacinta refused to admit Gabriela to her sister's presence, Andreas was able to place the portfolio containing Negri's jottings, along with other significant papers, on the table in the withdrawing room of the redoubt on the Giudecca, where he had arranged to meet Hedwiga.

It was a place where, later in the day, many of the most fashionable men and women in Venice would parade back and forth. When he arrived in the city, Andreas had once or twice penetrated to the main chamber of the building, which housed the gambling tables. He had too much presence of mind to lose more than a trifling sum of money when he played. But the spinning of the wheels and the dealing of the cards held an endless fascination for him, like everything he came upon which lacked a precise explanation. He had penned a treatise on the concept of randomness, but had never given it to be printed, because he could not make up his mind about the conclusion. Each time he returned to the manuscript, he would write a different ending for it. Or rather, he would struggle to stop himself from admitting his real feelings about the operation of chance, finding instead a new way to express the only view he could publicly acknowledge, namely that the overwhelming majority of events in the physical world are simply manifestations of chaos, devoid of any pattern or meaning.

Nine days out of ten, he could have put his name to this conclusion without any hint of dishonesty. But on the tenth day, which recurred with troubling regularity, he saw things differently. That alternative vision of the world left him breathless and excited, for then it was as if the hurtling of the dice and the shuffling of the cards, just like the restless seething of the waves in the chill stretch of water he had crossed to reach the Giudecca, or the battlements of clouds erected without apparent effort in the January sky, were a cryptic alphabet no one had yet learned to interpret. Everything was pregnant with meaning, looming but inaccessible. At the thought of it, Andreas would cradle his head in his hands and moan with fear and agitation, as if the weight of all the information the mad world contained was bearing down upon him and would crush him. And yet the world he intuited was not mad. It had a purpose, manifest in all its aspects, which meant that his actions, too, were taken note of, and reverberated through creation. He could not elude attention, he was trapped. The echoes of his enterprises reached the distant constellations. The idea made it hard for him to take a single step, as if the precise nature of the contact of the sole of his foot with the ground might unleash an earthquake or provoke a miracle.

That was how he felt today. He could not stop his eyes darting towards the doorway, to see if Hedwiga had arrived. Although it was the early afternoon, the redoubt was relatively busy. Masked figures passed in front of him, singly, in pairs, in groups of three or four. The absence of individual traits turned them into symbols for Andreas, making them more than human or, because they shared that enigmatic quality, fully human in a way he had never managed to be, guardians of a secret that had been kept from him. What would happen if he were to leap to his feet without warning and tear one of those masks away? He might be met with incomprehension, treated like a madman or physically chastised. Or would the face laid bare be precisely the one he needed to see? Perhaps the eyes in it would grow lively with kindness and compassion and, joining him at his lonely table, the person whose identity had been revealed so unexpectedly would explain what he wanted to know, the thing he could not even put into words, but which at that moment was more precious to him than life itself.

He was breathing so fast he could feel his heart beating at his chest, like a prisoner begging to be released from its confinement. It occurred to him he might be physically unwell, for he had never experienced anxiety or elation of this kind before setting foot in the lagoon city. Two things happened at one and the same time. Hedwiga arrived, impeccably dressed as usual, but subdued. And they brought him his mail. It was possible to do that in this sophisticated city, to have mail addressed to you at the redoubt, because you did not know where you were going to stay, or planned to change lodgings in the immediate future. Andreas received a steady stream of letters from acquaintances in Vienna and Salzburg, as well as a series of pamphlets from a bookseller in Nantes, who knew of his tastes and his scientific interests.

Seeing Hedwiga was an anticlimax after the speculations he had been engaged in. With the barest of courtesy, he gestured towards the portfolio on her side of the table and turned to his letters on their silver tray. His heartbeat speeded up again. The communication he had been waiting for throughout the last week, without being sure if it would ever materialise, had arrived. He broke the seal and held it up carefully, so that there was not the slightest chance of Hedwiga glimpsing even an isolated phrase from where she sat. The missive concerned her.

'I have managed to glean a certain amount of information about the individual who is the object of your enquiry,' he read, 'and whose name and title you correctly quoted to me as Hedwiga Engelsfeld von Nettesheim. The woman was of German language and birth, the eldest daughter of a landowning family in Curland, on the eastern shores of the Baltic Sea. They also had a town house in the merchant city of Riga. Engelsfeld was her father's name. She became a Nettesheim by marriage. She was lucky enough to attract the attentions of an elderly widower, whose estates stretch from the very gates of Riga to the boundary of the province, and beyond that into Russia. Rumour had it that he owned enough serfs to populate the city three times over. He became infatuated with her and married her within three months of their first meeting. There was a difference of forty-three years in their ages but I have come across no evidence that she was forced into the match. This conquest, and the change in status it brought with it, meant that all eyes were fixed upon her. Within a year she had a further claim to general notoriety, namely the cruelty and despotism with which she exercised her powers as mistress of the Nettesheim mansions and estate. I prefer not to commit to writing details of the punishments she visited upon her serfs. Suffice it to say that they came to the attention of the Emperor, and merited a personal rebuke from him, when the couple appeared at court in St Petersburg the following winter. This may explain why, when her husband died of a colic in the second year of their marriage, the rumours of poisoning which always circulate on such occasions were not allowed to die of their own accord. Baroness von Nettesheim was summoned to the capital for a formal investigation. Having been acquitted due to lack of evidence, by a special disposition of the Emperor the woman was banished from Russia and all its subject territories for the space of ten years, or as long as was his pleasure. The administration of the estate was entrusted to a government committee.

'All this happened more than thirty years ago. The individual in question set off for Prague, spending the remainder of her life in lands under the jurisdiction of our own much venerated monarch. She was not allowed to return home once her initial sentence expired. Confidential reports to the Emperor indicated that her conduct had not been blameless. He was especially displeased to learn that she had been seen in the company of a certain Gottfried Schwarz, a mountebank and conjuror whom the Emperor briefly entertained at court at the time of the woman's marriage, and who had since continued in his peripatetic mode of life. Her banishment was prolonged indefinitely, though she was regularly supplied with funds and produce from the confiscated estates, sufficient to maintain her in a lifestyle of some luxury. This brings me to the last and perhaps most crucial point in my response to your enquiry. What particularly surprised me in the letter I received from you was the implication that it concerned a living person. Hedwiga Engelsfeld von Nettesheim died in a coach accident in Lower Austria in 1752, and is buried in a village churchyard near Krems. I took the precaution of having a correspondent visit her grave to verify the inscription on it. The woman has not been of this world for nearly a decade.'

Andreas folded the letter carefully. He could not bring himself to lift his eyes and gaze at the figure sitting opposite. The air of Venice had transformed him beyond recognition. As little as two months earlier, he would have drawn the natural conclusion, that the woman was an impostor. Since meeting Hedwiga, however, and seeing Gottfried Schwarz's face shimmer on the surface of a bowl of water in her home, his concept of the possible had altered to such an extent that, rather than excluding the alternative explanation, he found himself favouring it. After all, why would anyone assume the identity of an exiled and execrated widow? What advantages could such an identity offer? In his present, exalted state, Andreas had no difficulty believing that he saw before him a creature who had been dead and was now alive, or rather, one who refused to be bound by such banal dichotomies, one for whom resuscitation would be no more troublesome a matter than her morning toilet. Had she not herself explained as much to him, however indirectly? 'Beginnings, endings, alive, dead . . .' He heard once more in his mind the weary tones with which she had pronounced the words, in that spectral town house in the Court of Darkness, as if those tiresome opposites concealed infinite gradations of possibility with which she would acquaint him, were he to prove a sufficiently adept and patient student.

It might be madness to have such thoughts. Even so, they filled him with exultation, with a sense of triumph he would not exchange for sanity. Here he was, face to face with an impossibility of a similar order to the one with which his life's journey had begun, in the cathedral square at Salzburg on that far-off December evening, when the wooden bird broke free of its restraints and flew into the sky. He was familiar with the episode in the Christian Bible in which the veil of the temple is rent asunder, at the very moment when the Son of God makes his ultimate sacrifice. Andreas had no notion what kind of sacrifice might be required of him in the future, or whether any part of him would survive the revelation he was aching for. The veil of his reality was torn apart. Raising his eyes inch by inch till they settled on Hedwiga's face, engrossed in the perusal of the documents he had persuaded Gabriela to steal on her behalf, he could not help speculating whether the emotion he experienced at that precise moment might be love.

23

Domenico was moved to tears when he played through Anselmi's opera for the first time, by the light of a pair of candles, sitting at the harpsichord in the unlit theatre, humming and half singing the vocal lines as he proceeded.

The libretto was a most peculiar piece of writing. Instead of casting the Spanish invaders as heroes and the Incas as savages, it created an aura of bleak fatality around Montezuma which must inevitably guide the listeners' sympathies towards him. The closing aria, which he sang before mounting the stake, offered a bitter catalogue of the humiliations and deceptions he had been subjected to since the aliens arrived. It ended in the major key, with a proud assertion of faith in his gods and his people. Last of all came a mixed chorus, again strange and daring, in which the Spanish soldiers exulted at the thought of the gold and silver that had fallen to their share, while the conquered Incas mourned their fate and plotted rebellion and revenge. Even when he had read through it several times, Domenico was unable to understand how Anselmi managed to combine such opposite emotions in a single structure, which nonetheless made perfect musical sense. The notes were not difficult. Indeed, it struck him as a relatively easy piece to sing and play. Getting the emotional register right would, however, be an infinitely harder task.

Limentani was eager to use Colombani's machinery twice, at the beginning and again at the end of the opera. The opening scene showed Montezuma receiving the Spanish invaders in his royal residence. The monarch of the Incas would be placed at the centre of the machine. Schiavoni was already busy with the construction of a moveable staircase which would allow the Spanish leader, in his glistening armour, to ascend to the foot of the monarch's throne. According to the libretto, the palace of the ruler of the Incas should be situated on an artificial island in the centre of a lake. Whether it would be possible to provide water, and have the Spaniards approach the foot of the staircase in a boat, was still a moot point. But even if this detail were excised, the effect ought to be magnificent.

The plans for the conclusion were more complex still. Schiavoni insisted that he could build a lightweight globe, which opened and shut without visible human intervention, to be situated at the back of the machinery. This would allow Montezuma to be led off in chains upwards, rather than to the side, a far preferable solution, given that his tragedy was to be the principal focus of the audience's sympathies. During the final chorus, the Spanish soldiers would be posted on the higher slats of the machinery, with the conquered Incas down below. The globe would open unexpectedly, revealing Montezuma in a sea of fire, whose colours were to recall those of the outlandish headdress he had worn when still in power. Its magical properties had been supposed to protect him while he ruled. The invaders bribed a native courtesan to steal it from him during a night of love. This visual echo was intended to bring a suitable touch of ambivalence to his execution, turning it into a kind of apotheosis.

Limentani explained all this to Domenico with enormous excitement. The younger man could not take the information in. He decided to shut his mind to the details of the production, and to concentrate instead upon the music, which had given him more than enough to think about.

The second, shorter opera was a pastoral love story. There was no question of asking Gabriela to memorise two such taxing roles in the limited time available. Anselmi agreed to let Domenico transpose the heroine's part into a lower key so that Donatella Reis could perform it. Donatella's husband had been overjoyed at the composer's defection to St Hyginus's. No more was said about the vexed question of how to carve up the major arias to be sung in the course of the season between the soprano and the contralto. When he learned that his wife was to have the chief part in the second opera, he beamed with pleasure, and behaved from then on as if Limentani were a hero in his eyes.

Domenico had not forgotten about the portfolio, or the mystery of its contents. However, it was well nigh impossible for him to find time for a visit to the nearby convent. Only by slipping away early from lunch at the tavern did he gain a brief interval before afternoon rehearsals started, and to no real purpose. Nobody answered when he knocked on the door of St Clare's and he did not detect any signs of life about the place. For all he could tell, the whole community might have been transplanted to an island in the lagoon, or have ascended into heaven. Time was pressing and he did not persist. In any case, he had no way of telling if Mother Hilary had recovered sufficiently to be in a condition to receive him, if it had been possible to gain admission to the convent.

Rumours were rife in Venice about the reasons for Anselmi's breaking his contract with St John Chrysostom. The first conclusion people jumped to was that the theatre had not paid him his fee, or had not offered him a large enough one. Domenico found this hard to believe, since there had been no mention of money when the composer arrived on the doorstep of St Hyginus's. If it were such a fundamental issue, surely he would have raised it with Limentani there and then.

Another story, which caused Domenico infinitely more concern, was that the composer had been discontented with the conductor at the larger theatre, had accused him of vandalising the scores entrusted to his care, and had sworn not to risk his own precious music in such clumsy hands. If this were true, it meant Pacifico would be scrutinising Domenico's every move. There might be storms on the horizon or, who could tell, even the prospect of a second defection, if his conducting did not come up to standard.

A third rumour was that Anselmi had been having an affair with the principal soprano at St John Chrysostom and that she had ditched him from one day to the next, in favour of the Piedmontese ambassador. The composer was so incensed he had taken the most savage revenge he was capable of, depriving her of a part any one of the principal sopranos in the peninsula would give a year of her working life to secure.

Domenico considered this explanation to be the most credible of the three, and observed Anselmi with interest and amusement to see if he would make advances towards their own soprano, Gabriela. That is, he did so until Limentani told him she had other fish to fry. The information tumbled out in the course of a long conversation the two men had in the tavern, after dinner on Tuesday night. Schiavoni, tireless as ever, had returned to the theatre to put the finishing touches to his plans for the staging of the pastoral piece. Tecchi and Iannelli had gone to bed. Donatella and her husband dined regularly with the children in their own lodgings, so that the impresario and the conductor were left to their own devices.

It was nearly midnight. Only a few hours earlier, the theatre had opened its doors to the public for the first time in seven years. The combination of Sarti's troupe and the Neapolitan farce had not been expected to draw a large crowd. Yet every seat in St Hyginus's was filled. Most of the tickets for Friday, when Anselmi's Peruvian opera was at last to be inaugurated, had already been sold. Limentani attributed their success on this first evening both to anticipation of Friday's momentous event and to the theatre's uncanny reputation.

'Many people wanted to come just to get a look at the place, to see the inside of a building which has so many stories connected with it. Did you know that the attic is supposed to be haunted?' he asked Domenico, with such a penetrating glance the younger man's cheeks reddened in confusion. 'Singing has apparently been heard coming from up there at odd hours of the day and night ever since the theatre was shut down. I have to admit to you, dear fellow, that I myself find the atmosphere quite eerie at times. Once all the excitement of the opening night has passed, and our season is running along smoothly, perhaps we could ask good Don Astolfo to proceed upstairs and carry out a full-scale exorcism. And, do you know, there are new mysteries to add to the already existing ones! Sarti, who is an extremely level-headed fellow, complained to me that the work of his troupe has been troubled by a ghost.'

'A ghost?' exclaimed Domenico, fearing the worst, namely that Angelo Colombani had started to wander from his perch next to the roof. He hated the idea of the poor fellow being discovered and expelled, or put on trial for murder, even though he personally stood to lose nothing in the process. He wondered if the moment had come to tell Limentani everything he knew about their hidden lodger. The turn the conversation took dissuaded him.

'You know that they kindly agreed to rehearse at odd times, mainly at the end of the day, once the musicians had packed up and gone home. Not that a great deal of preparation is needed. Improvisation is their trade and they are excellent hands at it. But I asked Sarti to make sure they put on an especially polished performance, seeing Venetian audiences are so notoriously demanding. I wanted him to think about sight lines and curtain calls, and maybe to try out a plot or two that people here would be unfamiliar with. A story that cannot be found in the traditional manuals. In any case, they ended up, through force of circumstances, using the stage when there was a minimum of light. Nobody could be bothered lighting more candles. Sarti insists that, each time they rehearsed, an additional character appeared.'

'What do you mean?' asked Domenico, wrinkling his brow. 'I don't understand.'

'It's perfectly simple. There are five actors in the troupe. At a certain point in each rehearsal, there was a sixth person on the stage.'

'And why didn't they stop right away and challenge whoever it was?'

'That's what I asked Sarti. He found it difficult to come up with an explanation. They are trained to work round any eventuality that may occur, so they fitted the girl into the story more or less instinctively.'

'A girl?' repeated Domenico. He could feel the hairs rising on the back of his neck.

'Yes, a girl, an extremely beautiful one, or so Sarti informed me. She sat in a chair to one side of the stage and combed out long red hair. She even sang on one occasion.'

'A Neapolitan song,' murmured Domenico.

'How did you guess that?' asked Limentani, quick as a flash. 'Has someone spoken to you about this?'

'No,' said Domenico, lying, and hating himself for it. 'It just came into my head.'

The impresario went on with his story.

'According to Sarti, it was only when they rehearsed for the second time that everyone realised she was a newcomer, and even then, not really till afterwards. The actors in the troupe took it she was an extra he had brought in without telling them. The most worrying thing of all, however, is that she does not confine her appearances to run-throughs.'

'In other words . . .' prompted Domenico, though he already guessed what was coming.

'There was no sign of her at the third and final rehearsal. But she was on stage tonight. I saw her with my own eyes. She must be barely twenty. I have to admit, I was taken aback by her looks. Beauty of that kind would be enough to fill a theatre on its own merits, without any need of further attractions. If it had been possible and we had needed to, I would have liked to publicise her appearances. But who can rely on the operations of a ghost?'

'And are you sure she is a ghost?'

'What other explanation can you think of? No one in the audience noticed anything untoward, though there was a gasp of admiration when she got up from her chair and strode to the front of the stage, before withdrawing. Instead of coming backstage, she literally disappeared. Sarti and his companions handled the situation admirably. They wrote her into the story as it was unfolding and even found a reason for her departure. In a way it is a pity the audience were not in a position to appreciate the extent of their professionalism.'

'What will happen if she interrupts our opera?'

Limentani shrugged his shoulders. The prospect did not appear to bother him unduly.

The conversation moved to a subject they had discussed several times, namely, the identity of the librettist of *King Montezuma and the Conquest of Peru*, concealed on the title page by what was obviously a pseudonym. Limentani propended for one of the younger brothers of an aristocratic family that had important connections with Spain, and had had a Spanish Jesuit as house guest two winters previously. The material was strikingly original. According to Limentani's informants, the Jesuit had visited South America and had access there to unusually detailed accounts of the rout and collapse of the empire of the Incas. His personal knowledge of the place led him to view the predicament of the conquered peoples with especial sympathy. While it was just possible that the Jesuit himself had written the libretto, Limentani considered it more likely that the supposed author had gleaned the necessary background information during protracted discussions of the situation in Peru, the conduct of the invaders and that of the churchmen they brought with them. The younger man was an excellent versifier with a long satirical poem in octaves to his credit. It was unlikely that such a polished libretto could be the work of a man coming to poetry for the first time.

'Why should he not want to put his own name to the opera?'

'Perhaps he fears the content will be considered too subversive. Or he may wish to protect his informant. If our calculations are correct, and Gregorio Calbo's third son is indeed the author, there could be no doubt in anyone's mind as to the source of the material. There are no other candidates. The priest's views would have been made public. Moreover he belongs to an illustrious family, which is extremely conservative by tradition. While it is perfectly acceptable for an aristocrat to dabble in narrative poetry, most literary men see writing librettos as hack work . . .'

'In spite of Metastasio?'

'In spite of that divinely gifted creature, yes. Remember that Metastasio is a priest of humble origins who, though his fame has spread far, is still dependent on the favours of the court at Vienna for his sustenance. That is a position no young man of breeding, accustomed to having independent means, would wish to find himself in.'

Limentani next enquired, half jokingly, if Domenico's religious fervour had abated, or if he continued his visits to the convent of St Clare. When he heard that Mother Hilary was ill, he looked worried. The news set him thinking of Donato Gradenigo. Since their first meeting, the old man's cough had descended into his chest, and now his lungs were being affected. He had been confined to bed for the last week. It was possible that he might be unable to attend the première of Pacifico Anselmi's opera in three days' time.

'We need to keep our fingers crossed,' he told Domenico. 'Though he is not yet at death's door, the state of his health is causing the doctors serious concern. If he were to die, the whole question of the estate and who inherits it would be thrown into disorder once again. He has no living heir.'

'What would that mean for us?'

'Maybe nothing, in the short term. In the longer term, it would place difficulties in our way if we wished to mount a further season.'

'You mean,' said Domenico, brightening considerably, 'that this is not to be the only season at St Hyginus's?'

'I have to tell you I have grown extremely fond of the place, with all its enigmas and mysteries. If my employer in Dresden can be persuaded to release me on a regular basis, I would not be averse to spending several months each year within the bounds of this small parish. Of course, I would be unwise to speak too soon or out of turn. This may be a passing enthusiasm, the temporary effect of working with such fine collaborators.'

Though he was familiar by now with Limentani's habitual courtesy, Domenico flushed with pleasure at these words.

'I mean, naturally, yourself and Luca Schiavoni. I have never seen him work with such fervour and excitement. And do you know what I attribute it to? The discovery of that machine. It is interfering with his sleep, just imagine! He lies awake at night thinking about it. In the process of overhauling it, he has discovered the solutions to problems that had exercised him for the better part of a decade. He is convinced no one else but Colombani could have designed such a masterpiece. When he mentions the fellow's name, it is in tones of awe, as if he were a saint and could work miracles.'

It was on the tip of Domenico's tongue to tell everything he knew. The impresario changed the subject.

'How is Gabriela Dotti coping with her part?'

Gabriela sang the role of the native courtesan, a captive from a neighbouring kingdom who was Montezuma's especial favourite. It was she who robbed him of his magical headdress, in a scene clearly borrowed from the story of Samson and Delilah in the Old Testament. Her part carried the main love interest of the piece, for in the second scene of the first act she fell for the son of the leader of the Spanish invaders, was subsequently seduced by him, and promised to betray Montezuma in the hope of persuading the foreigner to become her husband. In the last act, having been rejected by him yet again, she converted to Christianity and took the veil, in a ceremony which, though it was affecting, had an undertone of disquieting irony. If it had been placed differently within the opera as a whole, Domenico felt, a religious message might have come over. But occurring as it did just before Montezuma's execution, all memory of it was dispelled by sympathy for the dying king. Gabriela was coping surprisingly well, and he told Limentani so.

'I am glad to hear it. The woman has too many distractions. Did you know that she has found a lover?'

'Not at all. I was waiting for Anselmi to start paying court to her.'

'He's too late now. The man in question is German, or Austrian, to be precise. And I do not like the look of him one bit. She managed to smuggle him into a rehearsal yesterday, though I had expressly forbidden anything of the kind.'

'What did you do about it?'

'Nothing,' reflected Limentani, philosophically. 'It can cause no major harm, and the last thing I want to do is upset my leading singer in advance of her first night. But the matter causes me concern, let us say, on humane grounds. If you ask me, he has no real interest in her. I am familiar with the type. He intends to exploit her for another purpose.'

'What leads you to think that? And what might his purpose be?'

'She has been snooping round the building, as if searching for a lost or hidden object. I caught her rummaging in the cupboard upstairs, the one where all our scores are kept. When I asked her what she was up to, she invented a story about needing the music of an aria by Iommelli for a benefit night she is planning to hold between now and the beginning of Lent. She claimed to have left her copy behind in Parma. I didn't believe a word she said. While by no means stupid, the woman is not especially intelligent either. And she could have no reason of her own for ransacking a cupboard in that fashion. The Austrian man put her up to it. What his motives may be, I am in no position to tell.'

24

Domenico checked the cupboard the moment he got back to St Hyginus's that night, and found that the portfolio was missing. It took him ages to get to sleep. When eventually he did, the sleep was so deep the janitor had to shake him awake the following morning. Don Astolfo was waiting at the bottom of the stairs, eager to talk to him.

'Show him up,' said Domenico.

There was barely time to splash water over his face, towel it dry and slip into a fresh shirt before the priest was upon him. From his expression, Domenico could tell the man was in a state of considerable agitation.

'I called round last night but you were not in,' he said.

'Ansaldo Limentani and I stayed on much later than usual in the tavern,' Domenico answered apologetically. 'It was long past midnight when I returned home.'

'I visited Mother Hilary yesterday afternoon,' the priest began, sitting down without waiting for an invitation, and arranging his soutane around his knees. 'What she told me about the will is most important and most disturbing. I did not get a wink of sleep last night. Where is it?' he asked, with unusual abruptness, looking up.

'A will?' asked Domenico, playing for time. 'What will?'

'It was one of the papers in the portfolio you brought to the convent, for Mother Hilary to look through. She is a conscientious soul and sent it back to you before she had time to tell me about it. And now I am aware of its contents, I have come to discuss what action we should take.'

'But what was in the will?'

Domenico could not bring himself to tell the priest right away that it had been stolen. How could he have been so careless? He would need to prepare himself for that disclosure.

'If it can be shown to be genuine, and the person named in it can be found, then Donato Gradenigo no longer has an exclusive claim on the estate. He may have to renounce everything. And he is far from being in the best of health! The news will be the death of him. I hesitate to admit it, even to myself, but it crossed my mind that the best thing we could do might be to destroy the document altogether. Or return it to its hiding place. The previous lawsuit lasted seven years. If we get entangled in another one, who can tell how much time may pass before the issue gets resolved? I was so relieved when they told me everything had been settled, and that the theatre could reopen at last!'

'It's lost! Gone! Stolen!' cried Domenico, unable to contain himself any longer. 'It is too late for us to destroy it, even if we were to decide that was the right thing to do!'

'What are you trying to tell me?'

'I put it in the cupboard here, on top of the musical scores. I had a hundred things on my mind. I was already late for a rehearsal. That was on Sunday. I did not check again until last night, by which time it had disappeared.'

Don Astolfo surprised Domenico by the calmness with which he received the news.

'This may be the best thing that could have happened,' he said after a pause. 'Depending, of course, whose hands it has got into.'

'But what was contained in the will?'

'Mother Hilary and I put our heads together on that subject. I will give you the benefit of our mutual confabulations. Though I suspect that Angelo Colombani knows more than either of us about the business. It might be an idea for us to pay him a joint visit to see whether we can extract anything coherent from him. He was Alvise Contarini's closest confidante until the evening of his death. There is every likelihood he had a share in whatever secret ploys Alvise may have been engaged in.'

'You still haven't answered my question!'

'Alvise had a child out of wedlock. A son. His marriage, to Donato Gradenigo's cousin, was neither a happy nor a fruitful one. She produced a stillborn babe within one year of becoming his wife, after which he never visited her bed again.'

Don Astolfo caught the worried look in Domenico's eyes.

'Have no fear, I am not breaking a secret of the confessional. There were bitter and repeated exchanges between husband and wife on that account. As a result, every servant they had was fully acquainted with the sordid details of the business. Alvise tried to force himself upon her on one occasion, but she would have none of it. It was her maidservant, a particularly unpleasant individual by the name of Agatha, who heard her cries and came to the rescue. She must have been barely fifteen at the time, but she was lithe and energetic and pitched in without hesitation. Alvise bore the marks of her nails on his face for days afterwards.'

'What an ugly scene!'

'It was indeed. I reproached Alvise at length about it and imposed a stiff penance on him. But I suspect he paid no attention. He was never a regular attender at mass and, if he ever sought absolution for his sins, it was not from me. I saw him more frequently at the theatre than at church or in private.'

'You mean you came to see the operas here?'

'I did,' said Don Astolfo, with a grimace.

'And you saw the cloud machinery in action?'

'Naturally. I was here on the fateful night, as was Mother Hilary.'

The priest's features relaxed, and a smile played around his lips.

'If any of that man's manifold sins have been forgiven, it will be in large measure due to the joy he and his protégé procured their fellow human beings, thanks to those wonderful devices. I only wish we had known about this child at the time of his death, or long before. It would have saved much trouble and heartsearching.'

'Where is the child? Who is his mother?'

'The will was drawn up in the presence of a lawyer who is now deceased, so we cannot turn to him for information. The language of the document, if you want my opinion, shows the influence of Colombani. I would hazard a guess that he and Alvise drew it up together. The tale of the child reads more like a fairy tale than an actual occurrence. Yet I cannot bring myself to imagine they concocted it. The mother was little better than a beggar, a young woman who haunted the streets round St Hyginus's, selling flowers and oranges. It was the only one of Alvise's many liaisons to result in a child. That is presumably why his wife reacted so violently once she got to hear of it.'

'A violent reaction? What did she do?'

'She is dead as well, and has no chance to defend herself, or to give her version of the facts. So we must treat what Alvise wrote with caution. His account is undoubtedly biased. He was already estranged from his wife when he met the girl, and he never forgave her for what happened with the bastard child. He may have blackened her character unjustifiably in what he wrote. As for the maidservant, he conceived a loathing for her the very day she set foot inside the house. He claims the two women hatched a plot. They had the child stolen and its mother kidnapped.'

'But that is against the law!'

'Of course it is. Our law, however, offers little protection to either illegitimate children or their mothers. The girl already risked being prosecuted as a vagrant. I am not sure whether I can believe Giannetta to have been capable of such wickedness. It would be perfectly like Alvise to distort the facts, turning a sordid wrangle into a dramatic sequence of events which cast him in a tragic and heroic light. It is quite probable that all Giannetta and her accomplice did was find the girl a secure domestic position, somewhere in the hinterland, and place the child with foster parents. There would have been nothing criminal in that. It could even be interpreted as the expression of profound charity. After all, it is the duty of every lawful wife to separate her husband from both the occasion and the effects of sinning.'

Domenico looked keenly at the priest's face. It sounded as if he were quoting someone else's words, rather than voicing his own opinion. But he did not bother to challenge him on that score.

'And all of this was in the will?'

'Some of it was written there. The remainder Mother Hilary and I pieced together from fragments of gossip we remember. It strikes me as odd that we had never discussed the matter with one another. Both of us heard rumours of the existence of an illegitimate child without giving serious credence to them. Now I see that we were wrong. My vigilance over my parishioners has been proved faulty once again.'

'And is that all?'

'Alvise stipulated that he wished everything he left to go to the child, provided he could be found.'

'And is there any chance of that?'

'Very little, as far as I can see. Unless someone tracks down Agatha and persuades her to tell the truth about what happened.'

'How could the child be identified? What age will he be now?'

'Anything between twenty-five and thirty. The sad business occurred early on in Alvise's marriage and was followed by long and weary years of mutual hostility. Giannetta abandoned him in the end, much against my advice, and spent the latter part of her life in a convent on the outskirts of Padua.'

'But were no tokens left with him?' insisted Domenico, filled with foreboding, for the maidservant's name had rung out like a warning signal, and he sensed that he already knew what the priest would say in answer to his question.

'In the will, Alvise speaks of two, though there was no way he could be certain they had remained with the child. A small cameo portrait of the mother, with a lock of her hair pressed in beneath the glass. And a ring carved with the father's initials.'

'A and C,' said Domenico morosely.

'That is correct. Alvise Contarini.'

Domenico's tone was morose because he blamed himself bitterly for what had happened to the document, and because he realised he was not ready to share what he knew with Don Astolfo. The manner in which he had become acquainted with Rodrigo was too unorthodox, too far beyond the priest's conceptions or possibilities of understanding, for Domenico to risk even furnishing him with a falsified version, unless he had ample time to prepare himself. And although he was glad to see such unexpectedly grand prospects opening for Rodrigo, they filled him with sadness. There was no way what they shared could, in his opinion, survive a change in status of this magnitude. If Rodrigo were to regain what appeared to be rightfully his, Domenico would lose any claims he had on him. Their hurried lovemaking among the reeds, beneath grey skies the previous Sunday, took on a paradisiacal air in retrospect, as if it were an experience they could never hope to repeat. Don Astolfo broke the silence.

'Have you any notion who could have stolen the portfolio?' he asked.

Domenico nodded slowly, but did not say anything.

'You prefer not to tell me. I will respect your wishes. Indeed, as I have already said,' the priest went on, getting up, 'I cannot help wondering if this latest occurrence represents the hand of God moving in our affairs. Might it not be better to allow the thing to disappear without trace? Who can tell if the stolen child may not be living in perfect happiness, oblivious to his heritage, and better off that way?'

'But Donato Gradenigo is seriously ill. And if he dies . . .'

'The hawks will be out again, keen to dig their beaks into the carcass. No doubt they are sharpening their claws already, as we speak. Do we really wish to draw an innocent creature into such company?'

'What are you afraid of?' asked Domenico, almost fiercely. 'Why don't you want the truth to come out? Do you have something to hide yourself?'

The priest's voice quivered as he began his answer, but he managed to calm it.

'Yes, I am afraid. The word you chose is exactly the right one, and your reproach is fully justified. Ever since that fateful night, since people started murmuring about the activities of a certain individual in this parish, I have had the sense of a dreadful menace looming over us, a presence slumbering in this very theatre, waiting to be awakened . . .'

'Angelo Colombani is perfectly awake, above our heads, though his hours of rising and going to bed may be very different from those of ordinary mortals.'

'It is not Colombani I had in mind. I do not believe him capable of any evil whatsoever, on a lesser or a greater scale. The presence I spoke of goes by another name.'

'Goffredo Negri,' murmured Domenico.

'Then you know everything.' The priest made a gesture of rebuff, as if he had managed until now to wash his hands of the matter and wanted to continue doing so. 'I have no doubt that he was present on the night the machinery got stuck, and that he, not Angelo, was responsible for Alvise's murder. There was never clear evidence that he had been here, and within a month people claimed that he was dead. He was said to have poisoned himself, in an inn on the toll road near Mantua, because he had learned the police were on his tail. The unfortunate truth is, however, that certain things refuse to die. His presence darkens my parish still. Only in the cloister at St Clare's do I feel entirely free from it.'

'And that is what you are afraid to reawaken.'

An odd sound reached him from where the priest was sitting, like liquid trying to escape down a tube and not quite managing. He understood the man was sobbing quietly, while at the same time doing everything he could to suppress the signs of his emotion.

'But how can you be so afraid? Did you ever meet Negri?'

Don Astolfo shook his head mournfully from side to side. All at once Domenico understood.

'It is what you have heard about him from Angelo Colombani that frightens you so much. His story was enough to terrify you.'

The priest regained control of himself sufficiently to be able to speak.

'I am so ashamed, my son. Here I am, the representative of Mother Church, invested with the powers of Christ and of the angels, yet there is something in that man, or in what I know of him, that fills me with such panic I would merely turn and run if there were the slightest likelihood of coming face to face with him.'

'Then we shall have to find another means of dealing with him,' Domenico said gently.

What he was actually thinking was: I am going to have to sort out this mess on my own. It had just occurred to him that there was no way he could get in touch with Rodrigo or call upon his help. Rodrigo had promised to be in the theatre on the first night of the season, but that did not mean that they would see each other or speak to one another. The first night had been postponed twice, from Tuesday to Thursday and from Thursday until Friday. Would Rodrigo have succeeded in keeping abreast with the changes? What was more, seeing that he considered himself to be personally responsible for its loss, Domenico preferred not to see

Rodrigo again until he was in a position to give the will into his hands.

'We cannot just forget about it. The portfolio, to our knowledge, has not been cast into the fire or destroyed,' he said. 'I have a shrewd idea who may have stolen it, and who may have it now. Whoever instigated this theft would not have done so unless they wished to use the will for a precise purpose. And that is what has to be stopped. I do not think they have the true heir's interests at heart. Far from it.'

Domenico found his mind wandering repeatedly from the music during that afternoon's rehearsal. He was trying to work out what would be the best way of challenging Gabriela. She had never been the most attentive of singers. In the course of that week, he often had to remind her of the importance of maintaining eye contact with him at the harpsichord, however briefly or fleetingly. Today her gaze was constantly upon him, as if she were as preoccupied with thoughts of Domenico as he was with thoughts of her. It was she who requested a private interview in the office upstairs, once the players had laid their bows aside and everybody took a break.

She did not behave at all as he anticipated. There was no outburst of tears, no self-reproach, no appeal for understanding. She did not feel guilty about stealing the portfolio. All that bothered her was that she had done it for a man who proved unworthy of such dedication. She explained what had happened with a considerable degree of dignity. Oriana had visited her the previous evening.

'She is the younger of my sisters. I have two. The other is a nun at the convent of St Clare. How strange that we should all end up so close to one another! Oriana ought not to have left her bed, but she felt I was in danger and wanted to warn me as soon as possible. We have both fallen prey to the same seducer. Or rather, he has made advances to us both. Do not rush to misinterpret my words. I have not conceded the scoundrel so much as a kiss, though I cannot tell how far I might have gone if things between us had proceeded differently. His looks are such that very few women, especially here in Venice, would deny him anything he asked for, at a second or even a first meeting. That is what happened to my sister. His duplicity is equal to his beauty and he asked her to help him spy upon this theatre.'

Domenico wondered if he should pretend to be surprised about these words but said nothing.

'If I am not mistaken, he has been carrying on all this time, with a woman more than twice my age. Unless, that is, he has sunk to such a degree of depravation that not love, but a different, more obscure passion binds him to the creature.'

'What are their names?'

'His is Andreas Hofmeister. He comes from Salzburg. The woman is called Hedwiga Engelsfeld von Nettesheim. If Oriana had not fallen ill, I should have found out about it all sooner. But the deed was already done by the time I called upon her. I was so delighted to have found an admirer. Not a prospective husband, do not mistake me. That would be a mixed blessing. It is hard for singers like myself to meet a man who will tolerate this nomadic life, rather than demanding we abandon everything on the spot and fathering children on us, so we cannot work or move.'

'That is not what happened to Donatella,' Domenico pointed out.

Gabriela laughed ironically.

'The exception that proves the rule. What is she doing with a babe in arms? The only result of her marriage has been to give her extra mouths to feed. Her husband and children live entirely at her expense. Why should I take on such a burden? A man like Andreas, or such as I thought he was, would suit me perfectly. I was so excited when I called on my sister that I told her servant girl everything. But it was not to be. He is interested neither in me nor in Oriana, only in what he can learn through us about this theatre.'

'Where does Hedwiga fit in? And what has happened to the will?'

'The will?' asked Gabriela in puzzlement, without looking up. She avoided looking directly into Domenico's eyes at any point during the conversation. The contrast with the rehearsal could not have been more striking. 'I thought those were just scribblings. Mysterious signs and hieroglyphics.'

'There was a will amongst the papers. I suspect that is what your suitor was after.'

'She must have it. He sleeps in her town house now.'

'How do you know?'

'I paid a caddie to shadow him after our latest meeting. The man followed him all the way to a place known as the Court of Darkness, near the Ghetto. Afterwards he stopped in at the local tavern to quench his thirst. The people there were gossiping about the new arrival. Whether he has given it to the German woman or not, the will you speak of must be in the house. When I first learned about the deception from Oriana, I was so furious I thought of going to confront them both. But that would be a waste of time.'

25

He would go to the Court of Darkness and get the will back. That much was clear to Domenico, though he quailed at the thought of facing the perfidious Austrian nobleman and the German woman with the long name he found it so hard to pronounce. Gabriela told him where he could find the caddie she had used as an informant. There would be no difficulty in locating Hedwiga's house, for the man would be sure to guide him there in return for a sizeable tip.

First of all, Domenico resolved to pay Angelo Colombani another visit in the loft. Limentani noticed how preoccupied the young man was when they sat opposite each other over dinner in the tavern. He attributed this mood to the fact that the opening night of *King Montezuma and the Conquest of Peru* was getting closer and closer, and chose to ask no questions, in case by doing so he should increase Domenico's nervousness. Little did he suspect that the distraction was provoked by magical, rather than musical considerations.

When he got back to the theatre, Domenico's courage failed him. He not only decided to postpone his expedition to the Court of Darkness till the following night, but also to delay calling on Angelo. Having got into his nightshirt, he blew out his candle and curled up on the couch with a thick blanket on top of him. This was when, for the first time since he brought Rodrigo back after the opera at St John Chrysostom, he was disturbed by noises from upstairs. It began with the Neapolitan girl singing. Her voice possessed a haunting, oriental quality and, though it initially appeared to be coming from the attic, it moved around, so that for a moment he could have sworn she was in the room right next to him. Then she broke off and he heard Angelo talking in agitated tones, though he could not make out a single word the man was saying. Domenico sat up on the couch, clutching the blanket to his chin in an attitude of rigid fear.

Silence returned. He made an effort to calm the beating of his heart, still uncertain whether to carry out his original resolution of bearding the castrato in his den, or whether the best thing would be to try and forget about the whole confusing business of the murder and the will, to convince himself that, if he went tranquilly about his business from day to day, this mysterious tangle of events, occurring on a different but adjacent plane to his own, would leave him undisturbed and uninvolved.

He fell asleep for an hour or so but was woken once more by the singing. Colombani was practising an aria from Hasse's *Mithridates*, one of the most heartbreakingly beautiful pieces of music Domenico knew. He had heard it in the opera house at Bologna when barely ten, and it was his determination to understand its beauty, to grasp the craftsmanship of the writing and investigate the functioning of the harmonies, that led him to master musical notation. Colombani dispensed with the initial presentation of the vocal line and went straight to the reprise. His voice was clearly past its best, yet his ornamentations took Domenico's breath away, because of their daring and their stylistic appropriateness. Almost before he knew it, his hand was on the door at the bottom of the stairs. The cabinet which blocked access to the floor above was still in place. He was tired, and huffed and puffed at the thing before managing to get it out of the way. By the time he had kindled a flame, lit his candle and pulled the door back, the singing had stopped.

Once more, the costumes on their stands, clustered round the door at the top of the stairs, reminded him of a forest. He picked his way carefully through them as if they had been tree trunks with low foliage, all the more so because Angelo was engaged in a conversation, or perhaps a monologue. The person it was addressed to, if present, listened with the greatest attention, not interrupting even once. The monologue concerned the Neapolitan girl.

'The time has come to give her up,' Angelo was saying, in good-humoured, slightly wheedling tones. 'Fully seven years have gone by since you stole her. You know that is the term set. If you do not let her go of your own accord, she will find a way of freeing herself in spite of you. Then you will have lost all claims on her and may be exposed to whatever revenge she chooses to take.'

He paused. Evidently the other person was answering now, though no words reached Domenico's ears. Perhaps the castrato had gone completely mad and was having a conversation with himself after all.

'There is no question of my coming to your assistance. How many times do I have to tell you? If I had been in the least tempted by your promises and offers of reward, I would have given in when you arrived here. Why should I surrender so late on in the day? Come, Goffredo, stop being difficult. Admit defeat. Hand her over. It is the best thing you can do for yourself and for all of us.'

Shivers ran up and down Domenico's spine. Goffredo Negri was present! In this very room! No wonder he had felt frightened when he got back to the theatre that night. Despite his fear, he was aware of a tingling excitement at the idea of getting a glimpse of the man he had been told so much about. Neither Don Astolfo nor Mother Hilary had ever set eyes upon him! He edged his way forward and squeezed his head under the armpit of a heavy velvet robe, which he hoped would camouflage him sufficiently. If he were to attract attention, the conversation would come to an abrupt close, and he would lose his chance of finding out more about the girl and where she was. Her guest appearances with Sarti's troupe did not sound as if they had been planned by Negri. She was clearly beginnng to assert her own power. Moreover, he instinctively felt that he preferred to see the conjuror without being seen.

Angelo was sitting with his back to Domenico, at an angle. The mirror was on a low table in front of him. Because of the position it was in, Domenico could not see the reflection in the glass. He felt a stab of disappointment. The villain of the piece was not here after all. Angelo was merely staging a discussion with him. And that meant there was little likelihood of the Neapolitan girl taking material form in the attic, as he had found himself hoping she might do.

There was another silence, while Angelo waited for a response.

He cocked his head, as though listening to a line of reasoning. Domenico retreated into the forest of costumes and gingerly made his way through them so as to get directly behind Angelo. He could not have explained why, but he was extremely curious to look into the mirror for himself. It failed to occur to him that, if he were able to see into it, his reflection might also appear there, and his presence be detected. He edged forward so as to get a good view. What he saw gave him such a shock that he went weak at the knees. He grasped at the nearest stand to stop himself from falling over and knocked it down with a crash, which was followed by several more, because the costumes behaved like dominoes, toppling into one another. He had set a general avalanche in motion. Angelo leapt to his feet. A shrill sound like a cry of triumph rent the air. There was a gust of wind and all the candles were blown out.

The face in the mirror had not been Angelo's but Goffredo's. Domenico realised, in the split second before darkness fell, that the face had once been attractive. It inspired no sympathy in him, however, only terror at the idea that, if the mirror functioned as a window, then the eyes looking through it might light upon his own. There was a large wart in the hollow between the left eye and the bridge of the nose.

Domenico had fainted. When he came to, the candles had been lit again. He was lying on a battered chaise longue with the stuffing coming out of it, and Angelo was holding a handkerchief up to his face. The cloth gave off a repellent, fetid smell. Angelo had poured drops of a chemical substance on to it in order to revive Domenico, who pushed the handkerchief away, rubbed his eyes and yawned. Angelo gave no signs of surprise or anger. It was as if the accident that had just taken place were part of a pattern of events whose general design was familiar to him, however unpredictable its details should prove to be.

'Was that him?' asked Domenico, without any kind of a preamble.

Angelo nodded and smiled. He looked secretly pleased with himself. How could he possibly be pleased if Goffredo Negri had escaped at last? What on earth would he get up to here in Venice? Would anyone be safe?

'How can you be so calm about it?'

'There is nothing I can do. He has gone. All this is coming to an end at last. Can I get you a glass of wine?'

Domenico allowed the castrato to pour him some red wine and bring the glass to his lips. He sipped from it and sank back. He felt unbelievably sleepy, utterly exhausted, yet he knew that somehow he must find the strength to stay awake and carry on.

'How is that possible? I mean, that you look into a mirror and see another person's face?'

'He has been imprisoned in that mirror for seven years. I kept him there. That is how powerful I am.'

'And now he has got out because of me! What have I done?'

Angelo shrugged his shoulders and tilted his head to one side, birdlike as ever.

'It is a little awkward, yes. Not the kind of person one wants to set loose on the streets of Venice, especially during Carnival. If it had been Lent, that would be less of a risk. And were Easter within sight, we would have absolutely nothing to worry about. He could not raise a finger against anyone then. But just now he is extremely powerful.'

'Why did you let him out? Why didn't you stop him?' cried Domenico, who did not want to bear all of the responsibility for the accident that had happened.

'Talking to him is a dangerous business at the best of times. I can feel him pressing on me constantly, even when the mirror is turned towards the wall. And when I look into his face, it is as if my head were squeezed by fiery tongs. He brings me out in a sweat. It takes a lot of energy to keep him at bay and, as I am sure you noticed, he is not the easiest of individuals to hold a conversation with. Always trying to score a winning point. It takes me back to old times, actually. And he plays peculiar tricks. One night the glass in the mirror started rippling, as if it were quicksilver. I really thought he had got the better of me. All it needed was for my vigliance to falter for a moment. Unfortunately you provided the pretext for that.'

Domenico hid his head in his hands and moaned.

'Why did you decide to talk to him tonight?' he asked, after a pause, still unwilling to take all of the blame.

'Because of Eleonora. The girl from Naples. I take it you heard her singing.'

Domenico nodded, wide-eyed.

'I don't know where he has imprisoned her. But she is impatient to break free. She has been coming closer and closer all through the winter, frightening the nuns in Mother Hilary's convent, and those poor comic actors, too, by popping up where she is not supposed to be.'

'But please explain. I don't understand. Where does the girl fit in? What does she have to do with you and Negri and Alvise?'

'Do pardon me, I beg you. It is most inconsiderate of me to assume that you are fully informed about this whole complicated affair. In the last analysis, it can only interest a few people. Your involvement is entirely accidental. Let me fill your glass again, and block the hole in the window over there. Wait. I can feel a horrid draught blowing over my shoulders. I am extraordinarily suscep- tible to chills and, though I do not expect to sing in public again, it makes no sense to take unnecessary risks.'

Domenico had noticed the chill but not the reason for it. The window that looked towards the convent garden had lozenge- shaped panes. Four of them had been knocked out, leaving an aperture not much larger than a fist. This was the means of escape Goffredo had chosen. At that precise moment it did not disconcert Domenico in the slightest that a grown man should have slipped through a relatively small hole, as if he had been a gust of wind, rather than a creature made of flesh and blood.

'They have got my machinery working again, haven't they?' Angelo asked, taking his place opposite Domenico on a low stool. 'That Dalmatian fellow is a genuine wizard, to give him credit. Have no fear, I use the term metaphorically. There is nothing arcane about his craftsmanship. He could never have devised anything as complex as that off his own bat. But he was capable of reconstructing it according to my designs. That in itself is a task requiring huge technical expertise and a lot of imagination. Don Astolfo told me I should never have made the machine and perhaps he is right. It has led to a lot of trouble but it also gave me so much joy! You see, everyone thinks that clouds are accidental, insubstantial, that nothing is to be learned from them. Indeed, dear boy, if you and I were able to fly, as human beings one day will, we would pass through them without experiencing anything more than a passing and rather unpleasant damp flush. Make no mistake of it, however, anyone who apprehends the structure of clouds is well on the way to learning all there is to know about the architecture of the universe.'

'Who was your teacher in these matters? Where did you learn about such things?'

'From Negri, naturally. Even at this stage, the man is not entirely evil. When our paths first crossed, there was much good in him, but of a kind which it exceeded the capacity of ordinary men and women to appreciate or understand. He learnt still more by teaching me. The pupil leads his teacher on as much as he is led. That is something I understood at an extremely early stage, thanks to music, before natural philosophy began to fascinate me. Take it from me, if you stop learning, then you can no longer teach.'

'And did he teach you how to make the cloud machinery?'

Angelo shook his head vigorously.

'Not at all. By the time I designed that, Goffredo had gone beyond the point where he was capable of making anything. His skills had become exclusively analytic, and potentially very destructive. When we met again, he spoke of my stage designs with barely hidden contempt. It was partly jealousy. He thought, when I lost my voice, that I had lost everything, and it irked him that I had found a way of returning to the theatre, if in a less illustrious guise. For me as for Alvise, the theatre was a kind of a game, while Goffredo had lost his sense of play. The cloud machinery was a piece of barbarous frivolity in his eyes. But I did use what he taught me when I planned it. So a little part of the credit must go to him. That is why, when he turned up St Hyginus's unexpectedly, I was not prepared to send him away. He had a right to be there. Moreover, he had a right to be wherever I was, unconditionally, because he made me what I am. And though it may sound perverse, he has kept me company during these lonely years, there in his mirror. I could not have wished myself a worthier sparring partner.'

Angelo looked wistfully at the object in question. The glass in it had been blank as an unwritten page immediately after Goffredo's escape. Now it was filled with a pattern of swirling clouds, as if it were voyaging through the upper regions of the atmosphere. Domenico resolved not to look into it again. It made him dizzy, and he had no desire to encounter, through its agency, further mysteries to add to those already confronting him.

'So Goffredo was here on the night Alvise died.'

'Of course he was. He killed Alvise. Had you not guessed? How could you possibly have doubted it? Keeping him imprisoned in this loft was also a way of protecting him, from pursuit and from himself. Maybe these years of sacrifice have been worthwhile. He gains no happiness from harming others. His ill-will feeds upon itself, like a whirlwind spinning round faster and faster until it sets off on its journey of destruction.'

Domenico was trying to work out the implications of what he had been told.

'You mean he was your captive, and Eleonora in her turn was his?'

'Indeed. And now he has got his freedom back, perhaps she will get hers as well.'

'But if Goffredo was in your power, why couldn't you force him to release her?'

'I am unable to force Goffredo to do anything. And the nature of the barriers he set around her was unknown to me. That meant it was impossible for me to undo them. Persuasion was the only means and, as you can see, it failed.'

'How did she get here from Naples? Did he bring her to Venice with him? And if so, why?'

Angelo sighed deeply.

'That is a sad, sad story. If I had stayed in the seclusion of the Charterhouse at Parma, or rejected Alvise's proposal to come here and collaborate with him, then Goffredo might not have been tempted to undertake a task which proved superior even to his capacities. Call me self-centred if you will. I cannot help thinking he did it because of me. To awaken my envy, or to show his superiority. And when he got into difficulties, he came to me for help. I was the great love of Goffredo's life, you know. At least until he met that frightful German woman. He taught me everything he could during those years in Turkey.'

'Hedwiga,' put in Domenico, meditatively. Then he articulated the whole name as carefully as he could. 'Hedwiga Engelsfeld von Nettesheim.'

'Indeed,' said Angelo. 'A terrifying creature in her heyday, though now she is, in more senses than one, a shadow of her former self. Her dream was to possess him utterly. But she was unable to chase the last vestiges of love for me from his heart.'

Domenico found the man's vanity, and the tenderness with which he still spoke of Negri, disconcerting. He pressed on with his questions.

'And Alvise?'

'Goffredo was a severe and demanding master in matters both magical and musical. He was never satisfied with anything I did and always asked for more. He praised me so rarely that the days on which he expressed approval were feast days for me. Alvise was very different. The things I made were a source of unadulterated delight to him. His gift to me was that delight. I was happy in Alvise's company.'

'Why did he get killed?'

'You send me back to my list of "ifs" with such questions, dear Domenico. If he had never heard of me, he might still be alive today. If he had never loved me, or loved what I created, our association might have been wound up at an earlier stage, before Goffredo reappeared upon the scene. If we had worked less well together, St Hyginus's might never have become famous, and Goffredo would not have known where to search for me when he decided that he needed my assistance. But I have spent sufficient time repenting who I am and all that happened. Where is the man who can escape his life? The life we lead can feel like a diverted river, which should have run through different landscapes and into a different sea. Yet there comes a time when you stop regretting the life you should have had and come to look with pride on everything that is yours. Alvise and I were like two dancers improvising steps, to music only we could hear. This theatre was our stage, in more ways than one. Without a need for words, or any but the briefest of glances, we understood what might be possible, and brought it into being. Until our nemesis arrived, that is, in the shape of Goffredo Negri.'

Can I have that? Domenico was thinking, without articulating the words. Can I experience that delight? What must it be like, rather than interpreting what other hands have written, to bring into existence what has never been before?

'Goffredo made his proposal to both of us. It was December, and the cloud machinery was already functioning. This theatre, though small, and tucked away in an obscure corner of the city, had become the most celebrated in Venice. No other could compete with it. The owner of St John Chrysostom and the management at St Moses engaged a whole train of spies and saboteurs, to copy our designs or else to wreck them, but it made no difference. What Goffredo offered was much more than the chance to devise further and more wonderful illusions for our audiences. I have told you he considered such things frivolous, but he would have stooped to them, and infinitely lower, in order to induce me to collaborate with him. He had always insisted that the boundaries between individuals were frailer and more insubstantial than we all believe, that men and women can blend with one another and even become one another. He was obsessed with the idea of creating a single, androgynous creature which would dominate the world to come, combining the best qualities of men and women, reproducing itself without the need for nurturing or copulation. He announced to us that, after more than a decade of experiments, he had at last perfected a technique which would allow him to bring this creature into being. He was to be one half of it and Eleonora the other.'

'What you are saying makes no sense to me.' Domenico frowned. He could not grasp the concept of blending human beings into one another, nor did he like it. 'And in any case, if Goffredo had made his discovery, why did he risk sharing his secret with other people and maybe having to share the benefits of it, too? What point was there in bribing you to be his accomplices?'

'He needed me. He said the strength of one soul was not sufficient to set the process in motion. Our old partnership was to be re-established for just long enough to bring about the fusion.'

'And were you tempted?'

Angelo's voice quavered when he went on.

'I weakened. I had heard snippets of news about him in the intervening years. I knew of his association with Hedwiga, and that he claimed to have brought her back from the dead. Operations of that kind are naturally anathema to the civil authorities and to the church. They have to be conducted in the greatest secrecy. But if you have once been involved in occult matters, it is easy to get information about what is being done by other hands in other cities. I made the acquaintance of a Jewish usurer here in Venice, because of a foolish debt Alvise had entered into, which we were struggling to pay off with the money we made from the theatre. No sooner had I set eyes on the man than I realised where his true interests lay. I could say we became friends. When he discovered I had been an intimate of Negri's, there were no bounds to the reverence with which he treated me. Thanks to him I learned that Hedwiga was in Venice, even before Goffredo turned up at the theatre. The Jew also told me about Eleonora's disappearance. I put two and two together and realised that she was the raw material which would be processed as part of the experiment. Goffredo told me he had come upon her as an unexpected stroke of luck. Everything was ready.'

'And you believed him?'

'You have seen Goffredo's face, if only for an instant. A man like that does not lie about things which matter. Of course I believed him. He threatened that, if I refused, he would take Hedwiga as his assistant. I laughed when he said that. The woman is a bungler and he knows it. It was a different consideration which led me to accept his proposal, one so important to me I did not even mention it in our discussions, though I could not get the thought out of my mind, either sleeping or waking, throughout those days. It was so simple and so foolish. I hoped that, with Goffredo at my side, I might sing again.'

'But you still sing now, and wonderfully! Why did you need Goffredo?'

'What I mean is, sing upon a stage. I have never lost the power of singing alone, in seclusion, or with one or two listeners. But to do so before an audience, beneath the arch of a proscenium, had become impossible. And I longed for nothing more than that. Can you imagine what it would have been like to sing in front of one of my own machines? Or to descend in the midst of clouds I had myself designed and intone an aria, suspended in mid air?'

He paused, a rapt smile upon his face. Domenico was impatient for him to continue.

'So what did you do?'

'I played for time. We began the experiments, in the room where you are sleeping now, working at the dead of night. We were ready to start drawing her substance from the girl when the cloud machinery got stuck, during a trial run for a new opera. There was a minor defect in the design which I soon detected and believed I had rectified. That subsequent, fateful night proved me wrong. While I had deluded myself that there could be no harm in going a little way along the path indicated by Negri, all at once our work struck me as accursed. Alvise supported my decision to suspend the experiments, for he had been unhappy about the collaboration ever since setting eyes upon Goffredo, even before he had any notion what it would involve. When I told Goffredo I was not prepared to continue, a fierce argument broke out of the kind we so often had until our falling out in Florence. He was older by this stage, less patient and more desperate. He drew a knife and leapt on me. Alvise interposed his body and received the blow.'

'He gave his life for yours,' Domenico articulated slowly.

' "Greater love hath no man . . ." ' said Angelo, wiping his eyes. 'I was appalled at what my recklessness had led to and furious with Goffredo, incandescent with an anger I have never known before or since. It was beyond my powers to bring Alvise back to life. And even if I had been capable of doing so, I shuddered at the thought of committing such a sacrilege. But I found the strength to terminate my association with Negri once and for all. I overwhelmed him and trapped him in the mirror. Until that moment he had persisting in treating me as his apprentice. In the end the pupil proved more powerful than his master.'

26

Domenico lay awake until long after dawn. The peculiar little man in the loft had worn a relieved, almost euphoric expression when they had bidden one another goodnight. Goffredo's escape meant he no longer had to lead a clandestine existence. A surveillance lasting seven years had come to an end. Domenico, on the other hand, felt the burden had been passed to him. It was due to his foolish intervention that the necromancer managed to elude his captor's vigilance. Added to that was the responsibility of having lost the will, through distraction and superficiality. He could not think what had prevented him from glancing inside the cupboard to check that the portfolio was still there.

The rumours which spread through Venice in the course of the following day convinced him urgent action was required. During the middle part of the morning, a man in Turkish dress set up a stall near the Rialto, where he sold gleaming white masks of exceptionally fine workmanship at bargain prices. Word went round and soon people were queueing up to buy them. Those who tried them on when they got home, however, found to their alarm that they adhered to the face. No amount of tugging or shaking could get them off. What was more, when twilight arrived they started to glow, burning the skin and causing excruciating pain as they melted and appeared to fuse with it. The agony lasted for an hour or so, but fortunately Negri's victims were not permanently disfigured. The wounds healed in the course of the night. By the morning of the next day each face was restored to its original condition, though the individuals concerned were still wracked with terror at the thought of the pain they had suffered. Several proved unable to put on a mask for the remainder of their lives, so that the Senate had to emit a special dispensation allowing those victims who were aristocrats to appear barefaced in receptions and at the theatre, in contravention of the normal rules.

Next a miniature tornado made its way down the Grand Canal, upsetting boats of all shapes and sizes and sending waves into the ground floors of the palaces on either side. Reaching the open water beyond the Church of the Salute, it circled to and fro capriciously, capsizing some vessels while passing within inches of others, until, as if tiring of the game, it rose into the air in the guise of a thin column of smoke, and dissolved into nothingness.

At about the time the tornado wore itself out, a crier went through the streets around the Frari church, announcing that within the hour there would be an extraordinary sale of women's garments of superior quality, on the first floor of a house which had lain empty for several months. The people who arrived at the stipulated time were astonished to see the staircase swept and carpeted, while the reception rooms looked as if they had been inhabited by persons of considerable means only the day before. The clothes merchant was subsequently described to the investigators as a rather antipathetic character, who spoke Venetian nasally, with a German accent, and had a large wart in the hollow between his left eye and the bridge of his nose. He declared that, in accordance with the spirit of carnival, he would not take money for his garments, but would instead exchange them for whatever his clients happened to be wearing at the time.

The merchandise he produced from his coffers was fit for a royal family. It included silk underwear and lace bodices, of a quality of workmanship that meant they would be treated as heirlooms, handed down from generation to generation in the family of whoever was lucky enough to get their hands on them. All the menfolk in attendance were required to leave the building and the free-for-all began. A number of women possessed of sizeable fortunes were present in the company. Though they had no need of such things, they rushed to snatch whatever they could, merely to prevent their rivals getting hold of the items in question. The entire stock disappeared in a matter of minutes, as did the merchant, who lost no time in locking the garments he received in exchange away in his coffers, though no one paid any attention to this at the time.

The fun began when the company scattered and set off home. In contact with the outside air, the clothes which people had seized upon with such delight quite simply vanished. Lucia Bondi's breasts, which the Doge's brother was rumoured to have paid solid gold to have a glimpse of, without even being allowed to touch them, were exposed for all to see. Michele Calerghi's wife Alfonsina, who in her eagerness had donned four layers of underwear from the enchanter's store, relinquishing her bodice, her stays, and an embroidered blouse to get them, had to hurry home through the chill and sunny January afternoon with nothing but a shawl upon her back. Annalisa Zen, remembering the fur-trimmed coat she had stuffed without thinking into the gaping coffer, in exchange for a jacket of mink such as she had dreamt of possessing for the best part of a decade, fainted outright when she realised the trick that had been played upon her.

A group of eight women, friends and acquaintances, took refuge in a convent they happened to be passing, when the consequences of the merchant's devilish prank dawned upon them. One of them had two sisters who were nuns there. Messages were sent to the different homes for clothing to be brought with the utmost urgency. Even then, though their bodies were not exposed to general curiosity or scorn, as those of the other women had been, they hurried home with their heads hanging low, filled with fury at the deception they had fallen prey to.

A warrant for the culprit's arrest was sent out at sunset. More than a week later, a gondolier's pole collided with the coffers containing the stolen clothes, embedded in the stinking mud at the bottom of a canal by the Church of St Barnabas. Water seeping in had already transformed the garments into a mouldy, phosphor-escent pottage. They were ferried out into the lagoon beyond the Fondamenta Nuove and dumped. For weeks afterwards boatmen insisted that the water there glowed eerily after dark, and avoided the place.

These incidents took place on Thursday. That night the Neapolitan farce was to be performed for the third time, followed by a series of improvised scenes from Sarti's troupe. There would be no rehearsals at St Hyginus's during the afternoon. Limentani had ordered everyone to rest and gather strength for the dress rehearsal the next day, in preparation for the grand opening of Anselmi's opera on Friday evening. Domenico got through the morning in a daze, partly caused by sleeplessness, and partly by his unwillingness to think about the implications of what he had decided to do or where it might lead him. He foolishly assumed that he could make it to Hedwiga's, retrieve the will, and return to the theatre in time to conduct that evening's performance. As it was, within half an hour of setting foot in the Court of Darkness, he was ushered into the presence of Hedwiga and Andreas. The servants who caught him took the precaution of tying his wrists together behind his back. It was a foretaste of what lay in store.

The caddie who had spied for Gabriela had led him past the Church of the Holy Apostles, taking the same route Andreas had followed only a few days earlier, and left him at the point where he had to cross a still stretch of water in a flat-bottomed boat. Domenico found the isolated courtyard forbidding. He realised that he had very limited chances of entering by the principal door unnoticed. There was a narrow lane to the left of the façade, however, which took him to the back of the house. Oddly, given that the front was so secluded, this gave on to a busy thoroughfare which, although it was not long after lunch, presented a selection of the usual carnival figures, going about their ploys in twos and threes. The only windows looking on to the street at the back were high above, beyond the level of the mezzanine. At Domenico's feet, a grating let air into what was presumably a cellar. Further along, a wall about half as high again as a normally sized adult linked Hedwiga's house to the neighbouring one.

A low doorway was set into it. To his surprise, the handle of the rotting wooden postern turned when he tested it. He found himself in a small garden with a fountain at its centre. There were statues at the four corners which ought to have been cherubs but, on closer inspection, turned out to be dwarves. Domenico was peering at the distorted features of one of them, who carried a basket filled with coal on his shoulder, when it moved. The statue looked straight at him and croaked:

'What are you doing here?'

Domenico froze. The dwarf raised its voice and started shouting in shrill tones:

'Michele, Michele, come quickly! We have an intruder!'

The other three statues took up the alarm. Domenico rushed back to the door but it proved impossible to open now, even when he pulled at it with all his strength. He had begun to kick at it and shout for help when Hedwiga's servants overpowered him. One of them stuffed a knotted kerchief into his mouth to gag his cries.

Hedwiga and Andreas were discussing the will when they brought Domenico in. The bigger and burlier of the servants stood behind him, tugging at the cord around his wrists so that it cut into his skin. Hedwiga showed no signs of surprise.

'I take it this is what you came for?' she asked, indicating a scroll which lay upon a table next to the window.

Domenico managed to spit the kerchief out so that he was able to talk.

'You have no right to it. You got hold of it by fraud and I demand that you return it immediately.'

'And who might we return it to, pray? To yourself? What claim have you upon it? Or your employer, that fool Limentani?'

'Then let us take the whole matter before a lawyer and see what he decides,' Domenico said, with a bravado that sounded unconvincing even in his own ears. He could think of nothing else to say. After all, he had been caught trespassing on private property, and that itself was a punishable offence in Venice.

'We have the lawyer in our pocket,' Hedwiga told Andreas. 'There is no cause for concern. He will do everything we ask of him. And if I am not mistaken, our petty burglar shares a certain foible with Onofrio Carpi, as a consequence of which neither of them will so much as lift a finger to prevent us doing precisely what we wish.'

Domenico studied Andreas's features with curiosity and a certain sympathy. He could have sworn the man was uncomfortable with the situation in which he found himself.

'I should warn you that you have no right to detain me against my will. Hand me over to the appropriate authorities immediately,' he said.

The burly servant gave another tug at the cord, making him wince with pain. His wrists were already bleeding with the chafing the man had caused.

'First of all there are matters we should discuss,' Hedwiga told him. 'Take him down to the cellar,' she ordered the servants, adding significantly: 'And give him something to drink first.'

Domenico would not have let either food or drink pass his lips in her house if he had been able to resist. But they thrust a kind of funnel made of metal into his mouth, knocking out one of his teeth as they did so. The foul taste of the liquid they poured down it mingled with the sharp tang of blood from the wound. He wanted to retch but the pressure of the liquid from above was such that he could not. When they took the funnel away, what remained in his mouth spilled out and down the front of his body. It must have contained a soporific, for when he recovered consciousness, it was with the impression of having slept deeply for several hours.

He concluded he was in the cellar whose grating he had noticed from outside, for he could hear footsteps and the occasional clattering of a handcart behind him and far above his head. He tried to change position but could not. His hands and ankles were pinioned. He lay there for a while, hoping to gather strength, watching the reflection of passing lanterns shed through the grating on to the wall opposite him. When he tried to raise his arms again, he understood to his horror that what held him down was not cords, but a living thing, a long, lithe snake. Its strength was such that it forced his wrists back into contact with the couch where he was lying. His resistance seemed to have awakened it, and it rippled endlessly yet powerfully. The passage of the scales across his skin and the sense that he was in the control of an alien creature which he could not see made him want to vomit. And indeed, the contents of his stomach and his intestines were bubbling and seething, as if the storm Goffredo had released upon the Grand Canal had found its way inside him. Domenico moaned and then, in the darkness, began to pray, as he had not done since he was a child. The Latin syllables soothed him. He resolved to lie as still as possible, in the hope that the snake would calm down and cause him not quite so much horror.

That was when the door opened. A servant came in bearing two branched candlesticks, and set them on a table near the wall. Hedwiga and Andreas were behind him. Domenico could only just catch sight of them if he squinted from the corner of his eyes.

Hedwiga, who carried a candle of her own, made of black wax, which smoked and sputtered, strode over and stared down at the prisoner. He resisted the temptation to spit into her face. He was not in a position where he could afford to stir up her ill will needlessly, and he also feared that the attempt to spit might stir the demons cavorting in his abdomen to who could tell what kind of revels.

The door shut. The servant had gone, and the interrogation began. Domenico answered a series of banal enquiries about himself, about Limentani and about Gabriela. He felt sure Hedwiga already had this information. Then she put an odd question.

'Who is the person you most love in the world?'

His thoughts flew to Rodrigo, and he resolved to be silent. At that point his stomach began to heave, as if it had been a creature with a will of its own. It moved up and down, like a bellows sending air into a fire, and its contents made their way up through his body and began spilling out from his nose and his mouth. What emerged was a foul-smelling liquid filled, from what he could tell, with all manner of nauseous creatures, the kind that inhabit stagnant water or dank mud underneath a stone. The creatures had been so tightly packed together that when they emerged into his mouth they began to squabble and fight with one another. He could feel furry things and soft, multiplicitous feet passing over his tongue, while hard shells cracked against his teeth and claws and stinging outgrowths cut into the sides of his mouth.

The first rush was over. Another looked set to begin. He lost all hope of resisting, and murmured, helplessly: 'Rodrigo.' A silence followed. Hedwiga appeared to be ruminating upon his answer. She muttered to Andreas:

'I cannot reach the fellow. He is beyond my influence, for the power that protects him is hostile to mine. And do you know who his guardian is? That stinking cow of a flower-seller who crossed my path the day you and I first met! Unbelievable! It was outside the theatre, do you remember? Even then I sensed a force in her opposed to me. Didn't I tell you how I swooned when I came close and caught her fetid stench?'

Domenico, recovering from the bout of retching, quivered with anger, at himself for having given Rodrigo's name away, and at Hedwiga for her evident wish to injure him as well. He pulled his head up, with an enormous effort, and glared at his tormentors.

'Don't you realise?' he shouted at Andreas. 'That woman is already dead! She has no right to be in this world! You have allied yourself with a corpse!'

'Hold your tongue, if you hope to leave this place alive,' said Hedwiga. 'Remember that you do not enjoy the same protection as your friend. I can do with you exactly as I like.'

'Then it is true,' Andreas murmured, frozen with horror and admiration. 'You have been dead, and are alive again.'

'What a simpleton you are,' Hedwiga snarled, 'and what crude terms you use. Have I not attempted to correct you once before? This child we have caught, meddling in business he would run a hundred miles from if he knew its true implications, is alive, and will be dead before day dawns, if that is the end I choose for him. I can throw the fragments of his body as scraps to the dwarves who guard this mansion, if that should give me pleasure. And for him there is no possibility of returning. There is a limit to what he can suffer, in both pain and fear. Even now, were I to push him too far, he would expire in our presence, taking with him whatever dregs of knowledge he possesses, and which I can hardly find the patience to tease out of him. But as for me? Thanks to the arts of Negri, having been both dead and alive, I can never again be one or the other. I shall be Hedwiga till eternity, unless that villain's skill propels me into a fourth estate, releasing me from this one. You gaze at me wide-eyed, you Austrian doll, you porcelain figure, with all the beauty and premature corruption of your thirty odd years. Have no thought of abandoning me now! You are so deeply entangled in this affair that, were you to leave my presence, you would shatter like one of the creatures of baked, painted clay your charms so much resemble!'

'There is not a shadow of doubt,' cried Domenico from his couch. 'Negri will cause you further torture, now that he is at large! And your associate is a fool to believe a single word formed by your lying lips!'

' "Lying"?' repeated Hedwiga. 'Do you think that I can lie? Do you not realise that, in this respect alone, my condition is one with that of God's saints? I am unable to speak anything but the truth, and it is a truth so horrendous I would rather have been struck dumb till eternity than become its mouthpiece!'

Her mounting horror and anger powerfully affected the warring elements in Domenico's belly. A new onrush of stinking liquid and foul creatures began, more violent than the previous one. As his mouth jerked open, he lost consciousness.

27

That evening's performance was a shambles. Limentani could not accept that his musical director had quite simply disappeared. If Domenico was going to suffer an attack of stage fright, surely it ought to have happened on the following day, rather than when he was about to conduct, for the third time, a mediocre piece that presented him with no difficulties. Envoys were dispatched to hunt for him high and low, through all the hostelries and houses of ill repute in the city.

Half an hour before the performance was due to start, Limentani had still not made alternative arrangements. At this point his mood changed. He became deeply concerned, for what he knew of Domenico's character left him more and more convinced that nothing short of murder or kidnapping could have caused the young man to desert his post. It was left to the leader of the string contingent to come up with a substitute, a dissipated fellow with straggly hair, half librettist, half singing teacher, who was already well on in his cups when they extracted him from a tavern in the neighbouring parish, and seated him at the keyboard. Word of Domenico's disappearance reached the people working front of house, who judged it prudent not to admit any members of the public to the auditorium until they knew for sure the Neapolitan farce would go ahead. Limentani, with a nimbleness which was characteristic of him but which belied his years, scuttled up and down the stairs between the foyer and his office at least ten times in the hour before the evening's entertainment finally got going.

As a result, he did not notice Don Astolfo making his way to the attic to bring Angelo Colombani news of that day's outlandish occurrences. The priest was convinced that only one person could be responsible. While the thought that Goffredo Negri was on the loose filled him with terror, it also galvanized him into an active frame of mind. If anyone knew why the necromancer was on the rampage, and what could be done to put a stop to him, it was the retired castrato. Don Astolfo was determined to enlist his help.

They came downstairs into the foyer just when Rodrigo, who had been misinformed as to the timing of the première, and wanted to be present on Domenico's night of triumph, learned that the young director was missing and had probably been murdered. Such was the rumour running on eager Venetian tongues. Without having a clear idea of what he intended to do, Rodrigo headed instinctively for the office and the attic, and found himself face to face with the castrato. Don Astolfo had linked his arm with Angelo's, and was half leading, half dragging the poor creature back into the world.

Rather than three, five figures clashed with one another at the bottom of the stairs. At the very last minute, Limentani had the idea of changing the running order so that Sarti and his troupe could provide the first half of the programme, thus giving the new director time to look through a score he was barely acquainted with. He ordered the ushers to show the audience to their seats as quickly as possible, while also throwing open the doors to the standing accommodation on the ground floor of the theatre. Then he caught sight of Pacifico Anselmi, pushing his way determinedly through the excited throng, an expression of unbridled wrath upon his face. What the impresario most feared had already occurred. The celebrated composer, his cheeks shaded with only the lightest down of youth, had learned that the opening night of his cherished masterpiece was now in serious jeopardy. He was coming to expostulate.

Limentani paused at the bottom of the stairs, preparing to face the storm. He was too preoccupied with Anselmi to be more than mildly surprised when the parish priest, accompanied by a personage he had never set eyes on before, descended from an office that belonged to him, and which only he and Domenico had the right to use, or when a handsome, red-haired young man pounced on the stranger and demanded, in a strong Venetian accent:

'What has happened? Where is he?'

The impresario left the three of them to sort out whatever

business they had together and led Pacifico upstairs, muttering the most soothing words that he could think of. Their musical director was suffering a mild indisposition, he insisted, nothing more than that. And a conductor of his calibre would still be able to deliver a performance of the highest quality, even if he were not in the best of health. What was more, had the composer forgotten about the marvellous stage machinery which would be placed at the service of his music? It would render the audience oblivious to the hitches and minor upsets which were inevitable on any first night.

'You can come with me! You can help me save him!' cried Angelo.

'But who is this man?' asked Don Astolfo.

'He is the heir. The lost child mentioned in the will.'

Turning to Rodrigo, the castrato continued:

'Astolfo is too terrified to accompany me. The thought of finding himself face to face with Negri is more than he can bear. But you have never even heard of Negri, am I right?'

Rodrigo nodded, at a loss how else to respond. These names were totally unfamiliar to him. If Angelo was trying to explain himself, he was doing a very poor job, as far as Rodrigo was concerned.

'We may not have to confront him right away, you see. I do not wish to go alone because I may be tempted, just as I was tempted seven years ago. Everyone knows how much mischief has resulted from that. You have to keep me on the straight and narrow, that is all I require of you. And if he starts his magic, as long as you hold on to me, you will be safe. Catch hold of my sleeve, or a button, or even one of the curls of my wig. That will be sufficient to preserve you from harm.'

'I cannot understand a word that you are saying,' Rodrigo almost shouted. 'All I want to know is, where is Domenico? Is he alive? And are you able to take me to him?'

'He is alive, but in great danger,' answered Angelo, wringing his hands. 'Who would have thought he could be so unwise, so foolhardy, as to tackle Hedwiga single-handed?'

Don Astolfo's face, which had already lost its usual rubicund glow, grew paler still.

'You mean that woman is in Venice? And this youth is with her?'

'Where else can he be? The conclusion is obvious. He has gone to her house to retrieve the will, and they have made him prisoner.'

'Then we must rescue him,' cried Rodrigo, grasping the castrato's left arm no less energetically than the priest had grasped his right, to bring him thus far. Angelo shook himself free, not without a touch of indignation, dusted down his ageing, thread-bare jacket, and adjusted his wig so that it sat almost, but not quite straight upon his head.

'There is no call to take hold of me as if I were a criminal, and needed to be apprehended,' he said. 'After Goffredo broke free, I was filled with such exhaustion I slept for the remainder of the night and the better part of today. Hardly surprising, given the effort I had been making to keep him in that mirror for seven years. Now that darkness has fallen again, and I am sufficiently rested, I feel ready to enter the fray. I have been reflecting on the most suitable course of action since I wakened. It is not my fault if that young man decided to take matters into his own hands, and now faces the consequences. Yet he inspires a peculiar sympathy in me, and I should be sad to see him come to lasting harm. Given that I have found a suitable companion,' he concluded, darting a glance at Don Astolfo in which pity and contempt were mixed, 'there is no reason to delay our departure any further.'

'You do not know where to go!' the priest objected. 'Are you forgetting how much time has passed since you last set foot outside that attic?'

'My nose tells me,' said Angelo, tapping it with his index finger and making a grimace of disgust. 'That nauseous being spreads an odour of putrefaction around her that would reach my nostrils even if she were in Parma! Sad to say, she is a great deal closer. Is it possible that neither of you notices? What dull creatures you are!'

When Domenico recovered consciousness, the room was in complete darkness. He bent his head back, without thinking, so as to see the grating which opened on to the street. At that very moment there was a rustle of silk and a lady hurried by, scattering laughter as she went. The sound somehow gave him courage. Bringing his hands to his lips he discovered that, before leaving, his interrogators had wiped his face and clothes clean of the horrid mess that spilled from his mouth. That was, if it had been anything more than an illusion produced by a mean trick on Hedwiga's part. The snake had vanished, too! His whole frame shivered as he remembered what it had been like to be trapped within its coils. He sat up on the couch. His head was aching.

Strains of a mandolin reached him from the street above his head. The voice and the melody were familiar, though he could not identify where he had heard them before. A lantern was set down on the pavement next to his prison. The candle burning steadily inside it sent vibrations of light pulsing round the room. It was placed so close to the bars its flame seemed to dissolve them, as if the light were refracted through water rather than through a metal grille. Next came voices, and the sound of someone tugging at the grating.

'He's in here. There's no doubt about it,' said a man with a Neapolitan accent.

'Oh!' said a young girl, with a touch of exaggerated theatricality that made him think they might have been on stage. 'Such a handsome youth, and to be so unfortunate! All because he was headstrong! I am sure he can sing wonderfully.'

'And dance, no doubt.' The accent was from Bergamo this time. 'We'll have him hopping and skipping before he knows it.'

'What's this about him singing?' said the first voice. 'Are you looking for a new partner in that duet? How can you be so fickle? You had promised never to sing it with anyone else but me.'

Not quite able to believe what he was hearing, Domenico turned the upper part of his body round bit by bit until he caught sight of a long, pointed objected poking through the grating. He gave a cry of fright before recognising it as Pulcinella's nose.

'Yes, yes, I am in here!' he cried, leaping to the floor. 'Rescue me as quickly as you can.'

There was a wrench and the grating came away. Pulcinella, whose nose had got trapped between the bars, protested vociferously, to a background of raucous laughter.

'Now what are we to do?' the girl's voice said. 'How are we going to get him out of there?'

'We need something to lift him up with,' said the man from Bergamo.

'Is Pulcinella's nose not long enough?' put in a voice which had not spoken until now. 'Let us saw it off and lower it down into the pit, so that he can grasp hold of it.'

There was an outburst of sniggering and a prolonged yelping, as if the others had indeed latched on to the poor fellow's nose, and were doing their best to wrench it from his mask by force. After a few moments the tomfoolery came to a halt.

'Your shawl! Colombine's shawl! We can make a rope out of it and hoist him up.'

'You are too cruel for words! It was given to me by a young nobleman who made love to me in Cremona last spring. I held him at bay for at least three nights and got the shawl, a ring and a brooch as a reward for my forebearance. It is a love token and cannot be turned to such base purposes.'

'Is the memory of that man's love a year ago so much stronger, my dear Colombine, than the love you feel this very moment for a poor young fellow, trapped in a cellar through no fault of his own? Are you not woman enough to sacrifice one of the lesser trappings of your elegance for him? Who can tell how many shawls he will buy for you when he is rich and vindicated!'

There was a silence, followed by snuffling, then a giggle and a peal of outright laughter. Everyone present cheered. Evidently Colombine had decided to be altruistic. Domenico blundered across the cellar in the half darkness, took hold of the table Hedwiga's servants had placed their candles on and dragged it noisily over to the wall beneath the grating. The effort left him giddy. The effects of the potion he had been forced to drink earlier in the day had not entirely worn off, and he lurched backwards and forwards until his head stopped spinning round. When he felt sufficiently recovered, he clambered up on to the table and squinted at the opening where the grating had been. The idea that he might wriggle through it struck him as impossible. Though not particularly tall, he was stocky and broad-shouldered. At that moment, the knotted end of Colombine's shawl began to descend, for all the world like a feather floating down inside a sunbeam. There was such beauty in the sight of it he lost any sense of where he was and paused. When the fabric brushed against his nose and tickled it, however, he sneezed twice and took a firm grip.

The shawl went taut at once. With one great yank they pulled him off the table. Hands caught hold of his head, his neck, his shoulders. He thought somebody was sure to break a bone in the scuffling that ensued. Yet before he knew it, he found himself outside in the fresh evening air. They lifted him to his feet, let go of him, and he promptly collapsed in a heap on the ground.

'Darling!' Colombine whispered in his ear.

The scent of her skin was inexpressibly sweet after the horrors he had known that day. He placed his arms about her neck and clasped her, as if his safety depended on having her close.

'I have not had a new lover for at least a day and a half,' she said, then added, with a chortle: 'But you are scarcely in a condition to help me break my fast. I do not believe you could make love to a dried out water melon, never mind a woman of flesh and blood.'

Brighella and Pantaloon got him to his feet again and, half carrying, half dragging poor Domenico, the comedians hastened to put a healthy distance between themselves and Hedwiga's dread abode. Colombine went first, carrying the lantern and exchanging quips and insults with the merrymakers passing in the opposite direction. Bringing up the rear, Pulcinella strummed the mandolin and sang obscene refrains in a shrill, tuneless voice. There was no sign of Harlequin.

Twice they had to come to a halt so that Domenico could retch, without producing anything but thin bile from his stomach. It was disagreeable but reassuring. Whatever Hedwiga had put into his body had, to all appearances, been expelled, leaving only this sick weariness behind it. He was dimly aware of entering a broader space, with crowds of revellers in masks, and musicians playing to one side. It took his thoughts to the theatre at St Hyginus's and the performance he ought to have been conducting, but only briefly. He was living in another dimension as though, rather than providing music for the spectacle, he had become part of it.

All at once his friends broke forth in cries of recognition and delight. Harlequin had joined them, his shoulder bag stuffed with food. He had succeeded in gatecrashing a reception in one of the noble houses of the neighbourhood, and had helped himself to a sizeable share of the provisions before making his getaway. Pulcinella and his cronies polished the spoils off in an instant. They tried to get Domenico to eat but the very idea made him squeamish. The music was getting louder.

'Now for a dance!' cried Brighella.

The last thing Domenico wanted to do was wave his hands in the air, make an approximation of steps and move in and out of a figure to the unrelenting rhythms of the music. His rescuers were indifferent to his pleas. It had occurred to him that Paolo Sarti might be the agent of his deliverance. But no matter how hard he tried to identify the comedians, he could not be sure they were the troupe employed by Limentani. Who could tell how many Pulcinellas were roaming the canals and streets that night? He endeavoured to explain who he was and where he came from. They paid no attention. Instead, they insisted on sweeping him into the dance. He was so exhausted that he lost his footing several times. One of the group was always there to catch him before he fell and set him upright. It was part game, part torture, and it did not stop until he really fainted.

When he came to, liquid was being poured into his mouth. It reminded him horribly of what Hedwiga's servants had done that afternoon and he choked and spluttered. They were reviving him with spirits, which had a sharp, sweet, tangy taste.

'Enough play-acting,' announced Pulcinella. 'This man has business to attend to.'

'Business?' repeated Colombine, with wide eyes. 'Is he not going to join our company?'

Brushing her aside, Pulcinella peered down at Domenico, so that the tip of his long nose almost touched the young man's normally proportioned one. He thrust a coin into Domenico's right hand, and a key on a looped string into his left.

'With this coin,' he said, 'you will buy the loveliest potted rose in all the flower-seller's collection. Then you will make your way to the room whose door only this key can open, set the flower on the cabinet by the bed's head, lie down and go to sleep.'

'Flower-seller?' mumbled Domenico. 'Room? Bed? How am I going to do all this if I can barely stand up? Never mind set off in search of roses!'

'Harlequin!' ordered Pulcinella gruffly. 'You know where this chap needs to go. Take him to the stall but be careful not to touch the flower. His hands alone must bear it. Then go to widow Tursi's house and leave him outside the upper room.'

Harlequin grabbed Domenico's hand and, for all the world as if they had been two infants skipping on their way to school, led him off at a rapid pace. The crowds parted before them. Domenico had the sensation of flying rather than walking. His feet hardly touched the ground. His companion hummed or sang the whole time. Without any warning, a mighty presence loomed in front of them, like a cliff after a long voyage at sea. Domenico rubbed his eyes. When he opened them again, he saw the old woman whose oranges he had knocked over on his way to meet Limentani, on the day he got his present job. Her expression was softer now.

He remembered his errand and realised, to his relief, that he had not let go of either the coin or the key. He had no need to explain what it was that he had come for. Maybe it was his bewildered state, but she kept oscillating alarmingly in size, so that one minute she was hunched, smaller than Domenico, while the next she towered above him like a sheltering tree extending its branches in his direction. At the extremity of one of the branches was a banal terracotta pot with a rose bush in it. One blossom had opened, at the very tip. Scale was still varying dizzily, and Domenico was acutely aware of the drops of dew on the petals of the flower, as if they had been crystal goblets filled with a fresh elixir which he longed to quaff.

Without saying a word, he took the pot and held it in the crook of his arm. The old woman was giving him instructions that he strained to understand. She placed a phial in his free hand, the one that was not holding the key. If he was not mistaken, he had to empty the contents of the phial on to the earth in the pot before falling asleep. In this woman's presence (she might have been the slanting pole of a gondola, one side of an arch you walked beneath to go into church, or a graciously curved, tapering, feathery palm branch they would carry in procession on Palm Sunday) he was aware of a new weariness which was also a delicious inclination to rest, as he had not done since starting work on the operas for St Hyginus's, since getting the job as tutor in the Calerghi household, since leaving his parents' house in Bologna so many years ago . . . Indeed, he was unable to remember when he had felt as inclined to fall into deep sleep as he did now.

He lost all notion of direction, or of the distance he covered, trailing at Harlequin's heels with his precious burden, till he was more or less pushed up a twisting flight of stairs, coming to a halt in front of the door they had given him the key to. Harlequin was superstitiously careful not to brush against the flowerpot, and flatly refused to hold it while Domenico was fumbling with the key. In his somnolent state, it was no simple matter to unlock the door with his left hand while clutching the phial in the other, at the same time keeping the rosebush from slipping out of his grasp. He held it pressed against his body with his forearm. But eventually he succeeded.

The room could not have been more Spartan. Almost all of it was taken up by a double bed, whose linen smelt of sunlight and fresh air. There was a window to one side. Given that darkness had long since fallen, Domenico could not tell if the shutters were closed or not. Harlequin vanished. A candle was burning on the table at the bed's head. He placed the rose in its pot next to it, blew out the candle, and was about to fall asleep, when he realised he was still holding the phial in his hand. Uncorking it, he emptied its contents into the pot, and remembered nothing more.

28

The night was windy. It felt odd to be leaving a theatre just as the entertainment was beginning. Rodrigo was not a man closely acquainted with fear. The circumstances of his early life, the kind of love he was drawn to and the manner in which he found his partners meant he was accustomed to confronting a degree of danger in many of his doings. Rather than disconcerting him, it gave an edge to his existence he would not willingly have done without. Nevertheless, as he followed the castrato through the dimly lit streets and alongside canals plunged in darkness, the lapping of whose waters made him think of subterranean rivers, as if they had already been far beneath the earth, in search of a ferryman to take them into Hell, fear was his dominant emotion.

The contrast with Colombani's new found energy could not have been more startling. Though he had not left his eyrie for many years, the singer moved surefootedly through the Venetian labyrinth, whistling all the time, and hopping along so nimbly the other man had difficulty keeping up with him. It was not just their mood. The weather, too, was strange that night. If Rodrigo had had to describe it, he would have said that a wind such as swept across the lagoon on the grimmest days in December, bringing an Alpine chill in its wake, had been cut up like a piece of cloth, and the fragments scattered over the city. Halfway down a narrow lane, where the air was utterly still, a gust would catch them, so violent that it lifted Colombani's wig from his head, and Rodrigo had to clutch his three-cornered hat to prevent it being blown into the canal. On a broader highway which gondolas had once moved down, filled in with earth and paved over during the previous decade, a veritable gale was set loose without warning. Cloaks billowed out like sails. Hats and fans were swept up into the sky above the rooftops, and two caddies carrying a sedan chair, a rare and extravagant means of transport in that city, swayed and tottered, so mercilessly did the wind buffet them. Rodrigo heard the glass in a lantern shatter. There were cries of alarm, perhaps of pain, from those nearby, for needle-sharp splinters had flown in all directions.

He caught hold of Angelo, without thinking what he was doing, and was filled with wonder and still greater fear. The castrato was no more affected by the blast than a sculpture of bronze upon its pedestal would have been. Indeed, the force of the wind evoked a corresponding strength in him, which communicated itself to Rodrigo and coursed through his body, together with a warmth that ran down to the soles of his feet and back into the ground, as if that was the place Angelo drew it from.

When he glanced at the older man's face, a smile was playing on the lips, of recognition and, he could have sworn, enjoyment. He remembered the instructions he had been given, to hold on even to as little as the hem of the castrato's jacket, should they come face to face with magic. The thought that this unpredictable weather was the effect of necromancy, rather than of exceptional climatic conditions, did not please Rodrigo one bit. He placed a hand on his companion's shoulder and huddled close to him, in a manner incongruous for such a plucky fellow. The two of them made an unusual pair. But the other people abroad that night were far too preoccupied with getting safely to their destinations to pay them much attention.

The freak wind took a special pleasure in blowing out the lanterns which illuminated the major thoroughfares of the city and were a source of constant pride to its inhabitants. Rodrigo fell behind when their path led them through more or less complete darkness, though he still kept a grip on Angelo's jacket tail. When they reached the point where the lane petered out, the castrato stumbled forward into the flat-bottomed boat, producing a great splash. Rodrigo pulled him back out of it, thinking he had fallen into the water. Having worked out what had happened, they both got into the boat and pushed off cautiously. Within a matter of moments it grated against dry land on the other side.

Hedwiga's town house presented a most peculiar aspect that night. Candles had been set burning in every window, for she was aware of Goffredo's liberation and determined to welcome him with all the pomp at her disposal. Yet the wind had already found its way into the building and, as Angelo and Rodrigo gazed at the façade, the candles dimmed and sputtered. Several went out. Rodrigo was wondering what the castrato was going to do, whether he would ring the bell like an ordinary visitor and ask to be admitted, or wave his hand and make the doors disappear, in the manner of the genie in an oriental tale, standing outside the cave where a treasure has been hidden. A violent blast came from behind their shoulders, as if on purpose. The doors rattled madly, like a ship's hatch in a storm, and burst open.

They were met with the peculiar spectacle of a lackey flying past in a horizontal position, carried on a gust as if he had been no more weighty than a sheet torn from a drying line. Having gained admission to the house, the wind was doubling back upon itself, hurtling through the corridors till it reached the point where it had started, then setting off once more with renewed fury. Rodrigo noticed that the candles which went out were ordinary white ones, while a different class, of black wax, burned more brightly under the effects of Goffredo's magic. All sorts of debris was swept past them: wall-hangings, chair covers, tassels from curtain pulls, embroidered cushions, a painted fire screen, books and scrolls of varying dimensions. The carpet they were standing on inside the door rippled and arched its back like a snake. Another lackey came hurtling towards them, emitting a low moan. Overcome with pity for the creature, Rodrigo made the mistake of reaching out to seize him as he flew past and would have been lifted bodily into the air if Angelo had not caught hold of him. Once more that leaden steadfastness flowed through his limbs. His feet were rooted to the ground, but it was contact with the castrato that gave him stability, not the pull of gravity, or the floor of Hedwiga's hallway. More and more of its marble slabs were laid bare as, fluttering chaotically and tugging at the pegs that fastened them, the precious coverings soared off into the general hurricane.

'Feel no compassion for those beings. They are not human, but merely machinery,' Angelo explained. 'If they were ever living, they long since lost their right to air and sunlight.'

He made his way forward one step at a time, like a giant

plodding across a strait during a storm, or St Christopher carrying the Christ child over the river. He opened a door to their left, pulled Rodrigo in after him, and slammed it shut again. They were in Hedwiga's private suite, on the ground floor. The doors communicating with the adjoining room were closed. Voices raised in altercation could be heard coming from the other side of them. Rodrigo was unable to make out what they said, for they spoke in German. Angelo twisted his features in disgust, pulled a handkerchief from his breast pocket and buried his nose in it. Though Rodrigo smelt nothing, the stench of Hedwiga's putrefaction was evidently unbearable for the castrato at such close quarters.

Like an experienced criminal, with the utmost nonchalance, Angelo set to rifling the drawers of Hedwiga's cabinet, tearing open envelopes, emptying folders on to the desk, glancing briefly at paper after paper before he discarded it. A pile of litter gathered on the floor. Rodrigo noticed nervously that the wind had found its way beneath the door of the room they were in. It set the papers seething and churning as if it had been stirring a stew in a cauldron.

'What are you looking for?' he hissed to Angelo, though he wondered if there was any need to whisper. Loud crashes and the sound of broken glass came from outside. The voices from the room next door had fallen silent, or else the people there were talking so quietly they could not be heard. 'And where is Domenico? Have you forgotten that we came to save him?'

'The likelihood of our rescuing him from this maelstrom is small indeed,' replied Angelo, with an indifference that maddened Rodrigo. He had let go of the castrato when they entered the room but now prepared to lay hands upon him forcibly, if the creature put off hunting for his friend a minute longer.

'Anyway,' continued Angelo, 'he has already escaped.'

'How do you know?'

'They said so when they were shouting at each other. Didn't you understand? Oh, I had forgotten you do not speak German.'

He turned back to his papers.

'I am looking for a will. And since you are its beneficiary, I would advise you to assist me rather than interfering with me.'

'What about that scroll on the table by the window?' asked Rodrigo, who had had time to survey the contents of the room while Angelo was busy with his search.

'Ah!' The castrato seized upon the document, undid the knot that bound it and surveyed its contents. He gave a cry of delight. 'This is it! We have it! Now we can go!'

Rodrigo could feel a chill draught round his feet. The mass of papers on the floor was describing a wider and wider circle in its dance. The last thing he wanted to do was to go out into that corridor again. He looked at the window to see if it offered an alternative means of escape. At that moment there was a great howl. The storm threw open the door of the room they were in and hurled him bodily into the castrato's arms.

'Hee-hee!' tittered Angelo. 'Goffredo is on his very best form! I never knew him to come up with anything quite so impressive!'

'You mean Goffredo Negri caused this tempest?' shouted Rodrigo. It was no easy matter to make himself heard against the background of the hurricane.

'Caused this tempest? He *is* the tempest!' yelled Angelo, with a cry of exhilaration.

More slowly than before, plodding on step after step, the castrato made his way into the corridor and towards the main door. His power was sufficient to prevent Rodrigo from being blown away but not to keep his feet upon the ground. It was a very strange sensation. It occurred to him that this might well be how a flag would feel when attached to a flagpole in a high wind. The idea made him laugh. When he looked up, however, the laughter froze upon his face. The roof of Hedwiga's town house had disappeared. That was the rational explanation. But the grey turbulence above their heads bore no resemblance to the skies of Venice. The wind was drawing all the bits of debris into a vortex which grew smaller but no less intense as it receded into infinity. Servants, tapestries, tables and chairs all shrunk to tiny dots.

There was a cry of rage at their shoulders. The two intruders looked back. Hedwiga had emerged into the corridor. She caught sight of Angelo, and her features were distorted by a snarl of hatred such as Rodrigo had never seen in his life before. Andreas was behind her. A split second later, the tempest snatched up both of them as if they had been no heavier than rag dolls. Flying past, Andreas grasped Angelo's lapel. It sustained him for a minute or two, but his fingers soon had to release their hold. He hurtled after his accomplice, whirled up into the vortex above their heads. Despite the din of the storm, Rodrigo was able to catch some words:

'Save me!' Andreas cried. 'I did not know! It is not . . . too . . . l-a-a-a-te!'

As he strained his eyes to follow the black smudges the two figures had become, it occurred to him that there would be no respite for them, that they were condemned to circle eternally in the grip of that mad blast, which was the expression both of Goffredo's rage and of their own voracity. As he watched, there was a sound like thunder directly above his head. A crack appeared in the wall at his side and the masonry began to crumble. Everything went black.

29

The window faced east. The shutters had not been closed the previous night and the sun streamed into the room where Domenico lay asleep. The powerful wind had blown fitfully almost until dawn, clearing every wisp of cloud from the firmament. The day was of a clarity and brilliance rarely seen in that humid and mist-haunted city.

He opened his eyes, then shut them again because the brightness was so hard to bear. When he turned his head, his gaze fell on the rose bush. With a shock he noted that the single flower on it had disappeared. His surprise was even greater when he realised that he was no longer alone. A figure was stretched out on the bed at his side. It was a woman only a little younger than himself. She lay with her face upwards on the pillow, her breast rising and falling to the gentle rhythm of her breathing. A splendid head of auburn hair framed her features. There was no doubt in Domenico's mind as to her identity.

'Eleonora,' he murmured, leaning over her.

She opened her eyes and looked straight at him.

'Are you my betrothed?' she asked.

Domenico blushed so deeply his face practically took on the colour of Eleonora's hair.

'No, I don't think so. In fact, I am quite certain I am not.' He added, with a touch of pique: 'What makes you think I should be your betrothed?'

She did not answer, but turned to look at the rose bush in its pot. She laughed.

'Do you know, last night I dreamt I was the flower at the tip of that plant. And now I am lying here and the flower has vanished.'

She sat up.

'Where are we?'

'In Venice.'

'That explains why I sensed so much water close to me. I thought I might be in a boat but I could not understand why there were so many buildings round about. And who were all the people watching me?'

'What do you mean?'

'I combed my hair, and sang. Earlier, when I did it, it was in a high up place. There was a garden in the distance, with black-robed figures moving in it who once in a while caught sight of me. The last few times, I was one of a group of people standing or sitting behind an enormous arch. A sea of faces was observing us. I could not tell if I was visible to them or not.'

'You were visible. That was a theatre. They were looking at the stage.'

She looked alarmed.

'And I was on it? Did I disturb the performance? That was not my intention at all.'

'Oh, have no fear. They were pleased to have you with them, though they found your presence disconcerting.'

'I would have spoken to them if I had been able. All I managed to do was sing. And where is this?' she went on, pointing to the room around them. 'Whose house are we in?'

'I cannot tell. I was brought here last night. They said something about a widow Tursi, but I do not know her,' Domenico answered warily.

It struck him as preferable not to mention Harlequin because it sounded so outlandish. He decided he would have to go over the events of the previous afternoon and evening carefully in his own mind before giving anyone an account of them, in case they decided he was mad.

He moved on to the offensive.

'Where have you been?'

'Travelling, this long, long time. The last thing I remember from this world, the real one, where we find ourselves now, is the enchanter's eyes. A fire came next. How painfully it burned me! And yet my body gave off a fragrance as it was consumed. I can hardly believe I have it back. Look, touch it. Is it real?'

She took Domenico's hand in hers and gently brought his palm into contact with her cheek, her breasts and her belly. It was as if she needed reassurance of her physicality, that she was indeed materially present. Her own impressions were insufficient evidence.

'Yes, it is,' Domenico said quietly. 'You are really here.'

'I moved in a realm of shadows, walking, walking endlessly. All I knew was that I had an enormous distance to travel. Although I had the sensation of moving, I could not see anything of myself, and I wondered if I merely had the memory of once possessing a body. They say that, when a hen is beheaded, it will continue strutting around for several minutes, wanting to peck at grains with a beak it no longer has. Men and women who have lost a limb are supposed still to feel a phantom presence for days afterwards. That was how it was with me, as if I were my own ghost. Yet something stayed that was not a shadow. That was me.'

'How did you know which direction to walk in?'

'There was a light in the distance, like a star. At other times I could hear music far off. My ears guided me towards it. That was why I sang. Singing made the music stronger, so that I could be more certain of the path to follow. Perhaps I am falling into error when I talk of ears, since I had none, or of walking, since I had no legs. I can find no other words. Eventually I came upon a road, sat at the edge of it and waited. Before long, a cart came past. It was as shadowy as everything else, only a little more distinct. A man with a bowed head sat in the front holding the reins. At first I thought it was a hearse, but in it were three sisters.'

'What did you do?'

'I asked them to take me with them as a passenger and they agreed to do so if I would help them in their work. They were carding great bales of wool so that they could be spun into thread in another place. I asked them where the wool came from and they said it was the stuff of human suffering.'

'Did you have to learn how to do that? Surely the servant women spun the wool in the house you came from?'

'I was happy to be taught. It was like combing, and though I had a maidservant to comb my hair in my father's house, I loved to sit at the window and do it myself, on sunny days like this one, so that the light would bleach the locks and make them paler.

Though I could not see my hair, the sisters could, and took great delight in its colour. From time to time they would tell me to put down the wool and comb it while I sang to them. That was when I had my visions, or so I called them at the time. I mean, glimpses of the real world. The one you have always lived in. I asked the sisters if this was permitted and they answered yes, that was how it was meant to be. If I was patient enough and worked diligently, I would be able to leave the realm of shadows and return to the daylight world.'

'So they were kind to you.'

'Kind, yes, but very sad. It was odd, because though I always seemed to be alone with them, I knew other people joined us in the cart or got down from it. From time to time we stopped. Figures standing at the roadside took the carded wool and carried it away on their backs. But there was always plenty more for us to work on.'

'And how did all of this come to an end?'

'One day they set me down. It was at the sea shore. Everything was in different colours of grey, the beach, the waves, the sky. It was so beautiful! The rocks were nearly black while the sand glittered, as if it had been granite ground to a powder. The sea resembled milk, if milk could ever be grey, and the froth at the tips of the breakers came close to being white, though it was not quite bright enough. I started walking again. I had been sitting in the cart for such a long time it felt strange to use my limbs, and I have already told you I could see nothing. The noise of the surf rang in my ears like music and I sang to its accompaniment.

'Before long I rounded a headland. Right in front of me stood an orange tree which, unbelievably, had colours! I recognised it because, from the window of my dressing-room in Naples, I could see an ornamental garden at first floor level. It was paved with blue and white tiles and planted with orange trees. The one before me now was two-dimensional, like a painting of a tree on canvas, or like the banners they carry in religious processions. I reached up to touch it and one of the fruits came off in my hand, of its own accord, without me having to pull. I put my teeth to it and bit into the skin. It made me want to sleep. I remembered that, since my body burned, I had not slept. I had been awake through all those days and nights of travelling and labour. To tell the truth, there was neither day nor night, but merely an unending twilight.'

Domenico's attention had faltered during the last few sentences. He was counting the strokes of a church bell ringing from a tower nearby. He jumped to his feet.

'Noon!' he cried. 'We have to move. I am supposed to be conducting an opera this evening and there is a rehearsal scheduled for this afternoon. Is it Friday today?'

Eleonora looked at him with bewilderment.

'Why are you asking me? How could I possibly tell what day of the week it is, when I have known neither time nor sunlight for so long?'

'You will come with me, won't you?'

She smiled, with a sweetness and serenity which did something to calm even his agitated state.

'Of course I will. But where?'

'To the theatre at St Hyginus's. Angelo Colombani knows everything about you. He will be able to tell us what to do. Oh, what is going to happen if Friday has gone past, if we have been sleeping here for a week like the man in the fairy tale, and the première is over? What am I going to say to Ansaldo Limentani?'

30

People turned to look at them with murmurs of appreciation and admiration as they walked through the streets of Venice. Domenico had emerged from his ordeal chastened and thinner. The lineaments of his face took on a gauntness they had not possessed before, and the pallor of his cheeks made his black hair gleam in contrast, like the plumage of a crow caught in the sunlight. They proceeded hand in hand, as if still in a dream, and the throng parted to make way for them. A flower-seller broke off a rose and offered it to Eleonora, who accepted the gift with a majestic air that at once set people whispering how a princess had arrived from a foreign land, who had long, red hair the like of which had never been seen in the city. She had found a prince to marry her, they said, and the two were making their way to the Church of St Mark to be betrothed. They were not like the magnates who usually visited the city, and had no need of extravagant clothes, jewellery, or a trail of liveried servants. Simplicity was their garb, or so the story went, and their manners were humble, so that their beauty could more easily be manifest.

A housemaid fell to her knees, took hold of Domenico's hand and kissed it. The contact of her lips brought him to his senses, for until that moment Venice had seemed to him a wonderland, and he had been conscious of nothing but the sunlight on his skin, of the chill air when shadows fell upon him, and of the warmth and steady pressure of Eleonora's hand in his. He turned to a quack doctor, who was selling powder made from snakeskin and resinous ointments, and asked him the way to St Hyginus's. The man wore what looked like a red nightcap, had a pointed, grizzly beard, and was seated at a high desk, with his wares displayed in front of him. He got down, took off a pair of tiny, black-rimmed, perfectly round spectacles, and engaged in a lengthy discourse

Domenico made neither head nor tail of. The direction his hand pointed in was enough.

When they rounded the corner, Domenico stopped a water-seller who was carrying two brimming buckets on a shoulder yoke of wood and asked if they could drink. He then realised with confusion that he had no money to give in exchange. The woman, even more embarrassed by the beauty of the young couple in front of her, and by the silence of the crowd that watched them, set her burden down and, without a word or any thought of payment, dipped her wooden bowl into the water and offered it, first to Eleonora, then to Domenico. No sooner had they moved on than the onlookers besieged her, desperate to get a draught of the liquid which had been used to refresh the young prince's lips. Those were her richest day's takings in many a long while.

They were not the only source of rumours in Venice that morning. North of the Church of the Holy Apostles, an entire mansion had crumbled in the course of the night. It was unthinkable that the wind could have brought it down, however violent it might have been, and the authorities were more inclined to conclude that a defect in the architecture, never detected and sapping the structure with the passage of the years, had chosen that moment to reveal itself and bring the building tumbling down in ruins. But how then to explain what had happened to the statues in the garden, those peculiar dwarves, each of which was cleft right down the middle so as to reveal the ugly metal struts at its core? Could that be the effect of unsound foundations? The whole affair grew more bewildering when it emerged that the woman who rented the house was an impostor, that the person she claimed to be had died in a coach accident somewhere north of the Alps many years before, and that nobody knew from where she had recruited her plentiful troop of servants, or what had happened to them. Not a single corpse was discovered amidst the rubble.

A neighbour claimed that, in the hour before dawn, she had seen two figures emerge from the clouds of dust, a man of less than normal height half dragging, half carrying a youth whose face was bruised and bloodied. But there were no other witnesses, and the investigators dismissed her testimony as the product of too lively an imagination. They did, however, take the precaution of having the place blessed and abundantly sprinkled with holy water once it had been cleared, and before new foundations were laid. All the old stakes were removed and special care was taken in driving fresh wooden piles into the marshy ground, to avoid any chance of the awkward incident being repeated.

When Domenico and Eleonora reached St Hyginus's, they found a council of war, or perhaps a council of despair would be a more accurate description, going on in Limentani's office. On seeing the young conductor at the top of the stairs, the impresario felt all his anger melt away and was only conscious of an immense relief that nothing had happened to his protégé. With a quite uncharacteristic effusiveness, and without pausing to greet the young woman whose hand he was holding, he threw himself upon Domenico and hugged him energetically as if he had been a son. His eyes were filled with tears.

'You are safe!' he cried. 'You are safe!'

Liberated from Limentani's embrace, Domenico noticed Rodrigo propped up on the couch, looking distinctly unwell. His head was bandaged and his face was criss-crossed by streaks of dried blood where the falling masonry had cut him. There was a moment of awkwardness. Domenico was not sure whether it was appropriate to acknowledge him or not. Angelo, who had been deep in discussion with Luca Schiavoni, came to the rescue. He bowed solemnly in front of Eleonora and turned to Ansaldo Limentani.

'Allow me to present Eleonora Calefati, the youngest daughter of one of the noblest families in the realm of the two Sicilies.'

Next he winked meaningfully at Domenico, took his hand and led him over to Rodrigo.

'And this, my dear fellow, is the lost heir to the fortune of Alvise Contarini, a love child who is to be the future owner of the theatre.'

A voice broke in from the other side of the room.

'After due legal forms have been completed, that is. And provided the gentleman in question is able to produce the tokens specified in the will.'

It was Onofrio Carpi.

'You mean you found the will?' cried Domenico in delight, forgetting any thought of prudence or of concealing how much he knew. 'You got it back from Hedwiga?'

Onofrio, not Angelo answered.

'The document has been retrieved and is, as far as I can tell, genuine and legally valid. But naturally I cannot give a professional opinion at such short notice. The case is likely to require several months in the courts before a decision can be reached.'

'Nothing is to be said to Donato Gradenigo,' put in Limentani. 'At least, not for the moment. Though he has promised to attend this evening's première, which now, thank the Heavens, will undoubtedly take place, his health continues to be very poor. I would not be surprised,' he went on, looking at the lawyer with a measure of antipathy, 'if a sad decease were to obviate the need for extended wrangling before the judges, saving everyone the expense of protracted legal action.'

'The prospective heir,' said Angelo, 'has kindly agreed to let the matter rest, at least until the present season is done with and the carnival is over. He would be very unhappy were his good fortune to jeopardise the success of your operas or the future fame of St Hyginus's.'

'Do not say "your" operas, say "ours",' put in Schiavoni. 'If *King Montezuma and the Conquest of Peru* creates the stir we all expect, it will be due, in large measure, to the wonderful machinery which you devised.'

'And, of course, to the music of our prodigy,' said Limentani, gesturing towards Pacifico Anselmi, who was sitting in the corner, and whose presence Domenico had not noticed until now.

'What is to become of Eleonora?' he asked. He had not let go of her hand during all these explanations. 'Who is going to take her back to Naples?'

Anselmi leapt to his feet, made a pompous flourish with his hat, and pressed his lips to the hand Domenico was not holding.

'My next assignment is with the Theatre of San Carlo in that city. I shall set off south in a matter of days. It would be the greatest of honours to me to have the company of this fine blossom of the kingdom's aristocracy on my journey.'

Eleonora laughed so much her body shook.

'Who is this creature?' she murmured to Domenico. 'And why does he have a beauty spot on his cheek?' Then, in a voice that everyone could hear, she continued: 'Nothing would give me more pleasure than to accept such a gallant offer. But are we to make the journey alone? Like a young married couple on their honeymoon?'

'Madame Landowska, the great-aunt of the king of Poland, my benefactress and patron, will travel with us. You could not ask for a more highly placed or respectable lady to act as your chaperone.'

'Then it is settled,' said Limentani. 'Now, Domenico, we have to think about work. The rehearsal is to start in three hours' time.'

And indeed, three hours later, candles were burning all around the proscenium arch in the theatre of St Hyginus. As the final chords of the overture sounded, the curtain lifted, revealing the chorus assembled on the stage and, behind them, Angelo Colombani's wonderful machinery. King Montezuma sat in barbarian glory in the centre of it, at the summit of a ceremonial staircase the Spanish envoys would soon tread when they began their perfidious embassy. As he watched, Ansaldo Limentani felt sure that he was about to witness the greatest triumph of his personal career, one which would regain for St Hyginus's its position as the prime theatre in all the territories of the Republic of Venice. And he was right.

With thanks

to Matteo Ceriana and Corrado Anselmi, splendid friends and hopeless correspondents, beneath whose roof, on the edges of the parish of St Hyginus, the opening pages of this book were written; to Marco Fazzini, of Ascoli Piceno and Vicenza, and to Bianca Tarozzi, of the Sestiere di San Marco, for hospitality and encouragement; and to E. G. Del C., whose presence made the house on Campo San Ternita a home, for his love of tennis in all its forms, and for his admirable indifference to the ageing monuments of Venice.

The author gratefully acknowledges financial support from the Scottish Arts Council during the time this book was written.